THE DEATH OF HONOR

HONOR TRILOGY: BOOK 1

LYRA THORSSON

The Death of Honor
Honor Trilogy, Book 1
© 2021 FoxTales Press
Content and line edits by Victory Editing
Cover Design Copyright © 2020 by Biserka
Designs
All rights reserved.

ISBN for Paperback: 978-1-942023-75-3

ISBN for Hardcover: 978-1-942023-76-0

CHAPTER ONE

Rebecca

"Not again…"

I pursed my lips and felt my chest tighten as Nik sighed and punched in the combination once more, each finger bending farther than it should. Nothing happened.

Slamming his hand into the controls, Nik's emerald eye darkened. Luckily, he didn't break anything. This time.

Luck didn't come our way a few months ago when the computer stopped working, per usual, and Nik had thrown another tantrum. That incident forced us to replace an entire console. I hoped he would stop breaking things. We were already behind on a few payments, if I wasn't mistaken, and didn't want to waste money on repairs.

Nik cursed under his breath as he jumped up from his seat, then ran his fingers through his graying, ash-blond hair.

"*Scheiße* machine isn't responding again! I will have to manually drop us out of hyperspace."

Nik climbed around me to get to the passageway. We were used to the cramped ship at that point, and I didn't think about it as I tried to move out of his way. Nreff ships offered great craftsmanship but very little space and a tendency not to get along with nation-made electronics. This marked the third time in a month that the hyperdrive jumped us blind. We would need to pick up a new hyperdrive from the black market soon, since getting one the proper way involved exorbitant taxes. Hopefully our next one wouldn't be as faulty.

I wondered if ships from the Regit Republic dealt with this problem.

I hurried after Nik into the engine room, which lay less than five feet away from the cockpit. Taking the turn a little too quickly and not paying attention to my surroundings as I thought about the worst-case scenario, I hit my head straight on the doorframe. I touched the forming bump on my forehead and blinked a few times until my eyes made out the steel boxes bolted to the ceiling with what seemed to be a million wires spilling out of them. We should case them in for safety reasons, but we'd ripped away those panels long ago. They'd gotten in the way when we were forced to manually pull out of hyperspace.

And by manually, I meant rewiring the hyperdrive and going against the manufacturer's hazard warnings —not to mention the ship's safety laws everyone supposedly followed. But who obeys that crap, am I right? We couldn't stay in hyperspace forever.

The other problem with manually pulling out of hyperspace was that it sort of ruined a lot of the other mechanics. It couldn't, and shouldn't, be done more than a few times. Really, such an action should never happen since the calculations were complicated and supposed to run through a computer so one didn't end up somewhere they weren't supposed to be.

Like in the middle of a star, for example.

"What do you need me to do?" I asked, my head still throbbing. *Gott*, I hated having to watch where I walked. Pieces of metal hung all over the place. I figured I would have gotten used to it by now.

"Calculate how far we've gone past our destination and where we are in the system, if we are still in the system," Nik ordered as he pulled out a screen and started typing away.

"Got it!"

I spun to the other screen and took a deep breath of the ozone-smelling room. I could taste the metallic panels and wires. I focused on the numbers. Although I would use a computer, human error still intervened.

But what was life without a little Russian roulette? Except instead of a gun, we used a ship, and it could hurt something… or someone.

"Rebecca?" Nik's voice cracked a little.

I waved at him to stop fussing. He always got so uptight in situations like this—as if we had never come across a crisis before. "I got it. I got it. Still in the system; clear for twenty seconds. After that… Well… don't wait that long…"

He spun back around to face his screen. "Great. Twenty seconds."

"Fifteen now," I stated as nonchalantly as I could.

Nik tapped away on the screen. Nothing happened. "Work, you piece of *scheiße*!" He slammed his fist on the screen.

I grimaced when I heard the panel crack—the same sound my heart made when I worried about the extra payments we would have to make. He needed to stop venting his anger. I took a mental note to bring up his anger issues later when destruction didn't lie in our wake.

"Ten seconds!" I cautioned, my whole body beginning to shake. I held my breath—we usually never cut it this close.

Nik opened a drawer and pulled out the wire cutters.

"I don't know if that's such a good idea," I said. This wasn't a spy movie, and cutting the wires never seemed like the sanest choice.

"Do you have any better suggestions?" he shouted, as he headed for the hyperdrive.

I peered back at the screen. Five seconds remained. I waved. "Go right ahead."

Questioning for about a second whether it would work or explode, I nodded. I flinched as Nik cut the wires, and the force threw us forward as the ship dropped out of hyperspace before the regulators could respond. I slammed into Nik, and we both tumbled to the floor. I held back a few cuss words as I hit my head in the same spot again, but Nik cushioned the rest of my body.

We lay there for a moment, waiting to see if we dropped out in the clear or hit something we shouldn't have. After a few seconds, nothing happened. All seemed safe for the time being.

"Rebecca, you are getting a little heavy." Nik tried to crack a joke to lighten the mood.

I elbowed him in the stomach.

"Ow, I was kidding!"

I pulled myself up and licked my lips. The taste of copper filled my mouth. I must have bitten my tongue or lip. Holding out my hand to Nik, I helped him gather himself.

"You okay?" I asked as I dusted myself off. Why we always ended up in these situations, I couldn't say for sure.

He rubbed his head. "I'm getting a little too old for this *scheiße*."

"Yeah, you are. Two more years and you'll be forty." That meant only seven more years for me.

He raised an eyebrow and gave me a glassy stare that felt even scarier with just the one eye, as the other eye was covered with a patch. I smiled as we both turned to inspect the hyperdrive. The whole thing shut off; no power transmitted through it.

"Well, that's that." He let out a sigh and lightly slammed his head on the panel next to it.

Hurrying to the window across the corridor, I peeped out to find an asteroid alarmingly close. If we'd dropped out of space a mere ten meters to our port flank, we'd have been screwed.

"*Ach du liebe…* That was a little close for comfort," I whispered as I let out a deep breath.

Nik whistled. "That's a mighty big asteroid out there. Now can we buy a new hyperdrive? And this time one that works with the ship? Or better yet, a new ship? How many times have we been too close for comfort and escaped by the nape of our necks?"

I peeked up at him. His left eye scrutinized me. The black patch covering his right eye reminded me of how many times we'd barely made it out alive. Others didn't come out so lucky.

Letting those memories wash away, I smirked. "What would be the fun in that? Besides, this one reminds me of home. Granted, home is a place that I want to forget…"

He rolled his good eye and walked off toward the cockpit.

"Oh, don't give me that! You love flying with me," I said, following him. Just going into the engine room left grease on my hands. I wiped them on my khaki cargo pants and straightened my black tank top.

"I'm never trusting you to buy anything for this ship again," Nik said as he sat down.

I stretched my arms before I let my body collapse in the seat next to him. "It was a great deal, I swear."

He groaned. "That's what you always say. I don't trust you. I expect you just buy stuff on a whim, with no research, hoping to get some kind of adventure out of it. I'm guessing you enjoy putting my life on the line."

"Humph. I won't tell you if that's true or not, but realize that the next hyperdrive will be Nreff-made. That being said, we will need to visit the scariest black market that we can locate to find this hyperdrive. You've got an extra kidney, right?" I glanced over at him, biting my tongue with a smile. His frown showed to me he didn't find it as funny as I did. "What?"

"You laugh now, but I know that isn't far from the truth, especially since we're in Regit Republic territory. I wish this had happened when we were in YamaXie. At least there I can recognize that the parts are good. Can you promise me I won't lose another one of my organs, please?"

I took a deep breath, pushing away memories. "I can't make any promises, but I will try my best. Meanwhile, you should be working on that anger-management problem you have. Don't need you busting more of the ship."

"Well, maybe if you bought parts that worked, I wouldn't need to slam my fist into them, huh?" he shot back.

"Now, now, learn to be more like me. Calm and easy."

He raised his eyebrows at me.

"Hey, what's that supposed to mean?"

"You can't hold in your anger. You bite the head off of every person you talk to. People fear you, Rebecca. Admit it. You can't control your anger any better than I can." Nik leaned back and folded his hands behind his head. "We're just two freaks flying around all these systems on this broken ship."

My lips formed a small smile, knowing he didn't

realize the reality of that statement. He didn't understand how much blood covered my hands. He couldn't go back to the Nreff Nation because of the bounty on his head, but I couldn't go back for more reasons than that.

Nik stood. "But you're right. I should work on not hurting the ship. Maybe I should pick up a sport, like racquetball or something."

"How in the *'raum* are you going to play that on the ship?" I scoffed.

Nik shrugged. "Haven't thought about it that much. What, should I pick up something more practical? Like you did with your cooking?"

Right. My cooking. I guess I learned to deal with some of my anger and pain that way, though in reality it caused me to remember things I wanted to scrub clean out of my mind—things that still didn't go away with the medicine I took at night, although they helped with some of the pain. But Nik didn't know about the other way I took care of my anger issues.

I, however, could teach Nik how to cook and see if it helped him, but I hated it when someone else stood near me in the kitchen. "We don't need two cooks on a ship though."

"More like you don't like anyone in your kitchen."

I rubbed the side of my nose with my middle finger. "The kitchen is already too cramped for me, and it doesn't help that my partner always burns everything he touches. You've even somehow started a fire while making cereal the last time we were planet side. You're too much of a liability to be in a kitchen, never mind a kitchen in space where we can't escape the fire."

"Yeah, yeah, I get it. I'll come up with something. But as for now, we need to find a new drive when we land. I'm glad that there's a peace treaty across the nations so that trade is easy."

I shook my head. "We don't have enough for a drive, even on the black market. That's why I settled for the last one. Either we'll stay portside and fix the drive ourselves or we'll need to get real jobs to pay for one. Be like normal people."

He clutched my free hand, his thumb caressing the scars that went all the way up my arm. I bit my lip. I hated the memories those scars brought up and the fact that I couldn't get rid of them.

"You think you could last five seconds at a real job?" he asked with a little smile.

I took my hand away from him and folded my arms. "I'm just as capable of a real job as you are."

"Rebecca, you hate people. You make everyone around you uncomfortable."

That didn't stray far from the truth. The last job we took, the employer wouldn't even look me in the eyes. I hated people who did that. It was like they were trying to hide something or, even worse, saw me as inferior to them. My supervisor also tried to get me arrested, and I had to teach him a lesson. "Well, you stuck around and I don't see you complaining."

Nik gave me his side-eye look.

"Much."

Nik pulled me out of my chair and held me close, kissing my head. I closed my eyes, letting the warmth linger. Although we hadn't reached couple status, sometimes our passion impeded common sense. Being close felt natural, but baggage interfered with that.

"I'll always be here for you." He ruffled my short ruby hair and let me go. "Even when times get tough."

"Yeah, you might regret saying that after I try to fix the hyperdrive myself," I whispered under my breath as I pulled out my butterfly knife and started swinging the blade around—my favorite pastime.

"What did you say?"

I grinned. "Nothing. Let's get out of here."

"Right. You do that while I go to sleep. It's my cycle to rest since we didn't land on schedule." He yawned. "Much-earned rest too."

"Hey, I helped stop us from plowing into an asteroid." I joked but saw the truth of his statement. I had slept four hours before all the shit happened. Besides, Nik got cranky when he didn't sleep. "Go get some sleep; I have everything covered here. I will wake you when we get to the port."

He gave me a thumbs-up as he headed toward his cot. "Sounds like a plan. *Gute nacht*, Rebecca. Don't let pirates board the ship and kill me in my sleep."

I let out a quick guffaw. "That only almost happened once. Besides, there aren't any pirates in these parts. I assume… *Gute nacht*, Nik."

With that, Nik headed for his cot and I clicked buttons to put the ship into autopilot. I leaned back and took a deep breath that smelled of sweat, metal, and what I would call freedom. If only life had always been this simple.

CHAPTER TWO

Nik

The commlink buzzed, forcing me out of my dreams. I cursed under my breath. The hot chick just agreed to come back to my apartment after a drink at the bar. Why did I always wake up from a dream right before the good part? My dreams owed me better, as I never found a woman in bed next to me. Well, usually, but Rebecca left before I woke up, ignoring the fact that anything happened between us.

That was Rebecca for you: denying herself any happiness. But I understood. We both had demons to sort out.

The commlink buzzed again. I pressed the button,

mumbling, "Yeah, yeah, be there in a sec."

Blinking a few times, I tried to drag myself out of sleep. I wanted another hour of rest, perhaps two, but I didn't see that happening. Sleeping in seemed like a far-off fantasy, like the girl in my dreams.

My cot made up the entirety of my living quarters, so I crawled to the end and slid open the door. Nreff Nation ships didn't offer luxury because they focused on functionality. Quarters were only seven feet long, three feet wide, and about four feet tall. If you wanted to change in your quarters, you could, but as long as you were familiar with the person you flew with, such as Rebecca and me, changing in the corridor proved to be much easier.

I climbed out of my cot and opened the closet. Reaching in, I pulled out a pair of jeans and a gray shirt. I changed into them and placed my eye patch back on my right eye. Three years had passed since I lost my eye. I should have gone to a hospital right after the accident, but fear took the place of smart decisions. Now I kept a patch over the injury since we both feared a hospital would report us, even after all this time. Between the eye patch and Rebecca's scars, no one dared mess with us. Sometimes.

Wiping off the drool crust and popping two mints to get the taste of morning out of my mouth, I strolled over to the cockpit where Rebecca readied the ship to dock with the spaceport.

"All clear?" I poked my head in the cockpit to find the planet Unité below our ship. Seeing the beauty of every planet always made me feel warm inside. The planets gave the impression of serenity from so high up, although I realized that idea stood far from the reality of the situation. Crime filled the planets, between the swindlers, con artists, cheats, villains, and masterminds hiding around every corner. From here though, Unité appeared peaceful.

Rebecca nodded, her own deep sky-blue eyes observing the approaching planet. "Seems so."

The spaceport also came into view, the metallic object appearing as if by magic. Three dozen ships, if not more, took up room at the spaceport; each planet supported at least ten spaceports surrounding the planet. Not only did they house ships that came to the planet, but they housed military weapons and ships in case of an attack by a terrorist organization or another nation, not that anything ever happened.

Attacks from other nations didn't happen, as the Treaty of World Equality and Rights, TOWER, had kept each nation silent for over six hundred years. Though they re-signed the treaty every fifty years to make sure no government power went against the treaty and to make sure they didn't want to add anything. Now that I thought about it, the meeting should be coming up soon.

The two of us stayed silent as the spaceport got closer. Rebecca received the all clear to dock the ship moments earlier, and all seemed good to go.

Except nothing ever worked like that.

Something always went wrong during the docking process, whether it be the port needing to check out paperwork again, having us wait for at least an hour or two, or the thruster deciding not to turn off and us ramming into the side of the port, which made it appear like some kind of terrorist attack or something.

Yeah, fun times.

My muscles tensed as the thrusters stopped, and the port connected with our ship. The air equalized between the two like a sigh of relief. Rebecca and I started toward the port door, both of us still waiting for something to happen. Maybe this time we'd find ourselves in the clear.

Not a chance. We realized the moment we saw men starting to gather outside our porthole that trouble stood in our future. Four men, all dressed in dark red Regit Republic uniforms. A glance told me that none of them held any particular rank—just normal spaceport security guards, thank *Gott*.

They stopped in front of the door, and one of them slammed his fist against the glass. I wondered why they couldn't wait a few extra minutes until we opened the door. They either knew something or speculated. Why couldn't they ever greet us with women in bikinis and leis? Why couldn't my wish ever come true?

But I digress…

Rebecca pressed the communication button. "May we help you?" she inquired in a sweet, sarcastic tone—also known to me as her normal voice.

A stout man, a good decade or two younger than me, put his ugly face right up into the porthole. "Rebecca J. Smith, Nikolas K. Graham, by order of the Regit Republic, we order you to open your port door to be searched."

"All righty. Give us a moment. Kinda messy in here; don't want you to see our undergarments lying around." Rebecca switched the commlink off before we could hear any curse words, which I made out through the glass. She put the shield over the glass. *"Scheiße! Merde! Kuso! Tamade! Dermo! Shit!"*

"Wow, six languages. You must be frustrated," I commented, still amazed that she learned that many and kept them all straight in her head. She didn't just learn cuss words either but spoke fluently in each one. I only spoke English, German, and a little French, which explained why she only spoke in German to me, other than English.

"I will never say something was too easy ever again, even in my head," she murmured. *"Mierda."*

Ah, she forgot Spanish. So that made it seven. The burn of jealousy always lingered, though I could have studied while we smuggled items across the systems. While English made up the universal tongue, Rebecca's ability came in handy as the locals often used their native tongue to communicate things, assuming no one else understood them. We'd gotten out of some sticky situations because the locals figured Rebecca didn't understand what they were discussing. That normally happened in the YamaXie system because they didn't believe she spoke Japanese or Chinese.

I glanced back at the cargo and let out a breath. "We can't take long, and we have nowhere to hide the drug. If we get caught with Dasenni, we're screwed."

Dasenni didn't lie in the worst drug category in the galaxy, but the drug fell into the "If found in your possession, you will be arrested and put in jail for a few years" category. At small doses, one enjoyed a nice high. In large doses, well, that made for a different story. The liquid was also a pretty shade of sapphire blue, but that had no relevance over the situation. I thought it glowed an attractive color.

"We need to figure something out. I don't want to go to jail. If they run our prints, they'll see what happened in the Nreff Nation and send us back." Rebecca bit at her nails. "I'm not going back."

I didn't want to go back either. I could only imagine

what waited for us there—a few bullets to the head. Or worse. "I think we should have picked a less risky job if we didn't want to get caught."

She let out a brief laugh. "Not like we ever had a choice. Difficult to find real jobs when you are in a system illegally."

"But there isn't anything we can do now. Let's just hope they don't do a thorough search. We at least tried to mask it."

The soldier banged on the door again. Rebecca sighed. "Better open the door before he realizes something is going on."

"He already realizes something is going on; that's the problem." I leaned back against the wall in defeat, and I found no reason to stay proper with these folks.

"Who do you guess tipped them off?" she asked as she unlocked the port door.

"Who knows? Could be that we overshot the planet and came back. That looks fishy, not to mention having a Nreff Nation ship."

I mumbled a quick prayer to *Gott* who seemed to hate us as Rebecca opened the door. I held my breath, waiting to find the barrels of guns stuffed in my face. Surprisingly enough, they didn't go straight for their guns. The four men entered, their arms at their sides, a little too stiff for this neck of the woods. Something seemed off.

The leader of the four glared back and forth between Rebecca and me. His dark hair was gelled back and buzzed at the sides, a style few sported anymore. He couldn't have been in the military too long with that smartass look on his face, the same one I wore when I started out. *Gott*, why did I keep making myself feel old?

"Why were we not let in immediately?" he barked.

Yup, a smartass, young kid. If I still served in the military, I would have taught him a lesson for talking down to us. But alas, I wasn't, so I couldn't.

"As I said, I wanted to make sure none of my panties were out for your boys to see," Rebecca parried.

I rubbed my forehead. Even in the face of being thrown in prison, she still had that snarky attitude of hers. She had no fear.

The man slapped her. Hard. The action came out of nowhere, leaving me no time to react. It should have sent her flying to the ground, but after enduring the military academy and our old admiral, she had gained an immunity. Even so, she didn't deserve a hit like that. I stepped forward to retaliate, but the other three soldiers put their hands on their holsters, as if they would shoot if I made any approach to them.

"That was uncalled for," I grumbled.

"Shut your mouth!" the leader yelled back. "Or both of you will be taken in for obstructing an investigation!"

"We have done nothing. You are the ones who barged in here, spouting out orders and smacking innocent girls!" I yelled back, clenching my fist. Rebecca was right. I needed to learn how to stay cool like her. I found it surprising how calm she kept herself as she quietly stood there. Typically when dealing with people like this, she lost her temper and started yelling.

She started laughing.

"What's so funny?" The leader struck her again, but Rebecca caught his wrist right in front of her face. Oh *Gott*, her military background started to show its ugly head—that strict part of her that sent chills down my spine. She once held the rank of commander years ago. It came out when she faced people who gave her the most trouble, which in reality happened more often than not. That, and in another scenario that many frowned upon at the dinner table. She could be quite kinky.

"How dare you hit a ranking officer!" she shouted back as if he were a bug she wanted to squash under her foot. I gaped, confused at what *scheiße* she wanted to pull. But I said nothing, not wanting to ruin whatever idea swirled around in her head. It would end worse for us, but that was okay. If we kept distracting them, maybe they would forget to check our cargo.

The man's dark eyes widened. "What did you say?"

Rebecca pulled tags from out of her pocket. She

made the same conclusion as I did about these men: they were not from the Regit Republic but from the Nreff Nation. I tried not to glare at her, for what she was about to do would get us in more trouble than the Dasenni.

"I am Captain Franks of the Nreff Nation. I see that your men are undercover, trying to find something…" Rebecca threw down his hand in a violent rage. "But before you bark orders and slap women, you better make sure they aren't higher than you on the chain of command, Officer…"

"Jenson." His voice squeaked. He coughed. "Jenson, ma'am."

The other men froze, glancing back and forth at each other. They now found their leader harassed by Rebecca, who possessed a higher rank than any of them —and she did, three years ago. Now both she and I sat on the wrong side of the law. If they questioned all this, they would catch us as traitors to the nation, our act of treason coming back to bite us in the *arsch*.

So what in *der Weltraum* went through Rebecca's head? Then again, if they arrested us for the Dasenni, they would deport us either way.

She continued. "What are you looking for, Ensign Jenson?"

"It's lieutenant, ma'am."

"It will be ensign if you don't answer my question!"

I took a deep breath and leaned back against the metal panels. This wouldn't end well; things like this never did.

The soldier gulped. "The TOWER renewal is coming up. We're just making sure there isn't any reason it doesn't go smoothly."

I raised an eyebrow. Interesting concept, sending spies on each other to make sure all progressed according to plan, even though that in fact went against the TOWER. I found the irony amusing though. I could tell Rebecca felt the same because of the little smirk on her lips.

"All right. You're dismissed." She didn't let any of it affect the height of her stance. "If you let anyone know I'm here, you will jeopardize my mission and I will personally blame you. Do I make myself clear?"

He nodded. "Yes, ma'am, I understand." He spun on his heel and waved to the other three men, who jumped a little, startled, hoping the conversation wouldn't turn to them. "Move out men, we have the wrong ship."

I watched as they headed back into the port. In reality, they should have double-checked her numbers to make sure her story matched up. We could have stolen them or, better yet, committed treason, which we were. But then again, if Rebecca barked orders at me like that, as she once held the status of one of the most feared commanders in the Nreff Nation, if not all the systems, I wouldn't have double-checked the numbers either. Which she counted on.

But that didn't mean I forgave her for what she just risked.

Rebecca closed the port door after the men walked around the corner, then caught me staring at her.

"What's your problem?" she inquired with a bit of annoyance in her voice, which infuriated me even more.

I stepped away from the metal panels I was leaning against. "My problem? *Scheiße*, you know what my problem is. Why do you still have your tags?"

She held a relaxed posture, as if she didn't care. "Keepsake, I guess. Besides, they came in handy a few times now. You wouldn't believe how many Nreff Nation soldiers I've run into that are making sure the other systems hold up their side of the bargain."

I couldn't accept what she just said. For three years she threatened random soldiers by flashing her tags without even worrying about the implications.

I rubbed my forehead. "Are you kidding me? You've been committing treason by showing three-year-old tags?"

"Light treason, yeah. I guess if you put it that way. Didn't seem like a big deal since we're already wanted for treason."

I clenched my fist and tried not to overreact, trying to take her advice from earlier, but I reached my limit with this situation—especially since she'd kept it a secret from me all this time. "*Gott* damn it, Rebecca, if they found you aren't active, they would have killed you, or worse."

"They never check; you just have to act the part. I'm not stupid, Nik. I only use it on *blödmann* boys who assume they control the universe."

"Just because they are dumbasses doesn't mean they won't check your numbers. Think this through!"

Her face became more flushed. "Seriously? Why are you so worked up about this? Do I need to remind you what we have in our cargo hold?"

"But I asked you if you still had your tags the moment we left the nation. You told me no. You lied to me."

We'd promised each other no more lies so if anything went wrong, neither of us would be at fault. Though it would be a lie to say I told her all my secrets. But this was different—this could have gotten us arrested.

Her eyes turned cold. *Gott*, I hated it when she did that. Something clicked in her, and nothing I would say after would ever get through to her.

Slowly she answered, "I don't have my tags. Nothing would stop me from keeping his."

His. Chills went down my spine as I realized she told them her last name was Franks, not Kompen. Walrum Franks, our old comrade and Rebecca's former fiancé. I looked down, feeling like such a dummkopf. Of course she would have kept his, and I didn't have a problem with that, but she shouldn't have gone around recklessly showing them to any soldier she ran into. Nothing I could say would fix the tension that now filled the room, so I kept quiet.

Rebecca changed the subject as she swiveled around toward the cargo room. "Now, let's get this out of here before anyone else comes knocking on our door."

As if on cue, someone banged their fist on the port door. Rebecca took a deep, calming breath, but it didn't work. She slid the door open and yelled, "What?"

Rebecca's face turned white, as if she now stared at a ghost. I hurried to her side to see who came to our ship. As I stepped in the doorway, I understood why Rebecca found herself speechless.

"Oh, Jonathan?"

CHAPTER THREE

Rebecca

The man who stood in front of me was the last person I wanted to run into. Well, one of the last people, top ten at least. I stood in the doorway with my mouth open, looking like an idiot. Nik placed his hand on my shoulder, trying to calm me down. The action didn't work, as I started to shake.

"*Bonjour*, Nikolas, Rebecca." Jonathan stepped on the ship and wrapped the barrels he called arms around Nik and me. He smelled of thick cologne and sweat. I still found myself speechless, unable to respond to anything that was happening. Such a thing led to death in the field, so I was thankful we weren't in the military right now. I hated getting surprised, which made me want to hate him even more.

Laughing, Jonathan backed away from the two of us. "Aren't you going to say how much you missed me, Bex?"

I scowled at him for a moment longer, confused at the entire situation, then pulled my fist back and punched him. My knuckles cracked as if they had punched a metal wall, but I didn't care; it was worth it. He hit the ground with a loud thud. I hoped I broke something of his.

"*Connard!* Bastard!" I yelled down at him. After all this time, he showed up and acted like everything was fine—as if nothing had happened. His actions had led the Nreff Nation to consider us traitors and chased us out of the country.

And the reason I lost the love of my life.

"Rebecca," Nik began.

"*Non, non,* I deserved that." Jonathan pulled himself up. "And I know she didn't mean it."

Damn, he seemed fine. I ignored his last statement and started calculating all the events that led us here. When the job first started, I found it odd that someone called us out to here of all places. Now I understood. "You're the one who called us on this job, weren't you?"

He grinned that stupid smile of his I learned to hate

over all the years we had worked together. "*Mon ami,* still as smart as ever."

Rubbing my temples as a headache formed, I decided what I should do next. I knew I couldn't stay here, especially when I only saw red. Bad things happened when I saw red.

But that didn't solve what I should do next.

"You can help get the cargo ready with Nik." I shoved past him. "I'll be in the closest bar. Come get me when you're ready to go down the sky train."

With that, I left the two of them standing in the entrance to the ship. I would just deal with that *connard* later. I tried to take in a few more deep breaths, get my heart to stop beating so fast, but I didn't want to stop walking. His showing up brought back so many memories of a time I wanted to forget. I used him as a scapegoat for a lot of the hatred I gained over the years and blamed him for Walrum's death, but I knew the truth.

All that happened because of me.

I stopped in my tracks and stood in the middle of the corridor of the spaceport and took a few deep breaths, counting to ten each time. A few people bumped into me as they rushed past to get to their ship or to the sky train. I felt a tear in my eye. I wiped it away before it appeared on my cheek. If my fucking admiral taught me one thing, it was to never show pain.

Starting down the corridor again, I searched for the nearest bar. It shouldn't have been too far, as spaceports placed bars everywhere. It was the way spaceports made all their money, especially since people frequented them between layovers, after dealing with security, paperwork, and all that *scheiße*.

Glancing at the surrounding people, I noticed they were all families heading toward the cruise ships. Kids carried their little stuffed cartoon characters, probably going on a themed cruise. Most of the parents bickered with each other as their brats ran ahead of them. Although the thought of a cruise sounded enjoyable, I wouldn't go on one with a bunch of children. Then again, it would be a lie to say I never went on a cruise, but that involved capturing a pirate. It was a work trip and a stressful one at that.

I headed back down the corridor after locating the sign that pointed in the bar's direction. Thankfully I was able to calm myself down, and I didn't need to take one of my vials. I only had a couple left and would need to find some shady characters planet side without Nik finding out. Again.

Although I felt Jonathan would make that a little harder than I would like.

Just as I stepped into the bar, I noticed the four soldiers who had tried to search our ship turn a corner. Curious as to their real intentions, I followed them. Not one of my grandest ideas, but I wanted to distract myself from the ache that now formed in my chest.

Not to mention, their story sounded fishy, and I always feared the worst when I ran into Nreff spies.

I stayed a good number of meters behind them, walking as any other citizen on this spaceport. They didn't take notice since many people filled this area, and they headed straight to their destination without checking their surroundings. Foolish of them, but what could I have expected from such young officers? It surprised me that they received a mission like this at such a young age. The requirements to graduate from the academy must have lowered over the years, making me feel old, if I was honest. I turned thirty-three last week. Time just flew by.

The soldiers spun on their heels to face the door, and it slid open for them. Just as I approached, the door shut on me. I inspected the label: Communications Room. It was a small room, so if I stepped inside, they would notice right away. Hopefully no one had seen me before the door closed.

I needed to find another way to figure out who they went to contact since I knew it had to be someone in the Nreff Nation. A strange feeling about all this came over me, and I needed to know if my hunch was correct, as they had targeted us specifically.

I searched the rooms nearby and found a janitor's

closet. It was unlocked. Even if it wasn't, I could have jimmied the lock, but this saved me time. I entered the closet and searched to see if the room contained a ventilation shaft. It did—today was my lucky day.

I locked the door behind me, making sure no one would walk in on what I was about to do. Climbing up on the shelving units, I pushed the screen up and pulled myself into the shaft. I crawled over to the vent in the adjacent communication room where the four soldiers were.

The crawl didn't take that long, which I thanked *Gott* for since I could barely breathe from the tight squeeze. The sad part was that this didn't mark the first time, nor my last, I would have to crawl in a shaft. At least this time I knew I wouldn't fall into a firing range. Another reason I hated Jonathan: it seemed like whenever he came into the picture, I found myself in a vent.

I peered down through the slits, trying to get a glimpse of who they were video chatting with, but I couldn't see anything. I hoped that I could hear whomever they had called, then maybe I could identify their boss. Since it took a bit for the call to go through, they had just received an answer when I got above the room.

"Sir, we found her. She was on a ship that had just arrived to Unité. She was with another man, who I believe was Captain Nikolas Anders," the lieutenant stated.

So they recognized us. *Verdammt*.

"Very good. I want you to make sure that ship doesn't leave. I will send men to retrieve them soon," the other man said.

Closing my eyes, I felt my heart race and my entire body shake. *Scheiße*. I couldn't have an attack here. I had no room to maneuver my hand to get to my vials. Taking in a few deep breaths, tears fell from my eyes.

I knew that voice; I knew that gut-wrenching voice anywhere. How it was possible, I did not understand. I didn't know how he was able to reach his deadly claws all the way out here, but somehow he managed it. It didn't surprise me; it was only a matter of time before he found me and pulled me back into the special hell he had created just for me.

Sebastien Wilde, my old admiral, had found me at last.

My body shook stronger as memories came flooding back. It wasn't a full-blown seizure, but it was picking up like one. If I wasn't careful, they would hear and find me up here.

Not that I wasn't already screwed.

I wondered how many other Nreff Nation soldiers I had run into over the years he had hired. I messed up this time though, letting carelessness get the better of me. It didn't matter now. I wouldn't be finding a way out of this.

Who was I kidding? I would find some way. Four against one, it would take more than that to capture me, and Sebastien, or Bastien as he made me call him, expected that of me. He counted on the element of surprise, and now he didn't have that either.

"Yes, sir, we will port lock the ship. They won't be leaving anytime soon," the leader responded.

"Good," Bastien replied with a satisfying tone. I imagined his smile, and more tears fell down my face. "Keep a close eye on them. I don't need her slipping away again. If you mess this up, your next task won't be so easy."

The leader gulped. If he had worked with Bastien before, he knew no empty threats came out of Bastien's mouth. I had experience with his threats, and he took none of them lightly. I tried not to think about what he had in store for me after what lengths he went through to find me.

Because I was his little *Puppe*.

"Y-yes, sir." The man clicked off the video chat, and the four of them left the room.

I backed up and jumped down into the storage room again. Fumbling through my pockets, I found my little black case that held my vials. I opened it up and took one of them, quickly downing the painkilling medicine.

Sitting down and leaning my head against the

shelves, I took a few deep breaths, waiting for it to take effect. It would be a few minutes, but it was all I had.

Years had gone by since I first started taking this opioid medicine, back when I still served in the military. It was a derivative of morphine, known as morphine-B, that didn't dwindle in effects after long-term use, although they still used regular morphine on the black market since it was much cheaper. Sometimes drug dealers mixed this derivative with the old morphine to lower production cost and labeled it as the true deal. I stayed on the lookout for those, as that could end badly for me, with each dose having a lesser effect. Then I might overdose.

In the past, I took it for the anxiety of having to face Bastien every day and to help me with what I would consider to be PTSD. I lived in constant terror that he would find me, and now I knew my hunch was correct.

He could find me anywhere.

Now that I could rationally go through my thoughts, I realized what sort of *la shi* I was in. I was stuck here, our ship nonfunctioning, Jonathan sticking his grimy fingers in our business, with Nreff soldiers on their way.

What the hell was I going to do now?

I stood and opened the door, checked the hallway to make sure the four soldiers had left the area, then hurried out of the room and headed for the bar. Now I would have to order something nonalcoholic because the medicine did not interact with alcohol very well. Hopefully Nik wouldn't notice.

I debated going back and telling him what I had found, but I felt he would take note of my altered state and start questioning me. Since I never told him about the drug, I was too afraid of what he might do. I needed the drug to sleep at night—he didn't understand the horror Bastien put me through. So I took it when I lay in my cot right before bed, which might not be the safest way, but I wasn't that afraid of death. Nik made that clear earlier.

No, the fear of being caught outranked that of dying.

CHAPTER FOUR

Nik

I watched as Rebecca stormed off. I sighed, knowing how long it would take before she could see straight again. She usually kept herself calm, finding her own way to not let the anger get ahold of her, which she did by cooking, but that didn't always work. By the time I made it to the bar, she would have already started a fight with some innocent person, gotten the port guards involved, and all that fun stuff. Though was anyone innocent when it came down to it?

Turning my attention back to Jonathan, I studied him. Three years had passed since the last time we crossed paths, but he appeared the same, just a little scruffier.

His mocha-colored hair contrasted with his pale skin, and his olive eyes were bright, always seeming cheerful in even the darkest of times. I found myself a little jealous that his hair hadn't grayed. He grinned, as if tricking Rebecca into coming here had been the highlight of the century. Although I couldn't believe he didn't simply tell us to come here instead of having us transport an illegal substance. I did understand that Rebecca would never have agreed to come.

He stood in the corridor, waiting for me to speak. I realized what he needed me to do and the only reason he sought me out.

The Nreff Nation had reason to believe that they could find evidence against our old Admiral Sebastien Wilde and his affiliation with human experimentation, and they needed to arrest him before the re-signing of the TOWER. And, for some odd reason, Admiral Jacques Bardon still wanted me to help Jonathan capture him.

"Come help me unload." I motioned him toward the back of the ship, which was only three meters away. If those soldiers searched our ship, it wouldn't have taken long to find our illegal cargo. "And you can tell me what we need to do."

He laughed, entertained that I figured it all out already. He was always in a good mood, which solved the mystery of why Rebecca didn't get along with him.

She was a bit—how would one put it?—passive-aggressive. And sarcastic. And sometimes temperamental…

"*Mon amie*, can't get anything past you now, can I?"

I didn't reply to that remark, knowing that there was no place Rebecca and I could hide before someone would come looking for us and drag us back into the service. Unfortunately, what Jonathan came here for, Rebecca knew nothing about. It was one of those secrets I kept from her. And I felt terrible about it.

"So, Admiral Bardon still needs me. I don't expect Rebecca will be too happy about me leaving her." I lifted some boxes, one too many, but I couldn't confess that.

Jonathan grabbed a couple more. "Jacques needs her."

I about dropped the boxes. "Are you kidding me?"

He shook his head. "No. She's in as deep as we are. Besides, if this works—if we find his association with the human experimentations in the Nreff Nation and find where they are taking place—they will lift the charges of treason on all our heads. But in order for that to happen, Rebecca has to help."

I let out a breath. I didn't want to hear that. Rebecca had nothing to do with this. Hell, she didn't even know about the mission we received before we graduated from the academy. "You understand if she found out about that, the truth would shatter her heart. None of us told her, not even Walrum, and he was her fiancé. She's not one of us, and she's not part of the mission. She simply got caught in the cross fire."

"Is that why you stayed with her? You feel responsible for what happened?" Jonathan looked me over, as if searching for an answer.

I shook my head. "That's not fair. You knew I had feelings for her before Walrum made the first move. She doesn't deserve this. She did not understand that the admiral she served was under suspicion for crimes against humanity. If we had told her the truth—"

"It would have jeopardized our mission."

I took a deep breath. I found myself in the middle of a big mess, and I hated it. "She's not part of this, Jonathan. There is no way. We kept a close eye on Sebastien—whatever he is doing, he's doing it way, way under the radar. If he'd taken Rebecca with him on any of those missions, we would have been able to track him."

Jonathan didn't say a word but nodded. "Yeah, you are right. But that doesn't mean it was our fault she was on that mission. That *fils de pute* Sebastien was the one who sent us to die. If he'd known she was innocent, then he should have kept her out of it. Blame him, not yourself."

"No, he guessed she was with us—we were all so

close. We shouldn't have…," I began, but stopped, knowing I shouldn't go on.

"Let the two of them become a couple?"

Jonathan realized where I was going with the conversation. She and Walrum had become intimate and Walrum proposed. He shouldn't have blurted it out one night to Sebastien, because not long after that he sent us on the sabotaged mission. The proposal was the reason he thought she was one of us.

Jonathan went on, "We told Walrum that we wouldn't endanger her if anything happened. It wasn't our fault."

"Yes but she shouldn't have had to suffer for it either," I shot back. "But that still doesn't answer why you need her to help us."

Jonathan seized the other side of the box containing the rest of the Dasenni, and we carried it out to where he had two lifts ready. "We need her because she was the only one who could get close to Sebastien. They had a connection stronger than any of us knew about, and I have a feeling that after all this time, he would take her back as one of his close officers."

Touching my eye patch, I recalled the day they captured us and all the torture we went through. "No. I don't believe that. He almost had her killed. Why would he take her back?"

Jonathan pulled out a tablet. "I don't think he would kill her. Look what I found." He pushed a few buttons.

"You and me, we have wanted ads, stating dead or alive. It doesn't matter; whatever is easiest for the treason we committed. As for Rebecca…" He scrolled down. "Says they must take her alive. Even for the officers who arrest her, they can't hurt her or even speak to her. Our admiral wants her for himself."

I stared at the tablet. Why would he have gone through all this trouble after sending her on a mission that he himself had sabotaged? Did he know of her innocence, and if so, why would he have sent her on the mission? It made no sense, but that sounded like Sebastien—always a few steps ahead. "I don't understand…"

Jonathan motioned with his hands. "Neither do I. I just know that he doesn't want her hurt. She has a chance to get close to him and find the evidence we need. He wouldn't suspect her, not after all this time."

We stepped back on the ship, snatching the last of the cargo. "And how do we do that? I presume Jacques wouldn't want us to tell her the truth, just in case."

"We can tell her about the experiments and how we need to get evidence before they renew the peace treaty. We need to make sure a war doesn't break out. She would listen to us then. We need not tell her that this entire time we were spies for another admiral in the Nreff Nation."

He had a point; she didn't have to know that we were

part of another mission. She only had to know that time was of the essence. "Speaking of which, how did you get back on this mission without being killed or charged for treason?"

"I went straight to Admiral Jacques Bardon. He understood the situation and has kept me under the radar for the past three years. I've been helping him with missions, which is hard when they placed wanted signs everywhere in the system. But Jacques has sent me to get you and Rebecca to help us finish this mission once and for all."

Now that he mentioned it, he appeared tired, as if having to worry that someone could recognize him at any moment and he wouldn't be able to talk his way out of it. I didn't envy what he did. In fact, I admired his determination to finish this mission.

"Even if she wanted to help, she won't trust you. She assumes you were the one who sabotaged the mission—that you were a spy."

He raised an eyebrow. "*Pardon*? Why's that?"

There were many reasons, among the fact he disappeared the moment we got out of the prison. We never heard from him again, and now he's shown up out of nowhere. "Well, she knows it wasn't me or her or Walrum. That just leaves you."

He laughed, although I doubted it was out of true amusement. "Also leaves Sebastien."

I shook my head. "Never occurred to her he could have done it."

"She trusts that *pute*? How?"

Good question. "I've tried to bring that up before, but she just fidgets and changes the subject."

"Hmm. That's interesting…" Jonathan stood there, pondering for a moment. "On top of her wanted poster saying he wants her alive, sources tell me he is looking for her. Not us. Just her. He couldn't care less if they catch us."

I stared at him with my eye, rather surprised. "So you think there's something else going on? That she could know something or at least know where to find him?"

"I think for part of the mission we should leave her in the dark."

It made sense, but I didn't want to think of what that man might do. Rebecca was a strong woman, but that didn't mean she wouldn't be in danger. "So we would do this mission together, like a reunion."

Jonathan patted me on the back. "Yes, like a reunion but with other people that you and Rebecca don't know. We need a crew, after all."

Like Rebecca would agree to that. She hated working with others—I doubted she would even agree to travel with Jonathan. "But it's her we're using to get close to Sebastien? For whatever thing he thinks she knows?"

"Oui."

I rubbed my face. He was the last person I wanted near Rebecca, given the way she reacted to him. I couldn't even imagine what he would do to her, especially if he thought she helped us spy on him all those years ago. But all the clues pointed to him not wanting to hurt her. If that were the case, why did he let her become captured in the first place? "Fine, but it will not be easy getting her to agree, especially if there is a crew."

"Don't worry, *mon amie*." Jonathan smiled, which I knew always meant trouble. "I have a plan."

CHAPTER FIVE

Rebecca

"An alcohol-free beer. *Danke*." I sat down at the bar in the corner, away from any other customers. By the looks they gave me, they probably thanked the heavens I found a spot so far from them. Nik said I possessed an aura that made people nervous. I didn't understand what he meant by that, and he only laughed when I pressed further. The raven-haired bartender nodded and grabbed a bottle out of the cooler and poured the liquid into a glass. Thank goodness, as I didn't want Nik to see me with an alcohol-free beer.

Once he set the glass in front of me, I placed credits on the table, adding a couple extra for the man, letting him know I didn't want anyone to bother me again until the glass stood empty. He nodded again. A man of few words, I liked him.

I took a large gulp of the beer, wishing for a Nreff Nation lager instead. I missed drinking instead of always having to abstain due to the drug I took. Every time Nik and I ate out, I would offer to go to the bar to get our drinks, hiding the fact I couldn't drink alcohol.

At least I knew how to act inebriated.

There were a few times where I consumed alcohol, and the hangover of that was ridiculously painful. I hated dealing with hangovers, not to mention that mixing alcohol with morphine-B increased the risk of overdosing. I then couldn't take my next dose until the side effects of the drug withdrawal were noticeable.

I wanted to get the medication to wean me off the drug. That was easy nowadays as long as you went to the doctor first. My problem was that I was a wanted criminal and doctors would check my DNA before treating me. That, and the black market didn't sell the medicinal cure as they wanted you to keep coming back for more.

Taking another sip, I tried not to reflect on how this all happened because of my admiral and the things he had put me through. Now to discover after all this time that he'd never stopped searching for me and discovered where I was hiding.

I knew that that *drecksau* would find me eventually. He wanted me in his clutches, and I imagined how frustrated he has grown since I slipped away. The thought made me smile a bit, even though I realized he would punish me for running, just like the other times. This time would be worse as three years had passed. It was his own fault for sending us on a mission doomed to fail. That mission was just so he could prove a point.

That I was his.

Gagging at the image, I took another gulp, hoping the liquid would somehow erase the memories, even though the drink contained no alcohol. At least the morphine-B helped me to deal with the panic attacks even if my body was now addicted and went into withdrawal anytime I missed a dose. I gladly paid that price to get him out of my mind, even for only a little while.

When I saw Jonathan, I had been so afraid that Bastien had sent him. But that was wrong. It wouldn't make any sense for him to do that—not since I learned his backstory many years before.

"TOWER is for the safety of all peoples in our systems and those systems we align with—be proud to have a government that respects you and yours."

I glanced up at the screen in the bar and let out a quaint laugh. *Gott* why did they continue with that *scheiße*? People didn't care about the ads and ignored them. I hated hearing the ads as they were a big waste of everyone's time—not to mention I didn't give a damn. I doubted any system followed all the laws it contained. The Nreff Nation sure didn't.

Someone touched my shoulder, and I whirled around, flinging open my butterfly knife and placing the blade under my assailant's throat. Nik just smiled.

"We allow no weapons in here," the bartender ordered. "Put the knife away before I call security."

"Don't worry." Nik didn't move a muscle, knowing I still might cut him. He had seen how I reacted when people snuck up behind me before. I did not understand what passed through his mind to pull a stunt like that here. "She won't hurt me."

I held the knife under his chin a moment longer while my mind raced. After my fear of Bastien finding me overwhelming my senses, it took me a moment to realize I was safe at the moment. Putting the knife away, I glimpsed at the bartender. "And here I didn't think you could speak."

He muttered something about Nreff Nation people and headed over to where a new couple sat down.

Nik took a seat next to me. "How many drinks have you had?"

"This is the only one." I nodded to the pint that sat in front of me.

Nik tried to reach for the glass, but I grabbed it and

downed the rest. He couldn't taste the liquid or he would find it was nonalcoholic.

"Geez, you need to learn to be a team player and share."

I rolled my eyes. "Speaking of which, where's Jonathan?"

"Getting the cargo sent down to his facility. He wants us to join him and travel planet side for dinner."

He hadn't offered a yes or no question, but I answered anyway. *"Nein."*

Nik let out a sigh. "Rebecca, the mission wasn't his fault. There wasn't anything he could have done. Need I remind you we were there as well? None of us could have done it. We don't know who sabotaged that mission."

I brought my glass to my lips, drinking the last tiny drop. I knew the truth to his statement, but I also knew that his involvement with Admiral Bardon had led to that mission. "How did he get here?"

"What do you mean?"

"How did he end up in the Regit Republic, requesting illegal substances? Hell, how did he even figure out how to contact us?"

Nik shrugged. "I don't know. Looks like we will have to accept his dinner invitation to find out, huh?"

I already realized what the invitation entailed. Although I recognized I had a lot to do with the act of treason we committed, I still couldn't bring myself to forgive Jonathan. That, and I just didn't enjoy being near him, even when we had served together.

I debated telling Nik what I had overheard with the Nreff soldiers, but he wouldn't understand. He didn't know the things that Bastien and I did—the things I was "privy" to, as Bastien always put it. I didn't want Nik to learn the truth, and if I told him Bastien had been looking for me all this time, he would want to understand why. I couldn't bring myself to tell him all that, so I kept the information to myself even if we had promised each other no secrets. I would find a way out of this without Nik knowing that something had happened.

"Is he paying?" I asked.

"I believe so."

Standing up, I gave in to the invitation. "Fine, but I'm buying the most expensive thing—that's vegan anyway."

"That's my *mädchen*." Nik rubbed the top of my head, but I smacked his hand. I hated when he did that and he knew it. He always messed up my short hair, and it pissed me off. I shoved him forward to lead the way toward where Jonathan waited for us to take the sky elevator down. This would be a long ride, I could already tell.

I always found sky elevators an interesting invention

and one of the most used. The machine looked like a tram, but instead of running on land, it went from the spaceport to the station in the city. The spaceports rotated with the planet and almost appeared like pins sticking to the side of a ball. How the hell those worked engineering or physics-wise, I did not know. I stayed away from math-related subjects and focused on tactics and special-operations classes. My heart yearned for fighting and taking out criminals and pirates. Ironic, really, as I was now a criminal.

I took the window seat and waited for the elevator to get going. The planet Unité seemed calm below, shining blue and green, almost like the old photos of Earth. I knew, though, that the planet was anything but calm. Unité was known for its riots and drugs, which would come in handy for me later. The Regit Republic tried to keep problems under control, but mostly they let it be. They didn't want to waste the military men when the peace treaty signing was coming up.

Although a war hadn't happened in six hundred years, nothing seemed to slow down after they signed the piece of paper. They called it the New Space Race, which caused the scientific advancements, space travel, hyperdrives; all of it was to stay one step ahead of the other in case either side breaks the treaty and attacks the other. They might have claimed the war had ended, but I knew that such a thing never stopped in people's minds. The fear of war drove everything we saw.

I always wondered if this universe, this *Weltraum*, would be a better place if one power stood up to the others and defeated them. Everything underneath one rule seemed like a good idea, and the government could take a moment to worry about the people instead of their military power. So many people suffered, yet the governments did nothing about it on either side. But who would be successful in taking over this 'raum, I didn't know.

"I'm surprised you agreed to come to dinner, Bex." Jonathan sat across from me. I didn't turn my attention away from the window.

"Don't call me that. No one calls me that anymore. And I only agreed because you promised me food. Delicious, expensive food."

He scoffed at my comment. "You are as cold as ever, but yes, I will pay for dinner. But I do have one request."

"Of course you do." I swiveled around to face him, curious if he would tell me what all this entailed.

He leaned forward. "You listen to my proposal during dinner, think about it, then get back to me tomorrow morning."

"I can tell you now, the answer is *nein*."

Nik sighed. "Rebecca…"

Jonathan waved his finger. "Ah, ah. You can't give

me an answer until tomorrow, even while waving around the fact you can speak so many languages. We understand. Stop showing off, *ma chéri*."

I stuck up a finger at him. They couldn't blame me; Bastien made sure I possessed the same skill as he had for talking to different dignitaries. I always wondered why he never taught Nik, Jonathan, or Walrum, but the notion of him even trying to get the three of them to sit still long enough to learn a language made me understand why he gave up. At least they each spoke a bit of three languages.

Jonathan went on. "So, in the meantime, let's catch up. What have you two been up to?"

"Smugglin'. Better question is what have you been up to, Jonathan? Seems that you turned your back on the Nreff Nation, having a drug ring in Regit territory and all."

"I've been out almost as long as you have. I didn't have any loyalty to them just like you. I only served to get by. Pay was like no other, which helped my family out."

That wasn't why I served, not that he would ever understand that. I had loyalty to the nation, and I never sent a penny back to my family. He should have realized I never spoke once about them, but he would have had to listen to me while I talked to realize that. "Still doesn't answer why you are here."

"Friend of a friend of a friend got me transported out here. And since then I haven't had a worry in the world."

I knew how that went all too well. "Threaten everyone you meet. I get it."

He chuckled. "You are as lively as ever. Nik, you must have so much fun with her."

"Oh, tons," Nik sarcastically replied. I shot him a look. "You know I'm joking. We have fun, Jonathan, when the ship is working or not at gunpoint or not in a fistfight, or…"

"He understands," I interjected.

Nik smiled and leaned back. "It's better than the alternative, going back into the military."

"I could toast to that." Jonathan straightened up in his seat and leaned forward. "Word has it there will be a war and they will not sign the treaty."

I shook my head. Not that nonsense again. The treaty and war was the only thing people talked about nowadays. "The war would last two hours with one man down and lots of talking. You know how those things go. The threat is all that holds; no action ever takes place. No one wants to break that treaty."

"No, this is the real deal. All powers are ready for a full-blown war this time. Don't you feel the tension? Don't you hear the whispers?"

I sighed and recited what they taught us in school.

"Yes, but they are just rumors. There hasn't been a real war for over six hundred years. Once the groups developed into different powers, they searched up in the stars for more powers, and that is how the Gero-Euro-Russ Union became the Nreff Nation, the Americas and Australia to Regit Republic, Asia into YamaXie, and the Middle East and Africa to the Zalia Democracy. Each power had a system of planets they controlled, and every fifty years since the big war they have been signing the TOWER, and each time a threat that the paper won't get signed comes up, people scream war. We all took that same history class in the military academy. But it's not like anyone will know how to fight in an all-out war."

Jonathan shrugged as he leaned back in his seat. "I'm just saying there's been a lot of tension these past few years. It wouldn't be surprising if there were a lot of spies trying to find some kind of evidence for the treaty not to be signed. Then a nation can gain more power. We have been at an impasse for so long, Rebecca, can't you see that?"

I didn't answer because, if I was honest, I knew the truth of that statement. At first all the powers were striving to explore space, terraform planets, and claim systems as their own, but now that humans had inhabited all the ones that were within fathomable distance, what else could they gain? War seemed like the only way to win power and to take another system's area, but the way to do that was to find evidence against the treaty so they couldn't sign it.

I knew where they could find some of that evidence.

We arrived on Unité without another word about war. Jonathan filled out the rest of the paperwork. I didn't complain; I hated typing in all that *scheiße*. Everyone lied on it, and they knew it, so I didn't understand the point. I hated formality. Ask anyone I ever worked with. Things should just get to the point. One would waste less time, and everything would run efficiently for once.

Jonathan led us to a restaurant which, surprisingly, appeared pleasant. I thought he would just take us to a food truck like he used to back in the day. We used to laugh about it because every time he picked dinner, he led us down some weird alleyway with food trucks and we all thought someone might mug us, not that we kept anything in our possession. And if anyone crossed us, they would have one good wake-up call.

The waiter sat us down and handed us the menus on some nice-smelling paper. I sniffed the paper again. It smelled like fine chocolate. I didn't think you could find chocolate on many planets anymore. I would have to get my hands on some while restocking the ship for food. My mouth watered at the thought.

"This place must cost a pretty credit. Maybe you should tell us more about your enterprise," I commented as I saw one of the more expensive items on the menu. "Salmon, ah yes. I haven't seen that on the market. Too bad I don't eat meat."

Jonathan raised an eyebrow. "Are you still on that whole vegan nonsense? You do realize that any animal product or byproduct isn't an actual animal. Meat's made in a lab."

I shook my head. "No, there was that investigation where they found real animal meat on a few of the planets. Businesses have been lying."

"The odds of eating real meat are about a million to one, Rebecca. Get over it."

"I'd rather not worry that the meat I eat had killed an animal, thank you very much. I have been a vegan for years, and nothing you say will change that." Jonathan knew that he couldn't change my mind. No one could.

"Whatever," said Jonathan. "Anyway, let's order drinks before we talk business."

I had known Jonathan for many years, and we had spent many a nights drinking and laughing and having a merry ol' time. In these great times, I recalled that only one drink made him spill out anything you wanted him to say.

"Why don't we get a bottle of some scotch? Celebrate our reunion here," I suggested.

I hadn't drunk scotch for some time, since I hadn't been drinking anything for the past few years. It was an ancient drink and not actual scotch since you had to live on Earth for that, and the planet hadn't seen humans for centuries. But they named a region Scotland on the planet Charlottetown, so they kept the term.

Checking the time, I realized only two hours had gone by since I took my drug. Shit, maybe I shouldn't have suggested hard alcohol. I would just have to sip the liquor and keep pouring for Nik and Jonathan so they assumed I was drinking the same amount. After a few servings, they wouldn't notice a thing.

Jonathan smiled. "Well, someone is coming around. Why don't we do that? I haven't had a good scotch in years."

He ordered the drink, and we ordered our dinners as well. The waiter brought out the scotch and three glasses.

Nik opened the bottle, and I could smell the smoky undertones drifting from the fumes. It would go great with a cigar, but I felt this place didn't allow smoking, not to mention the price of cigars these days belittled that of even chocolate.

One could only imagine how much I paid for morphine-B. There was a reason I talked Nik into letting me handle the finances—he never noticed the missing money. That fact, however, was also why we never had enough to fix the ship.

"Here's to friendship." Jonathan held up his scotch,

and we knocked cups and took a sip.

I lifted mine up. "And here's to new futures, whether it be war or peace."

"Prost!" Both Jonathan and Nik agreed and knocked glasses again.

We set the drinks down.

Jonathan chuckled. "We better keep some drinking for later in the night, or I will not remember what I was going to propose to you two."

"Well, then why don't you just discuss the mission now? You know how I hate small talk."

Nik let out a brief laugh, then tried to mask it with a cough. I shot him a look, and he grinned but didn't add a word. I presumed he already knew about the proposal Jonathan would make since the two of them already had time to talk. They just needed to work together to convince me. And I was curious how they would go about such a thing.

Jonathan got right down to it. "I need you two to help me take a ship over the border into the Nreff Nation."

I raised my eyebrow. "You want us to smuggle some stuff over the border. That's all?"

"Yup. Easy as that." Jonathan took a sip of his scotch.

I studied him. When we used to play cards, he would always take a drink when he was lying. "Well, first off, you would be a raving lunatic to smuggle something into the Nreff Nation, especially if the three people doing so were wanted fugitives. Second, I call your bluff. Tell me the truth, Jonathan, or I will ask for my quinoa bowl to go and walk out of here." I put my hands on the table as if I was about to stand.

Jonathan held out his hand. "*Attente!* Fine. I'll tell you what's going on." He glanced at Nik, and they seemed to signal something back and forth.

I leaned back in the seat. "Trying to rewrite your plan through brainwaves or what?"

"Well, if you were just a little easier to talk to, we wouldn't have to try so hard," Jonathan spat back.

I raised an eyebrow, surprised by his lash of anger. Jonathan always remained relaxed in every situation. Whatever the topic entailed, it had to have been important. "Tell me the truth then. That's the only way to get me to listen."

Jonathan rubbed the scruff on his face and then looked me straight in the eyes. "You know of the TOWER being signed in the coming months, yeah?"

"Of course. We were just discussing it."

"Well, the nations are trying to find any excuse to start a war, and they might have it…" Jonathan let out a breath.

I glanced between the two of them. "And what's that?"

Nik was the one to answer. "Human experimentation. We have word that there is human experimentation happening on Nreff Nation soil."

My heart skipped a beat. Did they know? Did they know the truth? I took a sip of the scotch. "And?"

"And I know of a guy on Regenwelt who can get us evidence. If we can retrieve that evidence and give it to the Nreff Nation, we may stop it before word reaches the other systems." Jonathan stopped as the waitress came with our dinner. We all remained quiet as she placed the plates in front of us.

So they didn't know the entire truth. I took a deep breath, letting my heart stop feeling as if it would leap out of my chest.

The waitress left us, and we continued the conversation. I picked at my braised brussels sprouts. "So you need us to smuggle information within the Nreff Nation. How do we even know they would believe us? We're wanted fugitives, after all."

"Exactly. With this information, we could get our citizenship back, take away any bounties that are on our head. This could be our freedom, Rebecca. All we need to do is succeed and stop a war."

I peeked over at Nik. "What do you think?"

Nik stirred in his chair. "I guess it's a possibility that we should consider."

"You can't be serious. They will kill us."

"*Au contraire*, I expect we can win this." Jonathan placed his fork down and leaned forward. "But,

Rebecca, you have to help us. If you don't do this, then none of us can. All this is up to you."

CHAPTER SIX

Nik

"I don't know, Nik, this mission seems risky, and succeeding doesn't mean that we will get our names cleared. It only means that we will be helpless if they want to lock us up in prison for good." Rebecca slurred her words a little as we stumbled toward her room in the hotel.

Damn, I wished we had checked in a place as nice as the restaurant we ate at. Instead, we got a rathole of a hotel where only smugglers and prostitutes stayed.

I guess we fit in and found ourselves used to such accommodations…

A woman standing in the doorway to her room

winked at me, her teeth stained yellow from illegal cigarettes, hair appearing as if she hadn't seen a comb in over a century. Her clothes hung off her skeletal body, which was likely because of some STD. I stayed close to Rebecca, hoping none of the other women who appeared like her would try to hit on me. I mean, all power to women who wanted to express themselves, but they aren't going to express that sort of thing with my body.

I didn't even want to speculate about the things that happened in these rooms. I couldn't wait to get on with this mission so we could sleep in some nice ship—if Jonathan got us a nice ship.

Turning to Rebecca and trying to ignore the old man in the hallway, wearing just some boxers, I went on. "But wouldn't it be nice to go home? Where we belong? And away from here… I miss the nation."

She let out a short laugh, not even indicating the surrounding people gave her any discomfort. "You miss not having to pay a fortune for good beer."

I couldn't disagree with that, but my priorities stood a little higher than just beer. "I miss home, you know? I don't think I would want to go back into the military, but I would like to get a legal job. Make some money. If our names are cleared and with our military background, we could get any job we want."

Rebecca didn't say a word as she unlocked her room.

She kept her eyes away from me, as if deep in thought.

I bit my lip, debating if I wanted to push further. She hated to be questioned, took it as a trial of some sort, so I always tried to stay away from asking her too many questions. However, this time it appeared like she wanted to talk about something.

Clutching her hand, I squeezed it. "What's wrong?"

She shrugged as I followed her into her hotel room. Small, like I figured. The furniture consisted of a bed with crappy sheets, a thin blanket for a comforter, and a bathroom the size of a shower, like one of those all-in-one things. The whole room grossed me out. Even the beige paint peeled away from the walls, as if disgusted by what it had to witness. Another reason I wanted a better life—nicer living space.

Collapsing on the bed, which sounded like it hurt because of how boardlike the mattress was, Rebecca pulled her butterfly knife out of her pocket and swung the blade around. "I don't want to cause you any trouble, Nik, but I also don't want to be arrested again. I just need some time to think about it, okay?"

"But all this isn't just about the three of us, this has to do with stopping a war from happening. A war that could kill millions, if not more. You think any of the systems will hold back? I really doubt the Regit Republic would."

She looked up at me for a second and rolled her eyes.

"You have to be so self-righteous, don't you?"

Giving her my most offended look as I sat on the edge of the bed, I placed my hand on my chest. "Me? No, never."

Rebecca threw her pillow at my face. "Stop being such a dummkopf."

The pillow hit my face, snagging my eye patch string and pulling it off my head.

Rebecca got up and grabbed the eye patch. "Oh *Gott*, Nik, I'm sorry I didn't mean to—"

I placed my finger on her lips. "It's fine. Don't worry about it." I took the eye patch and put it back on to cover up my scarred-up eye socket. "See, all better."

We sat on the bed, inches apart. Time didn't seem to move, and I wanted to move in and kiss those pink lips of hers. I thought about it almost every time I saw her.

"Do you want some water? I could use some water." I stood up and snatched a bottle.

Rebecca ruffled her beautiful ruby hair as she set her knife down on the nightstand. "Yeah, I could use some."

I twisted open the cap and took a drink. As I handed it to Rebecca, I chuckled. "You know, this bottle of water probably costs us the same amount as the room."

She nodded. "Yeah, that's true. But I'd rather pay for the bottle of water than trust whatever comes out of the faucet."

I knew she had a point, especially since I even feared to shower with the stuff, but I hadn't had a real shower in weeks because on a ship there wasn't much room for water. It just misted, and that didn't leave you feeling clean at all.

Rebecca set the bottle down, and I leaned back next to her. "So, will you at least think about the mission?"

She placed her hand on mine. Her skin felt warm to the touch. I stroked the scars on her hands, scars from years of missions in the Nreff Nation. Looking me straight in the eye, Rebecca whispered. "I guess on the bright side, we would work close together still."

With that, she leaned in and kissed me. I was taken aback, surprised that she would do such a thing. She had a small amount to drink, so whatever this was, she had been holding it back for quite some time. I pulled her in closer, deepening the kiss. *Gott* I wanted her. I needed to press my lips against every inch of her body. But I had one problem—she was once my best friend's fiancée, a friend who died three years earlier. A friend I felt like I betrayed as Rebecca and I grew closer. Not only that, but I knew he still lived in her mind.

Rebecca pulled off her shirt, the black lace bralette she wore looking perfect against her milky skin. Even though scars covered her body, scars that she would never tell me the details of, I still considered her the most gorgeous woman I had ever seen. I traced my fingers along them, touching the uneven groves. *Gott damn*, if I wanted to end this, I would have to do so quickly. I knew I wouldn't have the willpower to stop if this progressed.

But then again, Rebecca was a strong, independent woman. If she wanted to do this, it was her decision, not mine. I mean, I wanted to, as I hardened the moment her lips touched mine. I would definitely have to make my mind up now or never.

Her hand slipped under my jeans and around my cock. So I guess this was happening then, again. She always knew how to make me want her.

I pulled off my pants and settled my body on top of hers, her warm skin pressing against mine now as we lay on the bed. I wanted this moment so bad, even though this didn't mark our first time together. A lot of time had passed since last time, not that neither of us didn't want to, the situation just never seemed to be in our favor. One of us had to stay in the cockpit or engine room at all times, so we couldn't sneak one in while traveling. Not to mention we found the size of the cockpit a challenge, and if we didn't pay attention and hit the wrong button, we were screwed.

Not that it never happened before…

Rebecca ran her hands against my chest, and I let out a small sigh as her touch soothed me. The craving for this had been suppressed for so long. I wanted no one else to touch me except her. She has always said she didn't mind us having an open relationship, that if I wanted to go have a meaningless one-night stand with some chick from a bar, that it was fine, but I never wanted to. All I ever thought about was her.

I placed my hand on top of her bralette and squeezed her breast. Damn, I was so hard right now, but I wanted this to last as long as possible. I wanted to enjoy every moment of us like this, to feel every inch of her body against mine and remember it forever.

With a small amount of force, she rolled me over and climbed on top of me. Rebecca pulled off her bralette and khaki cargo pants. The black lacy thong appeared to perfectly fit her. *Scheiße*, she had planned on doing this since her sleep rotation; even meeting with Jonathan didn't change her mind. She always wore lace underwear when she wanted sex. I learned that over the years.

She leaned forward and kissed me gently on the lips, then moved to my cheek and then my ears.

"*Sei hart mitt mir*," she whispered into my ear. My heart rate quickened. Every once in a while, on top of just wanting sex, Rebecca would get into these moods where she would want to be fucked hard.

I seized her by the wrist and pulled her face down on the pillow. I climbed on top of her, smacking her ass as I did. It was firm, so *Gott*damn firm. Even being stuck in space she stayed as fit as when she was in the military.

Tugging off her underwear, I spanked her again but harder. She let out a moan as I hit her again and again. She tried to move, but I wrapped my arm around her and fingered her nipples, my thumb with one and my index finger with the other.

"Fick mich jetzt," she murmured. *"Fick mich jetzt."*

I pulled off my boxer briefs. With her legs spread, I bit my lip as I slid into her, seeing her thighs twitch, gasping at the feeling I had been yearning for weeks. Thrusting harder and harder, I watched as Rebecca's back arched and she clutched the sheets.

"Fick mich durch! Fick mich durch!" she demanded with such authority I knew could only come from years of military service. Damn, I loved when she used that voice.

Clutching her by the waist, I tugged her closer and closer to me. I knew I could come at any moment, but I wanted more. Withdrawing from her, I flung her around.

I snatched her by the jaw and forced her mouth against mine. Kissing her, I wrapped her legs around me, lifted her from the bed, and forced her back against the wall of the hotel. Slipping my penis back in, I shoved farther and farther, keeping my mouth firmly against hers. I could sense each small moan she exhaled as I went deeper. I felt her bite my lip sharply, the metallic taste of blood on my tongue. She dug her nails into my back, and I felt my skin tear.

Gathering her wrists, I pinned them above her head. Pulling away from her mouth, I shook my head. "Ah, you don't get to play rough."

She bit at me playfully and tried to move her arms. I kissed her lips, ramming deep into her all over again. The bed shook, and her body made a loud thumping sound as she hit the wall. Moving across her cheek and down her neck, I kept my lips on her.

"Schnell! Schnell!"

Rapidly I went down her body, and the thumping got louder. I could hear the person in the neighboring room, banging his fist on our wall to keep it down, but I really didn't give a fuck what they wanted. I was about to come and Rebecca arched her back.

"Ich komme!" she cried.

I stayed in longer, making her jerk as she tried to get me to let her go. I pressed my lips on her, getting one last kiss out of her. I leaned my forehead on hers.

"Ich liebe dich," I whispered, meaning every word.

She blinked, as if I had caught her by surprise. Her sky-blue eyes stared at me, lost for words. She answered. *"Ich liebe dich."*

Moving down to the bed, she curled up against me. Her body still contained warmth and her skin moist with the mixture of both our sweat. I guess I wouldn't go to my room tonight, which I wish I had known earlier because then I wouldn't have paid for it. Oh well, it wasn't like we had to worry about replacing the hyperdrive now, and we could salvage the ship for some cash.

I lay there, my arm wrapped around Rebecca, listening to her breathe gently. I kissed her head one more time and closed my eyes. The last thing I remembered thinking about before drifting asleep was whether she paused because she didn't expect me to say that I loved her or if she thought about someone else.

CHAPTER SEVEN

Rebecca

He gently caressed the side of my cheek with his finger as he smiled down at me. My heart pounded in my chest. This was the end for me. I didn't know how he got here or how he found me, but my worst nightmare lay next to me.

He appeared the same as he always did, graying brown hair, those blue eyes that once seemed honest, but now I knew the truth—I knew the wickedness behind those eyes.

"*Meine liebchen*," he whispered in my ear, his hot breath sending shivers down my spine. "I'm never letting you out of my sight again."

My eyes shot open. My heart was racing, and my body was sweating and shaking. I took a deep breath. What I saw was just a dream—a stupid nightmare. I didn't know if my memories of the past inspired the image or if it was worries of the future. I didn't want to find out, so getting off this planet was my new goal.

Something moved next to me, and I grabbed the knife that lay on the piece of wood that served as a nightstand. I swung the blade around and stopped right before I stabbed Nik in the throat. Damn that was close. For a moment I thought that Bastien lay next to me. I regained my breath and placed the knife back down.

Nik didn't even wake up, which I thanked *Gott* for. I didn't expect finding me stabbing him would have left him in the greatest of moods. Such a scene wouldn't have been the first time either, which is why I didn't want him to see me now. He said I needed to work on not having a knee-jerk reaction to things. If he only knew how true my nightmares were, he would do the same thing.

Then last night's mistake hit me.

Rushing to the bathroom, I threw up in the disgusting toilet. I knew I shouldn't have had that whiskey. My body still shook, and I realized I would need another hit sooner rather than later. That would be complicated with Nik in the bed. Hopefully he wouldn't wake up anytime soon and I could sneak some from my pocket.

Normally I would take the drug before bed, but with the extra I took when I heard Bastien's voice, mixed with the alcohol, I would have to slowly wean myself down again and hope I didn't screw up the potency.

Letting out a sigh after I finished emptying the contents of my stomach, I stood up and turned on the shower faucet. I needed a shower. Bad. A week had gone by since I had a full-fledge shower with actual water instead of mist. It was one of the reasons I kept my hair short—so I felt less greasy while on a ship. That, and so I wouldn't be as recognizable. I also colored my hair red, which I preferred over my natural brown hair. Nik also liked the red, said the color made me look like a pixie. Not sure what he meant by that, but I never questioned his comment.

Gott, what was I going to do about Nik? I loved him, I loved him dearly, but our relationship was full of secrets and lies. He didn't know about my past. He didn't know the things Bastien had forced me to do. Nor did I ever want to tell him. He wouldn't understand, he couldn't understand, not when I couldn't even forgive myself. Not when he saw how much blood was really on my hands.

Forcing my mind off the topic, I thought about the mission Jonathan had presented to us. I had put up a fuss about the job, appearing as if I didn't want to help, otherwise Nik and Jonathan would have been suspicious. This could be my ticket to getting around those Nreff agents on the spaceport, and if we succeeded, then I wouldn't have to worry about Bastien ever again. He would be in prison. I could finally stop worrying about my nightmares coming true.

And they would clear my name of treason.

I laughed at the thought. Sure, my name would be cleared of the charges for killing a representative, but then my name would resurface as an affiliate of Bastien's. Nik would find out how close I was to him and how he had taken me on his special missions where I had to capture people and deliver them to warehouses, all to help the nation become a better power.

At least that was the lie Bastien had told me. He told me my actions were for the greater good and that those people deserved what we did to them. Never did I realize the horror that awaited them. Not until it was too late—not until I found out there was no going back from the deep crevasse I had fallen into.

That was why I ran away three years ago. It wasn't because I would be tried for a crime he had tricked me into committing: the assassination of a representative. No, somehow I knew that I would have been freed at the last moment and been under Bastien's thumb once more. And I didn't want that, so I ran as fast and as far as I could.

But no matter what, he still found me. He always

found me.

Which was why I had to stop this. I had to help Jonathan and Nik find the evidence against him, not only to stop the injustices that were happening but also hoping such actions will clean some of the blood that stained my hands. Either way, they would find out about me. I might as well help. Even if it meant I was going to prison for a very, very long time.

I shut the shower off as I heard a knock at the door to the hotel room. I wrapped myself in the cleaner towel on the rack. Nik would have to use the one with the hole in it.

Just as I stepped out of the bathroom, Nik opened the door.

"Eh bien." Jonathan grinned. "Looks like someone got *veinard* last night."

I stepped into the doorway. "I thought you wanted us to call you when we got up. You said nothing about a surprise visit."

He shrugged. "I was in the neighborhood. Besides, I had to know if you were sleeping together or not, and knowing you, you would have lied about it."

I began to shut the door. It was too early to deal with this *scheiße*.

Jonathan placed his hand in the way. *"Attendez,* I was just kidding. I wanted to let you know the schedule changed and I need to know your answer now."

"Couldn't have called?" Nik asked.

"I did. Multiple times. Neither of you answered."

I glanced at Nik, who shrugged. He slept through the communicators buzzing when I was in the shower. I let out a sigh. "Yeah, we will take the mission. Now, mind if we finish getting ready?"

He gestured forward. "*Oui, oui*, and *merci*. I will wait outside so that we can grab some breakfast and discuss the traveling arrange—"

I shut the door before he finished talking. It was too early in the morning to deal with his rambling. I turned to find Nik staring at me.

"What?" I asked.

He shrugged. "Didn't think you would agree to it. I guess you never cease to amaze me."

I rolled my eyes and pushed him toward the bathroom. "Just go get ready before I change my mind."

As promised, Jonathan was waiting outside. He apparently knew a good place nearby for breakfast, and although I didn't care for breakfast food, some hash browns sounded fantastic, even after sneaking a shot of the drug while Nik took a shower. Now only two vials remained, which meant I would need to find a dealer today.

"So…" Jonathan handed us some folders as he led us

to the restaurant. "These are your aliases. Memorize them quickly."

"Quickly?" I asked. "Don't we have a couple of days before we leave?"

He shrugged. "*Oui*, but you are about to meet the rest of the crew."

I stopped on the pavement, and I could feel Nik's hand on my shoulder, telling me not to start a fight in public.

"Crew?" I asked. "You never mentioned having to work with other people, Jonathan."

"I didn't? I thought I had. *Désolé, mon erreur.*"

I grabbed the collar of his shirt. "Oh, I will show you a mistake."

"Rebecca…," Nik began. "You are causing unneeded attention."

Letting out a deep breath, I let Jonathan go.

He straightened out his clothes. "And you haven't even met them yet. They are a smart group; you will get along with them very well."

Nik gave Jonathan a look this time, which made me a little mad. I wasn't that pathetic where I couldn't get along with everyone. It was just a good chunk of people. I got along with him just fine, and Walrum. But if I looked back on it, they were the only two in my entire life whom I got along with. That didn't include back when I was with Bastien. I didn't know whether that counted as "getting along." I decided it didn't.

"Fine. Whatever. They just better be skilled and have a lot of experience on missions." I flipped through my new identity. Natascha Weiß, a retired captain from the Nreff military. I could do that. I mean, the ranking was way beneath me, but that was okay. I was on a mission.

Nik flipped through his. He had a bit of a smile on his face.

"What's your name?" I asked.

"Gunther Davis." He laughed.

I rolled my eyes. That was an alias he had on another mission, a fake mission Jonathan had put us on for Nik's thirtieth birthday party. "I swear if this mission is a fake, Jonathan…"

"It's not, I swear. I just couldn't resist. But we're here."

Nik and I stepped into the restaurant. There was barely anyone there, other than an old guy eating cereal at the bar, a teenage couple in the corner, wearing all black, and a large group sitting at a table with three empty chairs. They were all staring at us, and I just stared back at them.

None of them appeared to be over the age of thirty.

"Something wrong?" Jonathan noticed my frown.

I shook my head. "No, just contemplating why you hired me instead of a real babysitter to watch over a bunch of kids."

"They are all very skilled in what they do, Bex, so stop getting your panties in a bind."

"It's Rebecca. And I don't doubt they are skilled, but being skilled and understanding how to sneak past the Nreff Nation are two different things."

"You care if something happens to them?" Nik asked, as if that surprised him.

I shrugged, not wanting to admit a soft spot. "No, but I don't want to be blamed when they are all killed."

Jonathan patted my back. "I'll take full responsibility, rest assured. You don't need any more blood on your hands."

I let out a chuckle. "And you do?"

"We sound like a bunch of war vets." Nik sighed.

I winked at him. "When in reality we're just a bunch of traitors. Yeah, I know."

"Until this mission is over, then our names will be cleared."

Easy for him to say. "Fair enough. But you both know I will not play nice, right?"

Jonathan patted my back. "Bex, I don't think I have ever seen you play nice. It's not in your nature. I don't believe you even played nice with Walrum, although he liked it that way. We're all Nreff commanders; that's what makes us perfect for this mission."

I smiled at his comment. "I was a commander. Now I'm just a troublemaker no matter where I go."

"Yeah, that hasn't changed though. Now come, wouldn't you like me to introduce you to the crew?"

I sighed. "Not particularly, but I guess I should at least try to remember some names. Then I will know who to yell at when all goes to hell."

"There's my friendly Bex."

"I told you that I don't miss your sarcastic comments, right?"

"You might have mentioned it once or twice." Jonathan led us to the table. "But I wasn't paying attention."

A young dark-skinned man was the first to stand.

"Natascha, this is the pilot, Samuel. Samuel, this is Gunther and Natascha. You can call her Tashy."

He held out his hand. "Pleasure to meet you."

"We will see about that." I shook his hand. "And my name is Natascha, not Tashy."

Jonathan patted my head. "Don't listen to her; she loves the name."

I grabbed Jonathan's wrist and bent it back. "No. I. Don't."

"Aïe, aïe! Je suis désolé!"

I let go of his wrist, and he rubbed where I had hurt the muscle. He was such a baby.

Samuel nodded. "So don't piss her off. Got it." He turned to Nik. "And he said you are Gunther, right?"

Nik nodded. "Yes. Pleased to meet you, Samuel."

"Call me Sam."

The two kids who were seated next to Sam stood up.

"This is Russ and Mary. They are your mechanics. This is Tash—" Jonathan saw the glare I was giving him. "Natascha."

I glanced between the two. "How old are you two?"

"Natascha…," Nik warned under his breath.

The boy pointed at himself. "I'm seventeen, and my sister here is fifteen."

I stared at them for a moment longer, then glared at Jonathan. "They are barely out of their diapers. Are you going to risk this mission with these two?"

"Hey!" Mary stepped forward, her head held high. "We may be young, but I can guarantee that we're the best mechanics in the 'raum. We can keep the ship in the air, no matter what."

She stood strong, and I appreciated the action. But it didn't change the fact she was too young. "Have you any experience with being boarded or shot out of the sky?"

"We were on the *Padrona*. We were the ones who saved the ship from blowing up in atmo. Yes, we're qualified for this job," Russ explained.

Nik and I glanced at each other. We had heard about the *Padrona*. I couldn't imagine that these kids had been behind the semi-success of landing her. Still didn't mean I trusted them with this mission. It was one thing to be there on the ship during a malfunction, it was another to stop a war from happening.

"So who else are we babysitting?" I asked.

"I guess that would be me." A woman with jet-black hair stood up. Something about her struck me. She seemed familiar almost. I couldn't place it, but she didn't seem to think anything about me, so it must have been something else.

She held out her hand to me. "I am Alexandra Mostovoi. Medic."

The name rang a bell, but I doubted she had any connection to whom I was thinking of. I shook her hand. "When did you graduate?"

"Last year," she said as she shook Nik's hand. "Top of the class, graduated in record time. My area of concentration was brain chemistry and nerve damage."

That was a coincidence—the two people I recalled also were experts in that field. Maybe I would have to monitor her.

"Impressive. How did Jonathan get you on this ship?"

She folded her hands in front of herself. "I have my reasons for wanting to be on this mission, as we all do."

I grinned. "Yes, we do, don't we?"

"And last we have Burt." Jonathan motioned to the last crew member. He was lanky with orange hair and a cocky look that I wanted to smack off his face. Just like

Jonathan. "He used to serve in the Nreff military as a pilot."

He held out his hand. "Hello."

Nik shook his hand, as did I. Jonathan motioned to the seats. "Now, let's sit down and get to know each other."

We all took our seats, and I sat between Jonathan and Nik. I didn't enjoy sitting down next to people I didn't know. It freaked me out and always made me feel on edge.

"So," I began as I looked at the menu. Yeah, oven roasted potatoes were the only thing on the menu that could be made vegan friendly. Jonathan hadn't thought that one through. "What're all our duties on the ship? I mean, I would like to know where these kids will be playing."

Nik nudged me, as if that would make a difference.

Jonathan clapped his hands. "Well, I was going to wait until after we ate, but I might as well tell you. Nik is in charge of the engine room, along with Mary and Russ; Samuel and I will take care of the piloting, Alexandra is the medic, of course, and Burt will be our captain."

"Meaning you get to do the paperwork." I winked. "You lucky devil you. So I presume I'm co-captain?" I asked as I took a drink of water.

Jonathan shook his head. "*Non, non, ma chéri.*

You're *le cuisinier.*"

I spat out all the water that was in my mouth on Burt. "I'm the cook?"

CHAPTER EIGHT

Nik

"So Rebecca is pissed at you for making her the ship's cook," I commented as we rode up the sky train.

Jonathan shrugged. "She'll get over it. She's a fantastic cook, or at least that's what Walrum always said."

"She is," I whispered.

He raised an eyebrow. "Oh? So she cooks for you as well? Why am I the only one left out of the group?"

"Well, it took a few months—she gave in because she got sick of me almost catching the ship on fire, trying to cook for myself. Either way, she came around."

"But she only cooked according to her vegan diet,

right?"

"Hey, you would be surprised what things you can cook that are vegan. I haven't eaten an unsatisfying meal in years. Well, until this morning. That breakfast was horrid. Jonathan, what were you thinking?" I asked. My stomach still hurt, and all I ate was a muffin.

"*Je suis désolé*, I guess I just missed finding random places to eat with you guys. You remember I'm great at finding gems."

"And you're great at finding crap houses like that one," I added. "Anyway, you think she's okay? With the rest of the crew, I mean. She's by herself with people she's not used to being around. Not to mention they are kids and will get on her nerves."

Jonathan motioned with his hand. "They're fine. It's Bex we're talking about. She knows her place. Besides, what trouble can they get into? They're at the market, buying food."

"Yeah… like that will go well… Also, you do realize she's going to only cook vegan meals on the ship. Is the crew okay with that?"

"Don't worry about them; they'll get over it. Besides, I doubt anyone will cross her about that. She's pretty set on her special little diet."

I rubbed my forehead. "That she is. Though it's better that she stayed on the planet, I expect she would have cried seeing her ship get sold."

Jonathan laughed. "Does she care about that ship?"

"It's not so much the ship as it is the symbol of freedom."

We arrived at the spaceport and went straight to the sales desk. In the line of space travel, someone always wanted to buy a ship, if not just to salvage for parts. Ours would probably be sold for scrap metal, and I sort of felt pity for it. It wasn't its fault it was a piece of *scheiße*. The problem was the hyperdrive, to be honest, but without that, it was useless.

Jonathan and I made our way through the line to get a sales ticket. There weren't too many people in line, just some sketchy folk who were probably on the run from the law, though I couldn't really talk.

"So, other than your and Rebecca's relationship, anything else interesting happen in the past three years?" Jonathan asked as the person in front of us got called to the teller.

I shook my head. "Not really. I mean, there was the one time where we ran into a samurai, or at least he called himself a samurai. Are there any samurai left after Earth was abandoned?"

Jonathan shrugged. "Beats me. But that sounds interesting."

"Yeah… But he lost to Rebecca. Any idea where she learned to use a katana?"

"She knows how to use a katana?"

"Apparently."

Jonathan scratched at his scruff. "Huh. That's… interesting."

"That's what I thought, but she said she had never used one before, so you know, lied through her teeth. I didn't press further, not like she would tell me the truth unless she wanted to."

"That's for sure."

The teller waved us forward, and we got our request ticket after she ran our numbers.

"The representative will be with you shortly. He will meet you at your ship."

Whatever shortly meant. Knowing the spaceport, probably an hour at least. I sighed as we strode out of the business area and toward the ship. "I wonder how much we'll get for it."

"Doesn't really matter. Jaq will cover our expenses, and once our names are cleared, we will get reimbursed some pay. So it's fine."

"Yeah, I know. Still, I paid a lot for that ship. I would like to see her get what she's worth."

Jonathan shrugged. "Whatever you say."

As we kept walking, I noticed that the Nreff soldiers who had boarded our ship earlier were staring down the corridor straight at me.

That was never a good sign.

Throughout my life, I had learned that if any person in a uniform looked at you for more than a brief second, you were up shit creek. This went with any uniform, really, even just a business suit. Staring meant they were up to something, and usually it wasn't something good. Although, if a woman nurse stared at you, that could have a little better outcome, but as I learned, that scenario wasn't as likely as I hoped.

They turned away and went about their business. They probably were just curious why I was back on the ship. Either way, I would keep an eye out for them.

I nudged Jonathan. "Hey, do those soldiers look familiar to you?"

He shook his head. *"Non. Pourquoi?"*

"They are really Nreff soldiers in disguise. I think they're up to something. Keep your eyes peeled for anything out of the ordinary."

Jonathan nodded. "That I will."

The representative showed up within fifteen minutes, which surprised me. He came faster than Jonathan and I bet, which meant neither of us got the five credits we wagered. I held out my hand to greet him.

"I'm Nik Graham. Thank you for coming out here."

He shook my hand, mainly because it would have been rude not to. "Yeah, yeah, just show me the ship."

We walked through the ship, which only took a few

moments since, well, it wasn't that big. He took heavy notes, which I wanted to read because I didn't understand how someone could write so much about this ship. I could barely write a sentence or two when I filled out the paperwork for the selling request.

Walking back to where the ship docked with the spaceport, the man tapped his stylus to his tablet. "I can do five thousand credits."

I choked. "Five thousand? I paid fifty thousand! It's at least worth twenty thousand."

He sighed and tapped the stylist again. "It would be worth twenty thousand if the hyperdrive was functional, but it's not."

I ran my fingers through my hair. This was not my day. "How about ten?"

"How about five and I don't report you for having so many loose wires in the engine room? You do realize that's illegal, don't you?"

I glanced at Jonathan. He shrugged. I turned back to the man. "Fine. Five thousand it is."

The man clicked a button on the tablet. "Great. You will have the check waiting for you at the register. Please leave all official documents with the clerk. Thank you and have a great day." He turned and left.

"Sunshine of a personality, wouldn't you say?" Jonathan commented.

"Yeah, well, doesn't really matter. Anyway, we better

get everything packed up. Rebecca and I have almost nothing, so it won't take too long."

"Right, just tell me what to do."

We started packing and clearing away any unnecessary garbage that was lying around, although I just wanted to keep it there for the spaceport to deal with. But I was too nice.

As we were about to finish, a woman showed up at the port door.

"Umm." She fiddled with her tablet. "Is there a Mr. Nik Graham on board?"

I stepped forward. "I am him. What is it?"

"There are a couple of things you need to sign before you can sell your ship. Can you come with me?" she asked. "It will only take a second."

I glanced at Jonathan. I didn't understand what it could be about, especially since I was supposed to go to the clerk for the rest of the stuff, but I would not argue with an employee. "Yeah, sure. You'll finish up here?"

Jonathan nodded. "Of course."

"Ciao," I said as I turned to the girl and nodded. "Let's go."

Ciao was our code to each other. If one of us was leaving with someone who we thought was fishy, we would say the code word, meaning the other person should follow to make sure everything was all right. I had a notion there was more to this than signing a few documents.

The young woman took me down a corridor I didn't recognize. I didn't know this port very well, but I was sure where we were going wasn't where my signature was required.

"Just up ahead, the door to your left. There is a representative expecting you," she explained.

So she didn't know the true reason behind the request. She was just a worker doing her job. "Thank you very much. What was your name again?"

"Penelope."

"Well, Penelope, you are fantastic at your job. But do keep in mind, when taking orders, to ask more questions. Got it?"

"Uh… okay." With a confused look, she turned around and hurried off, her blond curls bobbing up and down. She was very cute, especially from behind. I watched her walk all the way down the corridor until she disappeared. If Rebecca were here, she would have punched me.

Turning my attention back to the problem at hand, I needed to figure out my defense plan. They were waiting in the room, thinking I would really fall for that, or they were all around me, waiting for my first move.

I thought about what I could do. I could easily just turn around and start walking back, see what happens, be prepared for an attack. I didn't have any weapons on me; I wasn't Rebecca and paranoid all the time. Jonathan was also near, so I wouldn't be completely outnumbered. It would be at a minimum four to two, and we were trained better than they ever would be.

I also could go to the room and take them by surprise. I didn't think that would work though, so the first option it would be.

The moment I turned around, they were on me. It was the four men from earlier. Two of them grabbed my arms, pinning me against the wall. One was the leader. He wanted revenge on what Rebecca did to him. Men and revenge, I swore.

"Well, well, what do we have here?" the man asked.

"I don't know, what do we have? I just see a bunch of dummkopf boys who don't know what mess they are in. Need I remind you who I am?"

He rammed his fist into my stomach. *Gott,* I forgot how much that hurt.

"Oh, we know exactly who you are." He spat at me. "You are Nikolas Anders, wanted fugitive in the Nreff Nation. Wanted dead or alive for treason against the nation, killing Representative Beitz of Nash Mir three years ago. You wouldn't believe the price on your head."

I let out a laugh. I wouldn't show them any fear, mostly because I knew something they didn't know.

Jonathan was here too.

They must have known Rebecca was with me, and I wondered if they would bring it up.

The leader drove another fist into my stomach. "What's so funny?"

"Oh, nothing. But I can guess who you are working for. First starts with an *S* and last name starts with a *W* I presume?" I asked.

His eyes narrowed. "How did you—?"

"Obvious, really. He's the only one who's looking for us."

"Well, don't worry. You will get to face him soon. We aren't letting either of you off this station until he arrives."

I raised my eyebrow. "Either of us? Who do you mean?"

"Commander Rebecca Kompen. Don't pretend she isn't the woman with you. She's the one we're really after."

I started laughing. I would be on the ground if it weren't for the men holding me up. "Rebecca? She's not flying with me."

The man's eyes widened. "What?"

"She got a lift from a friend. Left a while ago. Sorry," I lied. I was mostly curious how they would react. That and I didn't want to endanger her later.

"Verdammt!" The man punched me in the face. This

time the men holding me let me hit the ground. "Where did she go? Tell me now!"

I spat out blood. "I don't know really. We got into a fight."

"Liar!" He kicked me in the stomach. "Tell me where she is or you are dead!"

"Can't get any information out of me if I were dead, you know."

Another kick. "Tell me, you *schwein*!"

I spat more blood. "How about you ask my partner?"

"Your what?"

I nodded behind him. "My partner. Right there."

Jonathan pulled back a punch and drove his fist right into the man's skull. He hit the ground, and I quickly got up to help take down the other three men. I grabbed one by the collar, driving a punch right to his stomach. Revenge, really, because I should have been aiming for his face, knocking his lights out. That was my next move, driving my fist into the side of his head. He hit the ground.

Two more.

One of them reached for their gun, but Jonathan was on him in an instant. He grabbed the man's gun and hit him against the temple with the butt. One left.

He tried to run for it, either to get port authorities or just because he didn't want to get knocked out. I grabbed the gun from Jonathan and threw it straight at the man's head.

Perfect shot.

All four had been taken down by us.

Jonathan and I high-fived, a ritual we did when we beat the odds, then a fist bump at the end.

"So, what did they want?" Jonathan asked as we hurried back to the ship to grab our bags.

"Oh, you know, sent by Sebastien, take us back to the Nreff Nation, torture us, same ol' same ol'."

"Hmm. I can't believe he was onto us this quickly. That or just bad luck. Either way we need to get off the planet fast. Also, I'd rather not tell Rebecca. This might spook her too much."

I nodded. "Agreed. It will be our little secret."

CHAPTER NINE

Rebecca

Jonathan left me to babysit. Stupid *connard.*

I only had to deal with three of them at least, as Alexandra and Samuel wanted to get other things they needed for the ship. Those two were the oldest of the bunch though, so now I found myself with all the youngest crew members. I would get Jonathan back for this, I swore.

Though, to be honest, I didn't feel comfortable around Alexandra. Something about her seemed familiar, and I didn't like that. Something from the past was trying to surface—back when I still worked under Bastien. She didn't seem to recognize me, so at least there was that. But even so, I couldn't shake the notion.

And it was all I could do not to take another vial.

Either way, I found myself in the middle of an outdoor food market with two hyper teens and a cocky military dropout. I had gone over the papers, and apparently Burt had been dismissed from the Nreff military for "not listening to authority." Great. I couldn't wait to get up in space with him.

At least he stayed quiet at the moment while the two engineers ran around touching and sniffing every fruit and vegetable that looked odd to them, the clerks freaking out because the engineers weren't supposed to handle the food. Evidently they had never seen a kiwi before. I pinched the bridge of my nose as a migraine formed.

"Oh, can we get this?" Mary held up a dragon fruit. "The sign says it's made of dragons!"

Her brother Russ grabbed the fruit from her and examined it closer. "Cool! Can we?"

I took a deep breath as the clerk snatched the fruit back. "Yes, we can. But I'll tell you now, it's not actually a dragon. It's just called that. Not to mention that I don't eat any animal products or byproducts, so don't think about taking any."

Burt looked like I had just committed a crime or at least another crime. "What?"

"You heard me loud and clear, soldier, so shut your

mouth before I shut it for you."

He threw up his hands, random people around us now staring. "That doesn't even make sense! Why the hell don't you eat meat? It's not real animal!"

I stepped forward, my back straight, staring him right in the eyes. "There have been a record number of findings that labels lie and that real animals were used for meat instead of bio-farming. I'm not taking that chance. So yes, it makes sense."

He folded his arms in front of him. "Well, there ain't no way I'm eating that monkey diet. What about you two, what's your vote? Are you going to stand by this nonsense?"

Mary and Russ glanced at each other. They appeared to be contemplating either making Burt more frustrated or crossing me.

"I mean," Mary began, "if we get to eat cool things like this dragon fruit, I don't see the problem…"

"*Sí*, and that thing called a kiwi. It was cool and fuzzy," Russ added. These kids really were entertained by the darndest things.

"Well, there you have it," I said. "You're outnumbered."

Burt shook his head. "This isn't fair. What about the others? Don't they get to vote?"

I shrugged. "Gunther'll vote for me; he'd be stupid not to after all this time. Jonathan knows that I won't cook meat no matter what, so his vote will be mine. That makes five against three, if the other two were on your side. So get over it. I'm not cooking anything having to do with an animal."

Burt let out a huff but didn't say another word. By all his logic, I won the argument, not to mention I was the cook, so even if we bought meat, I wouldn't touch it.

"So between Samuel saying he can't consume nightshades and my hatred for mushrooms, ordering food will be fun."

"I…," Burt began. "I'm allergic to nuts. Except pine nuts. But yeah, they give me migraines."

I sighed. "Okay, I will make a note to spike your food with nuts if you're being a pain in my ass. But as for this list, I expect we'll manage. Russ, Mary, pick out all the strange fruit and vegetables that your hearts' desire. But no nightshades."

It was like I told them it was Christmas, though to me all this seemed more like Krampusnacht. The two of them turned around and sprinted through the outdoor market, bumping into two others on the way and apologizing.

"And when you're done, meet us by the beans! And don't touch the food, just write it down on the form!" I yelled at them. I wasn't sure if they heard me, but either way I could call them on their communicator. At least they were out of my hair. I turned to find Burt still standing there. "Didn't want to join them?"

"Sorry, I don't get that excited about cucumbers."

I made a little smirk.

His face turned red. "That's not what I meant and you know it! I was talking about vegetables. God, and you call us children."

Letting out a little laugh, I started toward the beans-and-grain section of the market. There was every kind of bean that one could ever dream of, along with grain, pasta, rice, nuts, and so on. The prices were cheap, so I decided it would be best to order anything that could last a long time here since it wouldn't get moldy or rot, and then I wouldn't have to worry about it later on in the mission. We had over two weeks of traveling to do, so times that by three and then eight people.

That was a lot of food. At least twenty liters of grains and another thirty of beans or some kind of protein like lentils. Good thing Jonathan had some money. At least Nik was getting something for our ship, though I was sad to see it go. She had served us well these past three years. I guess more like satisfactorily. She didn't kill us, and that was good enough for me.

"So," I began as I wrote down the order I would need to give to the clerk. "Which commanding officer did you serve under?"

I hated small talk—I really did—but I also hated awkward silence.

"Oh, Commander Kisicaa. She was a hard-ass, a little like you actually." He gave me a little sarcastic smile that I ignored.

"I know the name. She serves under Admiral Bardon, am I correct?"

Burt nodded. "Yeah, she does. That was how I got the job. Admiral Bardon sought me out."

"Even though you were dismissed from the military?" I asked. "Seems a little odd."

He shrugged. "Guess he realized even though I didn't enjoy listening to authority, I know what's right. This mission will bring peace—or keep peace anyway. I don't want to see the systems start a war."

That sounded fishy, especially since I had run into Admiral Bardon many times over the years. Bastien always said to keep an eye out for him. Guess he was right. "Very few people do, yet if there's one little mess-up, it seems like everyone is quick to pull out their gun. Interesting, really."

"What, do you think there will be a war?"

I shrugged. "If the right person wanted to and was clever enough, they could get a war started with a snap of his fingers. However, there are plenty of other clever people who can stop him." At least that was what I hoped. The man we were after was smarter than most gave him credit for.

"Like us?"

"We will see, won't we? Now…" I motioned to the pasta. "Which do you think would be best for our trip?"

He shook his head. "Like it matters. Can't have meatballs with our marinara."

"Can't have marinara anyway. Tomatoes are a nightshade."

Burt looked as if he would pull out his hair. I laughed. Causing him anguish would be my new favorite hobby.

Burt and I waited another hour before Russ and Mary came back. They had a long list for what they wanted to order. I narrowed it down and told them I would get the other stuff at the next stop. I assured them that we would have plenty of time to try a square watermelon.

That left snacks and sweets to purchase. Since it was a larger group, I didn't mind buying a pie for dessert since I didn't have to pay for it.

"Well," I said as I stepped up to the bakery counter. "Anything look good to you?"

Russ and Mary were drooling on the glass. Luckily there weren't that many people there because I had a feeling it would take them a while to choose. Burt stayed back, his arms still folded.

"What's your problem?" I asked as Russ and Mary argued which pie looked better.

"I just don't care for pie. Except shepherd's pie. And

chicken pot pie. And—"

"I get it. But not eating meat will not kill you. Just get over it."

"Whatever. I didn't even want to do this mission. Admiral Bardon just promised that they could reinstate me in the military if we succeeded."

So that's what they offered him. Why Admiral Bardon would want this guy in the military, I did not understand. I guess if it motivated him and got the job done.

"And you would want to go back?" I asked.

He shrugged. "Yeah, why not? The pay is good, and it was the only place where I felt like I could belong."

Somewhere one could belong. I didn't know if I could relate. There wasn't a place I ever felt like I belonged, at least not right now. Even with Nik I didn't feel like I belonged but more like I was lying to him, as I had kept secrets from him for a very long time. Maybe, when all the truth came out, if he still wanted me, I could feel like I belonged somewhere.

"What about you? Why did you take this mission?" Burt asked.

The question took me off guard for a moment. It wasn't like they knew the truth, how Jonathan, Nik, and I all had served under Admiral Wilde, tricked to commit treason, and had been in hiding for the past three years —that this was the only way we could reinstate ourselves and be free.

"I just don't want a war to start and think that the human experiments are wrong and whoever is behind them needs to be punished," I said. It wasn't a lie, but it wasn't the complete truth either.

"Yeah, there's that. I mean, whatever's going on, if it's really going on, it has to be bad for them to go to all this trouble, right? I can't imagine that these human experiments are really happening. No one has any evidence, yet the fear still stands."

They were real. I knew they were real, but it wasn't like I could tell him that. Once they knew the truth, they would question me on how I knew, and I would have to face the fact that the dark crimson blood still stained my hands. And they would arrest me. Maybe they wouldn't charge me as harshly since I helped gather evidence, but I doubted that. I had committed a crime, and I needed to face the consequences.

I debated coming out and telling the truth to Nik and Jonathan, but even if I did, I didn't have any proof. I couldn't remember any of the doctors' names, and Bastien would deny it. Or, hell, he would break me out before I could testify against him, then I would be one of his new test subjects. So this mission had to succeed to the very end—it had to find evidence, otherwise there would be no proof.

"I have a feeling we will find the answer to that soon.

As for Mary and Russ, I think they have finally picked out a pie."

Burt turned to find Mary and Russ holding up a large white box.

"What did you get?" Burt asked.

"Key lime pie!" Mary beamed. "With coconut milk and avocados, so no animal byproduct, per Natascha's request."

"That sounds disgusting," Burt added.

"No," Russ commented. "It's fantastic! They let us try a sample. It's better than the real thing."

Burt shook his head. "No, you just don't know good food."

Russ and Mary glared at him.

"We're from an Italian family," Mary exclaimed. "We know good food. What are you? English? Like you would know good food if it hit you in the face."

I let out a laugh. I was starting to like these two, just a tad. Though the real answer to whether I liked them would be when I saw them keep the ship flying. If they could do that, then I really didn't have a problem.

But that was an enormous if. I had a feeling if Bastien found out about this mission, he would come barrels a-blazing. And it would be damn difficult to keep the ship flying against him.

So let's just hope he didn't find us.

* * *

I had the others go ahead and board the ship while I finished getting the orders ready for delivery. And by orders, I meant my morphine-B.

It wasn't like I could let the crew know about my drug, especially the doctor. I didn't want to be lectured about the dangers of getting morphine-B on the black market. I already knew that and learned how to tell the difference. I had a special liquid I could drop into the drug, and if it turned a color, it meant they had contaminated it.

Venturing down to darker parts of the city, I found what I needed. In these types of cities, it wasn't hard to find a shady-looking guy who had the right connections. The man led me down an alleyway, then down stairs, through a laundromat, and into a cramped room full of boxes and vials of drugs.

If I wasn't mistaken, business here was doing well.

"What's the order?" a man in a fancy leather chair asked. He leaned back and smoked something in his pipe, probably an illegal substance.

"I need thirty vials of missy-B." That was the street name of the drug. "And don't sell me the contaminated stuff. I can tell the difference."

The man placed his pipe down and smiled. "Well, lads, bring her the goods."

Two men fumbled around and brought me a wooden case.

"You do understand what you are asking for is expensive, right?"

I nodded. "I do, and I have enough credits for it." I did now, as Jonathan gave me some extra spending money. It made me wonder if Bardon knew about the drug I was taking. Jonathan said nothing, and I didn't ask.

The man held out his hand, and I gave him my cash card. It was a throwaway card anyway, as none of this could be tracked. He placed it into his tablet.

"You weren't mistaken. This is enough." He nodded to the man who handed me the box.

I opened the box. "There are only fifteen in here."

"Right, we have a higher price for our premium product."

"Twice as much as other planets?"

He shrugged. "It is what it is."

I let out a sigh. There wasn't much I could do. "Can I open one to check the contents?"

"Do as you wish, but you will find that it isn't contaminated."

I didn't care what he said but opened a random vial and squeezed my drops into the vial. It didn't change color.

Closing the box, I nodded. "Thank you for your business."

The man nodded, and I left the building before I got

into any trouble. Sometimes these transactions ended with me punching someone in the throat.

Yeah, this went a lot more smoothly than normal. I just hoped the rest of the mission did as well.

CHAPTER TEN

Nik

So yeah, Sebastien knew about the plan.

How the hell that *arsch* learned about the plan or knew where to find us, I did not understand. Did he still suspect us after all this time? I couldn't believe that. No, he must have known Bardon would find evidence again and sent out his minions to find us first.

"We need to leave, *bientôt*," Jonathan said as we hurried down the corridors toward the sky train. "There could be more of them, and when they figure out we're on a different ship, they will try everything to stop us before we can even get started."

Wouldn't that just be swell to have a mission

thwarted before it even began? And if this was Sebastien's doing, it impressed me. He seemed to always know what's coming before we even did. "Agreed. I can go down to the planet and get the crew ready while you get everything for the ship all set up to leave straightaway."

"That sounds like a plan. Rebecca should be done picking out the food. We'll just have to do a rush order, get it shipped up here, and we should be *bien*."

"The entire ship is all set to go? And navigation?" I asked. Usually that took days to get ready, especially when the hyperdrive acted up.

Jonathan nodded. "Yes. I figured it would best to set up first just in case something like this happened. Guess my worry was right."

He could say that again. Even now Sebastien was still two steps ahead of us. Hell, he knew about the mission before I did.

"Better safe than sorry. We learned that the hard way," I commented. "I just hope the crew doesn't ask too many questions. Mainly Rebecca, she always has questions."

"That's because she understands that knowledge is power. But I think she will understand even if we don't tell her. She knows how he can be and that this mission would bring him down once and for all."

"But she isn't even sure he's part of the human

experimentations. I mean she, for some reason, thinks he is innocent."

"Yeah, that's what she said, isn't it? Well, she'll know that someone is trying to stop us and that it would be best to leave sooner rather than later. As to what made us decide this, well, we'll have to lie a bit."

I let out a sigh. It wasn't easy to lie to Rebecca; she was good at asking the right questions to find out the truth. It made her a great partner but a horrible enemy.

I wouldn't have to worry about her being an enemy. But I did still find myself pissing her off every once in a while. She didn't like to show mercy either.

I wondered what would happen if she found out the truth of what a horrible *arsch* Sebastien was. I mean, she knew he had a dark side—we had all faced that when we messed up a mission—but to see the crimes he has committed, that will be another thing entirely.

"What gate number are you at?" I asked as we came to our split-up point.

"G569-83. Keep me posted on how long it will take them to get ready so I can get an estimate to the departures department."

"Will do!" I yelled back as I turned toward the sky elevator to get to Unité. I just hoped Rebecca didn't have too much trouble with the crew. Knowing her, she probably had already punched Burt for talking back at her.

* * *

Well, to my surprise, Rebecca had punched no one. Yet.

Burt commented on how Rebecca, or Natascha rather, didn't eat meat. I would need to remember not to call her Rebecca since it had been so long since we used fake IDs. I mean, after we had run away, we switched just our last names—there was no point in changing our first names when they were so common. I couldn't even remember how many false identities I had now. I had lost count.

We all stood in the hotel that Jonathan had booked for the crew, as it was our meeting spot after everyone got their supplies. It surprised me how nice the hotel was and wondered why he didn't mention it the night before. This was so much nicer than the place Rebecca and I slept in. It even had a pool.

"We got a pie!" Mary, the youngest exclaimed. "It's key lime and doesn't have any milk, but it tastes delicious!"

Rebecca gave me a look of *See what I put up with while you left me here.* "Yeah, and they got to pick out fruit and vegetables. It was such a wonderful day."

I raised an eyebrow. "You let them pick out food? You rarely even let me help pick anything out."

She crossed her arms in front of her. "Yeah, well, your taste buds suck. Besides, it got them out of my hair for a while. This is the last time I ever babysit, by the way. It's your and Jonathan's turn."

I laughed. "Right. I will keep that in mind."

"Speaking of which, where's Jonathan?" Alexandra asked.

"He's finalizing the departure. We've decided it would be best if we left before scheduled. This mission is of the utmost importance, and since Natascha and I have agreed to join you, we have a full crew and can leave. Does anyone have any problem with that?" I asked, trying not to look at Rebecca, but I could tell she was giving me a suspicious look.

"Well, I need to get my things ready, but that will only take two hours," Samuel said. "So should be able to leave tonight."

Alexandra nodded. "Yeah, I should be ready by then."

"Us too!" Russ added.

Burt shrugged. "Not like I have anything to get ready."

I turned to Rebecca, who was still giving me a disapproving look. I tried not to sweat, to not appear as if anything was wrong, but that was impossible.

"Natascha, what about you?"

"The orders for the food will need to be updated for a rush shipment, but I think other than that, it should be fine."

I clapped my hands together. "Great. Well then, off to

it. We don't have any time to waste."

The ship was almost ready to go. Everyone had brought their stuff on board and were unpacking in their bunk bedrooms. They were about the same size as the ones Rebecca and I had, but the ship was a lot bigger to accommodate the number of people.

Rebecca's bed was on top of mine, and she sat on the bed with the door open, her feet dangling down where I was finishing folding my clothes.

"So," she began. "Have anything to tell me?"

I shrugged. "Our ship only got us five thousand credits."

"What?"

I hoped that would get her off the topic of having to leave on such short notice. "That's what I said."

"But it's at least worth twenty thousand."

"I also said that. The buyer said it was five, or he would report us for having wire exposed in the engine room."

She sighed. "Guess that's fair. So then we get some money after the mission is over, right? And compensation for having our names slandered like they've been?"

I nodded. "That's right. Then we can start anew, however we want."

"We can buy a new ship."

I let out a laugh. "You want to spend more time in space? Don't you want to slow down? Stay on a planet for more than just a couple of weeks?"

Rebecca looked up at the ceiling. "I guess… I guess I never imagined life to ever settle down. I don't even think I could handle life being slow like that."

I climbed up the ladder and sat down next to her. I wrapped my arm around her. "It will be fine. I will be there, so it will be fun. And believe me, you can get into all sorts of trouble on planets; you don't just have to be in space. And we could get to know a planet, go hiking, have hobbies that we could never do on a ship. It will be fine."

She let out a little laugh. "Yeah, then you can play that racquetball you were talking about earlier."

"I could. And you could play too. We could join a league and—"

"Whoa, hold your horses. I didn't say I was agreeing to your imaginative future. We first have to finish this mission, and then maybe, just maybe, our charges of treason will be lifted. If we're lucky."

She didn't know that Admiral Bardon had promised that to us, as we had been under his command since before we graduated from the academy. He could drop the charges since it would have been for a top-secret mission. And he could fudge it and say Rebecca was in on it too. "Luck will be on our side. I wouldn't worry about that."

"And do you think Bastien will go down without a fight?" she whispered.

"I—" Wait. Did she just call him Bastien? None of us called him that—we all called him by his full name, mostly because he yelled at us if we called him anything else. Maybe it was a slip of the tongue. I wouldn't push it, not when I was hiding my own secrets. "I think we can beat him. I mean, there's three of us and one of him."

"And all the people he has under his thumb. He's been getting away with these crimes for years now with no one catching him—if he is behind them, I mean."

I knew in my mind that he was behind him. He was a sociopath, everyone knew that. He used people as simple play toys and nothing else. He didn't have a real human feeling in his body but took pleasure in destroying other people's lives, just like he did ours.

Johnathan smiled. "Aw, how *mignon*. You two look like two school kids sitting by their lockers, waiting for classes to start."

I gave him a look before grabbing Rebecca. I could tell she was about to jump down and slug Jonathan in the face. Again. You would think being over thirty she wouldn't still act like a schoolgirl with a crush. I guess some things never changed, especially since she did the same thing when we teased her about Walrum. I wondered why that was.

"What's going on here?" Burt came around the corner of the ship.

Rebecca rolled her eyes and leaned back on her bed. She still didn't like the fact that there were others on this mission.

"Oh, just making fun of these two *amoureux*. Have you checked on Samuel and the engineers?"

Burt glanced up at Rebecca and me, then turned back to Jonathan. "Yeah, they're ready to go. So whenever the departure time has been approved for, we're set."

"We'll leave in less than an hour. Natascha. That gives you time to start dinner."

Rebecca didn't sit back up. "Good, then *je peux vous empoisonner*."

"You aren't going to poison me," Jonathan commented. "Then how will you torture me the rest of the mission?"

"Never said the poison would kill you. It would just make you really, really sick."

He laughed. "Right. Well, I guess I will just have to switch plates with Gunther."

I gave him a look. "Like hell you will. I wouldn't doubt she'd spike your food with something."

He clapped his hands together. "Then off to it. We have no time to spare. Gunther, why don't you go check on our young engineers and make sure they've got everything under control."

I jumped down from the bunk bed. "Right. See you later Natascha. Have fun getting dinner ready."

She waved her hand, and I laughed. She still wasn't too happy about having to cook for others on the ship, though deep down I knew she was a little excited about it. After all, she finally would get to share her hobby.

CHAPTER ELEVEN

Rebecca

Nik was keeping something from me. What that was, I did not know.

My instincts told me that I didn't want to find out and that Jonathan was behind the lie. Unless I got them drunk, there was no way I would get anything out of either of them. I guess I would just have to go on not knowing.

Yeah, like that would happen.

I would have to wait though, before I could find any clues as to what they were up to. There was no point in bringing it up now, not when we were so far from the border. But when we got closer, I would figure it out.

Especially since I had a feeling it had to do with the Nreff soldiers.

Did the two of them know those soldiers were after me? Did they know the truth of everything and this was just a setup to get me arrested? To get me to bring out Bastien and the evidence? I didn't think so, especially since Nik would never betray me like that.

Jonathan on the other hand…

That is if he knew anything. I doubted he would know, especially since Bastien was clever to cover our tracks or anything that led back to him. That didn't mean Jonathan didn't have his suspicions, or Admiral Bardon. It wouldn't be the first time Bardon was hot on Bastien's trail.

I diced up the onions, getting them ready for the meal. I decided that I would make something Mexican themed, without tomatoes or peppers, to go with the key lime pie. Pretty much everything called for onions, so I had quite a lot to dice. Good thing they didn't bother my eyes. I couldn't say the same for others, especially Nik. They always made him cry like a baby.

The door to the mess hall and kitchen slid open. I glanced up to find Mary peeking in.

I sighed. "What do you want?"

She stepped in. At least she was alone. "I was just wondering how dinner was coming along."

I glanced up to her. Was she wanting to help? Did

Jonathan put her up to this? He knew I didn't want anyone around me while I worked. "It's coming. I'm making Mexican food."

She scurried through the room like a puppy that wasn't sure if she could do something. And she was one of the best engineers in the system. That seemed a little hard to believe at the moment.

Mary leaned against the opposite side of the kitchen table and looked at what ingredients I had lying out. "Why do you have peaches if we're having Mexican?"

I hated questions while I was cooking. I really did. "Because Samuel can't have tomatoes, I thought substituting peaches would work. Not sure how it will taste though. It's going to be a little experiment."

"Oh? What all are you going to make?"

"Guacamole, bean-and-corn salad, and lentil with cauliflower tacos. And the pie the two of you picked up."

"That sounds *fantastico*. Can I do anything to help?"

I set the knife down. "Don't you need to help Gunther with the engine?"

She shook her head. "Nope. Everything is taken care of, and Russ is watching over the engine as we speak. It's my shift off."

"Meaning you should sleep."

"But I'm not tired. *Per favore*, I used to help my mother all the time in the kitchen. I miss it."

Gott, she sounded just like a kid. Oh wait, she was one. If I said no, she would keep bothering me, but if I said yes and Nik or Jonathan walked in, I would never hear the end of having a soft spot. Whatever, I could just threaten them for a bit and they would quit it. "Fine, you can help me."

She clapped her hands together and hurried to my side of the table. "What do you want me to do?"

"Just cut up the peaches into small chunks while I get the onions and garlic sautéing. The lentils are already cooking, so once those are done, we can start the tacos."

"Sounds like a plan," she said as she began chopping. I monitored her, afraid that she would cut herself and get blood all over the peaches, though to my surprise she was good at cutting. All the pieces were consistent. So she wasn't kidding about having helped her mother.

"So," I began as I turned the heat down on the stove as the onion and garlic were almost ready. "Does your mother miss you when you are on missions? Then she doesn't have you at home helping cook and everything."

She shook her head. "No, my mother and father passed away a few years back. It's just been Russ and me for a while now."

Now I felt like a bitch and at a time I didn't want to be. "I'm sorry, I didn't kn—"

She held up her hand. "It's fine, really. Russ and I have come to terms with it long ago. But that's why we like to travel so much. It keeps us from lingering on such thoughts. But assisting you has felt good. I haven't cooked a real meal in ages."

I nodded, feeling a little better that I had let her help. It explained why they could do what they do without worrying about the consequences—there was no one waiting for them, hoping that they would come back. They only had each other.

I guess Nik and I were a little like that. We had each other and didn't care about anything else—or at least not until Jonathan came to us with this mission. I kind of wish I hadn't taken it, that Jonathan had never found us, and Nik and I would still be doing our whole shady smuggling enterprise. We would still be happy and minding our own business without a care in the 'raum.

That is until Bastien caught up to us.

So I guess it didn't matter because that bastard would always find me. It was just that sometimes he could find me faster. I tried to push away the thoughts of what he would do to me if this mission failed, if for some reason Nik and Jonathan failed at finding the evidence, but the memories kept flooding to the present. So much pain, so much torture. I couldn't go back. I wouldn't go back.

My heart was racing, and I was losing the sense of

where I was. All I could see was his face, his cold eyes and smile as he strategized the best way to hurt me.

My hands shook. No, I couldn't do this here. Not right now.

"Natascha, are you okay?"

I blinked and realized I had almost burned the garlic and onion. People would have been pissed since that smell would have lingered for quite some time. "Oh sorry. Just was thinking. Didn't mean to space out."

"Don't worry, happens to me all the time."

I wanted to make a witty comment but decided against it. I wanted to point out that I was not like a teenage girl. Hell, even when I was a teenager, I wasn't like any other teenage girl. I was one of the best fighters in the military academy.

And that was why I had very few friends. None, to be exact.

I got the rice and tacos going while Mary worked on the guacamole and bean-and-corn salad. Dinner was almost ready when the door to the corridor opened. I glanced up at Burt and rolled my eyes.

"Oh, it's you."

He looked around. "I was just wondering if food was almost ready. I'm getting hungry."

"If it was ready, then I would have announced over the commlinks, now wouldn't I've?"

He collapsed onto the couch. "It was just a question,

geez. No wonder Jonathan said you were a hard-ass."

I raised an eyebrow. "Oh? You think that's why he calls me a hard-ass. Just wait until you see me when we're closer to the end of this mission, then you'll know the truth to his statement."

"Great, I'm so looking forward to that."

"Or maybe I'll just—"

Mary interrupted. "It's almost done if you want to get the others or at least those who don't have to watch over the engine room or navigation."

Burt sighed as he stood up. "Fine, but just make sure she doesn't poison my food. I have a feeling she will sneak something in there."

I gave him a big sarcastic smile and watched as he left the room. *Gott* I hated dummkopfs like that.

"You know, if you just lightened up a little more, people might like you."

I let out a brief laugh. "Now why would I want that?"

She said nothing but finished mixing the beans. I cooked up the rice and tacos, and after we got everything prepared, Burt showed back up with Alexandra, Russ, and Samuel.

"So, I take it Jonathan and Nik are watching over the ship?" I asked Samuel.

He nodded. "Yeah, they said they will come get some food later."

"Like hell they are reheating my food. I will go take

them some. Eat as much as you all want; there will be plenty of leftovers for lunch tomorrow." I made up three plates and headed out of the mess hall. There was no way I would be left with people I didn't know. So either they were joking with me or they wanted to talk alone.

I found Nik and Jonathan in the cockpit. They smiled when they saw me step inside.

"We were taking bets on how long it would take you to blow a fuse and come eat out here. Nik said about ten seconds, and I said five," Jonathan said.

I glanced over to Nik, shaking my head. "Nik, you should know me better than that to bid so high."

He shrugged. "I know, but I felt like I had an unfair advantage. Had to let Jonathan win at something, now didn't I?"

"No, not really." I handed them their plates. "Now eat up. I didn't cook so you two could just heat it up later. Defeats the purpose of having me be the cook."

"Maybe you could just have Mary cook for you, then you could do whatever you want," Nik whispered as he took a bite of his taco. "Oh *Gott*, this tastes weird. What is that?"

I punched him. "That was for commenting on Mary." I punched him again. "And that was for saying it tastes weird."

Nik rubbed his arm. "No, seriously, what's in it?"

"Peaches instead of tomatoes."

"Why in the 'raum would you do that?" Jonathan asked.

"Samuel can't have tomatoes, so I thought I would experiment." I took a bite of my taco. "It's not bad; it's just a bit different."

Nik kept eating his. "Yeah, different."

"Isn't there pie? Why's there no pie on my plate?"

I shot a look at Jonathan. "Because that's for dessert. Wait a bit, will you?" I sighed. "Anyway, how much time until our first stop?"

Jonathan answered, "About three days."

"So then we will stock up and refuel before we hit the border. I presume you have a plan to get the three of us past the border with no problems, right?" I eyed Jonathan.

"Of course. You know I always have a plan." Jonathan winked.

Nik and I glanced at each other, shaking our heads.

Nik was the first to respond. "No, no, you don't. You wing everything, and then we have to clean up your mess."

"Please tell me Bardon came up with the plan," I added.

Jonathan nodded. "He did. We will discuss it later though. First I need to get something to wash this weird taste out of my mouth."

Before I could do anything, like punch Jonathan in the face, Nik pulled me back and laughed. It almost felt like old times, and even though I smiled, I could feel my heart hurt. Walrum wasn't here to enjoy this, he wasn't here laughing or telling me to calm down, and he never would be.

CHAPTER TWELVE

Nik

Other than that first dinner, Rebecca's meals were great. Now that she had a larger kitchen to work with, she could make all sorts of food. She could prepare meals like pesto pasta, tarts, and casseroles. Her cooking even impressed Jonathan, and although she wouldn't ever show it, I could tell she appreciated others enjoying her meals. I didn't understand why she always tried to hide her hobby. Maybe she was just a perfectionist and couldn't stand getting something wrong.

Like adding peaches instead of tomatoes.

Either way, three days passed, and we had arrived at Libertas. Rebecca and I were heading down the sky elevator. She stared out the window, watching as we grew closer and closer to the planet's surface.

I put my arm around her, and she made a little smirk. She didn't think I would show any PDA when we were around people. She still didn't turn to face me though.

"What are you thinking about?" I asked, not sure if she would give me a straight answer. There was a lot going on for the both of us, and I had a feeling I wasn't the only one who was keeping a secret. But what secret she was keeping from me, I wasn't sure.

"This place is *Gott*-awful. Reeks of drugs, sex, and some other odor I never placed last time we were here."

"We're only here for a few hours to restock. Just get over it."

I never cared for any of the Regit Republic planets either. They all were run-down and not as interesting as those in Nreff Nation. There seemed to be more culture on Nreff planets; they also seemed more… clean and eco-friendly. Regit planets felt as if the people couldn't care less what was going on around them. As long as there was money involved, who cared, right?

Then again, some people in the Nreff Nation only cared about money. Money and power, that was all that mattered to some people. People like Sebastien.

Rebecca went on. "Yeah, well, I don't want it to be the last planet I see before they kill us at the border."

Ah, so that's what it was.

The next stop was the border, and none of us looked forward to that. Jonathan had promised that our paperwork would be fine and we wouldn't be recognized as, well, ourselves. He got on the Regit side to find us, so I had to take his word for it. However, as both Rebecca and I recalled, none of Jonathan's schemes ever went according to plan. It was like he always tried to have something go wrong, or he just was that unlucky. I was surprised that Sebastien kept him around as long as he did. It was likely because he wanted his enemies where he could see them.

Which means he had to have known from the very beginning.

That seemed strange and scary to think he had been planning this since the moment he had met us. We hadn't even graduated from the military academy when Admiral Bardon came to us with this mission, to gain Admiral Sebastien Wilde's trust and find out if he was part of the human experimentations ring. Every time we thought we were getting close, he threw us a curveball.

Like setting us up for treason.

Admiral Bardon knew that we were innocent, that we were tricked, but he couldn't do anything without Sebastien finding out he was trying to bring the bastard down. Then who knew what would happen?

"We will be fine." I tried to assure her, but I didn't even feel that positive about it. We could be caught at the border. It was the most crucial point in the mission, other than getting the evidence of course. If there was one slipup, we would be screwed.

Rebecca let out a laugh. "Easy for you to say. You haven't pissed off as many people as I have."

That was true. Even on our missions, she always pissed off the wrong person. But the odds were slim for seeing someone that she knew—I mean there were billions of people living in each system. It wouldn't happen.

Yet I knew we would find some problem.

And I could tell Rebecca felt the same way. We always seemed to find trouble, no matter where we went. With this mission being of the utmost importance, whatever issue we would hit, it would not be pretty.

"Maybe you should work on that personality of yours then. If you were a little nicer to others, you wouldn't be in this predicament," I said jokingly. It was the only thing I could think of since the atmosphere was getting negative. Neither of us liked it when that happened.

I expected her to punch me or even give me a nasty look, but she did neither. She stared out the window, still caught up in her thoughts. This was bothering her —which was weird because it was rare for Rebecca to show such worry. It had been such a long time since she was this open that I wasn't sure what to do.

"Look, if you want to leave the mission, you can. I

wouldn't blame you."

"But would you leave the mission with me?" she asked in a whisper, as if it had been something she had been thinking about.

I paused. I would want to. I would want to stay with her no matter where she went, but I knew I couldn't. Not when so much was at stake this time. Not when I had run away from this with her to begin with and it had all caught up with me. There was no way I could run again, not when Bardon was watching.

"I can't…," I whispered.

She turned to me, a little surprised. "Why? Why after three years Jonathan shows up and you do whatever he says? I mean, I understand this mission is important and that we could be free, but at what cost? What if it doesn't work? What if we're killed or arrested again?"

"I—" I didn't know how to answer. She didn't understand that this mission had been going on for twenty-one years. That was how sly Sebastien was, how well he hid his tracks and the tracks of anyone who worked with him. *Gott*, I couldn't even believe that we had been working on it for that long—kind of made me feel like a failure if I was honest. That was a long time to come up with nothing.

And that was a long time to keep a secret from Rebecca, a long time to be lying to her. Of those twenty-one years, she was only a part of the group for sixteen of them, but that was still a good chunk of our lives.

I felt like I should tell her the truth, that Jonathan, Walrum, and I had been working for Admiral Bardon. This mission was important, and Rebecca should know what all the factors in play were. Besides, if we got killed on this mission, I didn't want to die knowing I had lied to her.

Jonathan was going to kill me.

I decided it would be best to tell her soon. Then she could decide whether she wanted to leave the mission before it was too late.

Now I just had to muster up the courage to tell her.

We landed on the planet and headed toward the food market. Mary and Russ wanted to come, but Rebecca got Jonathan to have them go find supplies for the ship. They were pretty bummed, but Rebecca promised to get some of the things from the list they had made from our last stop. That cheered them up a bit.

"So, will you need much time to look up what food you want?" I asked as we made our way through the crowd. Everyone seemed to be in a hurry, as if there was no time to take pleasure in anything. Then again, this city wasn't that great. I was glad we weren't staying long.

"It won't take long. I already have a list, and I just need to drop it off. Probably will get more fruit and make a chia pudding. Has a lot of omega-3 and fiber.”

It was amazing how much of a nutritional nut Rebecca was, but I guess it made sense—she wanted to stay in perfect health so that no one would have an advantage over her. Even in the small ship that we had, we both stayed fit by working out. I mean, it wasn’t like we didn’t have time to kill.

She glanced over and saw the smile on my face. “What?” she asked.

“Nothing, you’re just funny.”

“You know I have my butterfly knife in my pocket. I can stab you with no one seeing.”

I rolled my eyes. “You’re so quick to threaten. What did we just talk about? You need to lighten up and stop making enemies.”

She folded her arms. “Fine, instead I’ll say I have a cute pet butterfly that wants to flutter to your face, care to see it?”

I laughed. “That’s not any better. In fact, I think that’s worse.”

“Well, maybe I just can’t change. It’s who I am and have been for decades.”

“Even before you joined the military academy? I find that a little hard to believe.”

“Why do you think I joined? For fun?” she commented, her tone a little low. Now that she mentioned it, I didn’t know what her life was like before joining the academy. She never mentioned her family or her childhood, and if it ever came up, she diverted the subject.

So I just wouldn't push it.

"Because you knew you would be partnered with the three of us and then we all would have merry good ol' times." I winked.

"Heh. Like right now?"

"Of course. Didn't you think in the academy you would be out picking food to cook on a ship? I mean, your dream came true."

She laughed. "Yeah, I guess it has. And what about you? Was your dream to be out here stuck with me finding shitty food?"

"Ja." I leaned in and kissed her, taking her by surprise. She shoved me away.

"That's not funny."

"Who says I was being funny. I do enjoy being out here with you."

She rolled her eyes. "Whatever. Help me find the register so I can order the food."

I watched as she walked off ahead of me, smiling. Her cheeks were a little red, embarrassed that I had said that about her. She hated to show affection, but at least with her reaction I knew she felt the same about me.

We found the register, and Rebecca gave the elderly man her order. He smiled at her, which I could tell

Rebecca didn't know how to handle. She was too used to dealing with black market thugs, holding her own against them. Now with someone gentle, she didn't know how to behave, her stance awkward.

He handed her the receipt, and she checked it. "Hey, we've got some extra credits leftover."

"What do you have in mind?" I asked, curious what she was getting at. I had no idea what she wanted to buy.

She nodded down the street. "I saw a store up there that sold some chocolate. Expensive but I think I can get enough for a dessert."

"Or a snack for yourself?" I knew she had a weak spot for chocolate. Though buying real chocolate was hard, and she always liked the bitter stuff since she ate nothing with milk. It was a real pain.

"*Nein*, I would share, I swear. Now come on, we don't have time to lose. I want to get off this stupid planet."

I sighed as she grabbed my hand and dragged me to the store. It was large, or at least bigger than what I was expecting. It carried not only chocolates but also different types of alcohol. I thought about grabbing something for the three of us while we were off duty, mostly because I missed our nights drinking and having a good time. But it wouldn't be the same without Walrum.

There weren't many people in the store, just another couple, one man who looked like he was about twenty, and the person at the register. Rebecca went straight for the chocolate, drooling. With no one to overhear us, I knew this would be the only time I could talk to her about the mission and tell her the truth.

"So what do you think?" she asked as she grabbed two bags. "These are both superb companies, but I'm not sure which one is better to cook with."

I shook my head. "I don't have a clue. But Rebecca, there's something—"

"That's about to go down, yeah I noticed it too."

I had no idea what she was talking about. "What?"

She nodded over at the guy that was standing in the back. "Him. He's going to try to rob the place."

I glanced over. He didn't appear like he was doing anything, just looking over the different beers. "Rebecca, I don't think—"

"I bet you tonight's dishes he's going to rob the place. If you win, then *ich werde deinen schwanz lutschen.*"

I coughed. Just the thought of that made me want to go punch the kid to make sure he did nothing. "Seriously?"

She nodded with a little smile. "*Ja.* Now, I will count down to when he's going to do it." She put one of the chocolates away and pulled out her butterfly knife, hiding it in her hand. *"Zehn, neun, acht, sieben, sechs, fünf, vier, drei, zwei, eins…"*

As if on cue, the boy turned to the register and pulled out a gun. "Load up the credits on this device, now!"

Rebecca gave me a little smile. "Told ya."

CHAPTER THIRTEEN

Rebecca

Nik was such a sore loser. I could tell by the way he frowned that he wanted to win the bet. And could I blame him? But at least I didn't have to worry about dishes tonight. Though maybe I would surprise him tonight and reward him after all.

The boy trying to rob the place was such an amateur, probably just looking for some extra cash. He didn't think that the other two people in here nor Nik or I were a threat. Well, I couldn't speak for the other two, but I was. And Nik would be my backup if need be. He usually didn't get involved until I made him, probably because he knew I would get mad at him if he was in my way.

I stepped up behind the boy, who didn't even realize I was there. As the woman at the register started loading up the credits, I spun my knife in my hand.

That he heard.

He twirled around to find me smiling, satisfied that he had noticed me.

"Good day, young lad. Seems you are trying to rob this place."

Looking at me with complete disbelief, he waved his gun at me. "You think that you can go up against someone with a gun with that silly knife?"

I shrugged. "No, not really." I snapped the knife closed and threw it to my other hand that still had the bag of chocolates. "I don't even need a knife."

Grabbing him by the wrist, I moved the gun away from any target as he fired it. The other couple and the woman at the cash register screamed. I kneed the boy in the stomach and wrapped his arm around his back, making him release the gun.

"Now apologize to the young lady for scaring her." I turned him to the cash register.

"I-I'm sorry."

"And now apologize to me for having to deal with this kind of crap."

"I'm sorry?"

"That didn't sound sincere, but I will take it. Good

boy. Now, I can't have you running away, because you might get some buddies to come after me, so…" I moved my knife into my other hand but kept it close. All I needed was the hilt that I jabbed into his side, immobilizing him. He collapsed to the ground. "Stay. Good boy."

The civilians who witnessed this just stared at me as I twirled the butterfly knife in my hand. It would intimidate them to listen to what I was about to say. "Now, I presume you have already called the police?"

The woman at the register nodded.

"Well, I can't stay around for that, nor can I have cops searching for me. So here is what will happen: the two of us will leave here, the three of you never saw us. Some masked vigilante came and saved you, and you have no idea what they looked like, got it?"

The three of them nodded. I shut my knife. "Great. Now, how much do I owe you for this?" I held up the chocolate.

The woman shook her head. "Nothing, just take it."

"Cool. Let's go."

Nik nodded and followed me out but not without grabbing a bottle of schnapps. "I'm taking this too. Thanks!"

We hurried back to the sky elevator before any of the police showed up. Then both of us collapsed on our seats, laughing.

"*Gott* that was a close one." Nik sighed. "How come you always run into trouble no matter where you go?"

I shrugged. "Who knows? I'm just special like that."

Nik laughed. "You could say that again. You even had it down to the second. You're good at reading people, Rebecca. That's definitely a talent."

I just wished that I had been good at it before I met Bastien, then I wouldn't have gone with him all those years ago. I would have taken a different admiral's officer, probably Bardon's. Though it was Bastien who taught me how to be so talented at reading people. Who knew how he got so good at reading humans? Especially since he didn't know what it was like to have a real human emotion in his life.

Except jealousy and selfishness. He had those emotions for sure.

Sighing, I ripped open the bag of chocolates. With the thought of Bastien, I needed one to keep me from shaking and having to take another vial. I would finish the bag in no time. Too bad I knew I should keep some for dessert for the rest of the crew. And people acted like I was selfish.

"Hey, what were you going to say before I changed the subject and stopped a robbery?" I asked.

"Oh," Nik began, casting his eyes down. "Nothing. I was just going to say we should grab some alcohol, which I did."

I didn't believe that, but I didn't press further. It was apparent he didn't want to talk about it. "What kind did you get?"

"Apple, of course."

I smiled. "Of course."

Everything else went according to schedule, and we were on our way to the border. It was only about a day out, but it was better to fill up with supplies before rather than later, just in case they held us at the border longer than expected.

I had already made dinner, some stir-fry on rice, spring rolls, and edamame with chia pudding for dessert. Samuel and Mary were on duty, so Russ took them both some food. He was quickly back to eat more.

Alexandra smiled. "This is a *chudesnyy* meal, Natascha. It reminds me of my mother's cooking when I was young."

"She was a cook?" I asked. It seemed like everyone's mothers were cooks. Mine sure as hell wasn't.

Alexandra nodded. "Yes, she was. Until my parents were killed, that is."

Everyone became quiet. Damn, why did everyone's story have to have a crappy ending, but I guess that would include me. I said nothing.

"How old were you?" Russ asked. I guess he could relate.

"Twelve. They were killed right before my eyes. Some people wanted them to do a job for them, but they refused. So they were killed just like that."

Everything felt like it stopped. *Gott*, I knew where I had seen her before; it was that night—the night Bastien made me kill those doctors because they wouldn't join his enterprise.

Gott in himmel.

Did she remember me that night? I doubted it, because if my parents' killer was standing before me, they wouldn't have time to react before I killed them. Well, that wasn't true. I hated my parents. But if someone killed Nik, I would be out for vengeance.

Unless that was why she took this job.

It all made sense now. She remembered Bastien—how could you forget such a coldhearted smile?—but I had changed since then. I had to hide my appearance—it was amazing what a hair change and a little makeup could do. But it would only be a matter of time before she put two and two together.

I had no idea what else everyone talked about at dinner. I couldn't remember. I was too involved with my mind, replaying the night I killed those doctors and trying not to have a shaking fit. I kept taking deep breaths and hoping that the others didn't pay attention. They all kept laughing and talking, so I doubted anyone thought anything of it.

There had been a little girl in the cupboard. I saw her through the slit. I didn't get a good look at her, but she resembled her mom now that she was older. Bastien didn't see her though, so I said nothing. He would have made me kill her, and there was no way I would kill a little kid in cold blood.

Burt, Russ, and Alexandra retired for the night, or at least for the time being. I didn't know if it was really technically night. Nik was in charge of washing the dishes since he lost the bet. He had hoped I had forgotten. I didn't.

I played with my knife, twirling it back and forth, practicing.

"I should go relieve Samuel of his post. Care to join me?" Jonathan stared me right in the eyes, noting that it was an order, not a request.

I got up and followed him out toward the cockpit. "Bye, Nik, come get me when you are done."

"Hey," he called over the suds. "That's not fair!"

"Too bad, so sad." The door shut between us, and I frowned. I had a feeling I knew what Jonathan would talk to me about, and it would not be a pleasant conversation.

We made our way to the cockpit to find Mary and Samuel both there. In the same seat. Making out.

"Hey, no making out while on duty." Jonathan slammed his hand on the chair.

Mary jumped up quicker than I thought possible. Her face was beet red. "I'm sorry, I just wanted to run something past Samuel—"

I threw my hands up in the air. "I didn't know you needed to touch lips to talk. Damn, I've been talking to people all wrong all these years. Well, to most people."

Jonathan laughed. "Me too, apparently. Now get out of here, both of you. I'm taking over the shift."

Samuel got up. "Whatever."

"And Mary," I added. She turned to face me. "Don't date a guy much older than you. It's not worth it, am I right, Jonathan?"

Jonathan gave me a suspicious look but didn't say a word. Mary and Samuel could tell the tension between Jonathan and I was growing and left the cockpit before they found themselves in the middle. Jonathan shut the door, and both of us sat down.

"I didn't think Walrum nor Nik was that much older than you."

I shook my head. "You know who I meant by that, just like I know who your lover is."

He leaned back. "Really?"

"*Oui*. But don't worry…" I gave him a little smirk. "I never told a soul."

"Because you knew Admiral Wilde would have killed me?" he asked with a straight face. He and I both knew what kind of monster he was, even to his own men.

I nodded. "And he would have made me do it."

There was silence between us for a moment as Jonathan checked a few of the controls. "Jacques knows that you were close to Sebastien and suspects you were involved in some way with the human experiments."

Damn Admiral Bardon and never minding his own business. He thought it was his duty to make sure there was justice in the system—which was why Bastien wanted me to always keep an eye out for him. "I know, he has for a long time. And Sebastien knows that."

"So you won't deny it?" Jonathan added.

I shrugged. I was surprised myself that I hadn't denied it, but knowing where we were heading, it was only a matter of time before the truth came out. "Is there a point to deny it now? Not to you, not when you and Admiral Bardon are *les amoureux*."

He stared at me for a moment longer, his eyes full of dread. He kept up such a happy appearance, but that was long gone now. Jonathan sighed. "I had hoped he was wrong."

"I wish he was too, but that won't change the fact that you brought me in here to talk about something. What does Admiral Bardon want me to do?"

Jonathan nodded to my pants pocket. "You can take a hit if you need to keep yourself calm."

I froze. "Did Bardon tell you?"

"He saw on your medical records that they prescribed

you morphine-B a while back and that you took nothing to wean off of it. He doubted you went to a doctor after the incident, so he gave me that money I gave you just in case."

I took the case out of my pocket and opened it. "It's strange, not even Nik knows, and yet here you are, spilling all my secrets."

"Yeah, well, it comes with our line of work."

I popped open a vial and took a dose. "Now, tell me what Bardon really wants me to do."

"You aren't going to like it, but only you can pull it off."

Jonathan gave me the details, and he was right. I didn't like it.

CHAPTER FOURTEEN

Nik

I woke to find my arm around Rebecca. She was still sound asleep, her warm, naked skin against my own. To my surprise, I still got the reward for the bet we made, even though I had lost. I had no idea what got her to have sex on the ship, but whatever it was, I was thankful for it.

And I was also thankful that these cabins were soundproof. It was so that some of the crew could sleep while the rest of the crew could go about the ship without having to worry about disturbing them, along with the engine noise. But it came in handy when two crew members had sex.

Jonathan and I knew that after being on the same ship as her and Walrum.

I tried to push back those memories and enjoy the present. For whatever reason, Rebecca was showing more emotion toward me, and I wondered if it had to do with the mission and her thinking that this could be our end or if it had been something else. I wasn't sure and knew better than to question it.

Wondering if Jonathan knew about our romantic night, I hoped he wasn't waiting outside. I could just imagine the remarks he would make and how he would piss Rebecca off. Then she wouldn't want to sneak in bed with me ever again. Damn, I would probably punch him if he caused that.

Rebecca stirred, stretching and almost punching me in the face.

"Geez, you're violent even when you're asleep," I commented as she woke up.

"Yeah, well, can never be too careful."

I guess she had a point. It wasn't like we had never been ambushed while we were asleep before. "Well, are you ready to get to the border?"

She didn't answer but leaned forward and glanced around. It was almost as if she had forgotten where she was. I could tell it all came back to her, and she realized we were on a ship.

"Right, that's coming up, isn't it? Great…"

I stroked her back. "Don't worry. Jonathan's paperwork will work. It has to; he got us this far, didn't he?"

She gave me a look, then laughed. "Yeah, I suppose it should be fine. It's not like Jonathan ever threw monkey wrenches in our missions before."

We were silent for a moment, then I shook my head. "Not this one. He wouldn't try anything like that."

She rolled her eyes. "Whatever you say. Anyway, we should get going, or Jonathan will make some comments."

"That is too late to stop, but you do need to get breakfast ready. Anything good today?"

"Sweet potato hash with lentils. I started it yesterday so just have to heat it up. Should be ready in about half an hour." She crawled out from under the blanket and grabbed her clothes. I smacked her bare ass real quick, because I had a feeling I wouldn't be able to again for a while.

Rebecca turned back and kicked me in the face. I should have seen it coming; she was predictable like that.

"Dummkopf," she spat back as she changed.

"You didn't complain last night," I commented with a little smile.

"Yeah, well, shut up."

I grinned as she threw me my clothes. I pulled them

on, and she slid the door open and climbed out. I waited a moment and climbed out behind her.

Of course there was someone in the corridor.

Burt glanced us both over and groaned. "God, I don't even want to know."

"No, you don't," Rebecca replied. "And don't mention it to anyone. Especially Jonathan."

"Like I wouldn't find out." Jonathan laughed.

I turned to find him grinning ear to ear. Rebecca and Jonathan held each other's gaze, and after a moment she turned away and headed toward the mess hall.

"What was that about?" I asked him.

He shrugged. "Probably just didn't want me to find out about your quickie."

I gave him a smile. "Oh, that was anything but quick."

He patted me on the back. "Yeah, I don't want to know, *mon ami*. Now get to the engine room. Russ is itching to be relieved."

I nodded, then headed straight there. I debated going to the kitchen to grab a snack beforehand. It wasn't like it was that far on this ship.

We were almost there. I could see the border patrol outside the space shield.

It was massive, as many ships lined up in different lanes, getting their paperwork checked and hoping that nothing was wrong. Nreff patrol wasn't as forgiving as others.

Jonathan, Rebecca, and I stood there, staring out the glass, all wondering if this would be our demise. I hoped that it wouldn't be, but with our stroke of luck…

"You promise everything is foolproof, Jonathan? That we won't get caught?" I asked once more.

He nodded. "*Oui*, everything should go according to plan."

Rebecca didn't say a word but watched as we got closer to the patrol. She appeared to be more nervous than either Jonathan or me. Placing my hand on her shoulder, I tried to comfort her, but she shrugged it off.

"I will check on the engine room. Let me know when you get word from them when it's our turn for inspection." She turned and headed toward the engine room.

"That's strange. You think she's okay?" I asked Jonathan.

He shrugged. "Seems fine, just nerves. I wouldn't worry about it."

I knew he was probably right, but that didn't mean I felt any better about it. We were coming up on the border, and I didn't want her to be off guard in case anything happened.

An hour passed, and it was our turn to be inspected. Burt, who was listed as captain, was already undergoing the typical questioning of "Why are you coming to the Nreff Nation, and what is your business?" The rest of us just waited our turn, although it wouldn't be as lengthy for us.

Rebecca leaned against the wall next to me in the waiting room. If it weren't for the fact weapons were illegal in this area, she would have been playing with her butterfly knife. It was fun to see the reaction of people around her as she flung that thing back and forth, twirling it between her fingers. It surprised me she had never cut herself that badly with it with all the tricks that she does. Then again, she had used many other dangerous weapons over the years; this was hardly anything new. I bet that the knife was in her pocket though. I just prayed that she wouldn't be searched.

Instead, she bit at her nail, not ripping it or anything but more just gnawing on the edge. It was her backup thing to do when she was nervous.

"Don't worry, it's fine. Burt will answer everything, and we will be on our way."

"Yeah, whatever."

She kept biting at her nails. She didn't appear to be stopping soon. I leaned back and closed my eyes. It had been such a long time since I had gone through Nreff border patrol, I'd forgotten how long it took.

Another half an hour went by, and the soldier came

back out with Burt. Nothing appeared wrong, as Burt didn't look distressed. I didn't want to jinx it though.

The soldier went through his tablet, checking our identification to make sure we matched up with who we said we were. He went around the room, clicking the screen again and again. As he went to Jonathan, I held my breath. *Gott*, this was nerve-racking.

Jonathan seemed to be fine as the soldier moved on from him. He got to me, and I tried to act casual, as if this was no big deal. I felt like I was doing a horrible job at it but knew that my Special Forces instinct had to have kicked in. I should have been used to this.

He passed by me and I let out the breath I had been holding. When he got to Rebecca, he froze.

Scheiße.

It really impressed me how fast he pulled out his gun. And if it wasn't for it being pointed straight at Rebecca, I would have clapped. Instead, I stepped forward and raised my hands.

"Whoa, whoa, whoa! What are you doing?" I asked.

"This woman is a wanted criminal of the Nreff Nation. There has been a recent posting for her immediate arrest."

My heart skipped a beat. No, this couldn't be happening. How was there a recent posting for her but not for Jonathan or me? "No, this is Natascha Weiß; she's a friend of mine."

"Sir, she has either been lying to you or you have been cooperating with a fugitive. If you do not stand down now, I will have to bring you in."

I glanced at Jonathan, and he shook his head. He was right. If I kept pushing this, then none of us would walk out of there free.

But either way, Rebecca would be arrested, and I couldn't let that happen. I just didn't know a way I could help her without sabotaging the rest of the mission. This mission was important, but so was she. Or at least she was to me.

"You're right. I am the wanted fugitive you have been looking for," Rebecca said as she turned to me. "I'm sorry, Gunther, I lied to you. I ran away from the Nreff Nation three years ago. I didn't think they would still search for me. I'm sorry."

What was she doing? I couldn't believe what I was hearing. She would let herself get arrested? After all this time?

Jonathan was quick to come to my side, knowing I was about to do something. He leaned forward and whispered in my ear, "Don't."

I let out a deep breath as I watched the soldier call for back up and shove Rebecca toward the wall. "Both hands on the wall. Now."

Rebecca leaned forward and put her hands on the wall. She wasn't speaking, wasn't even trying to escape. Was she going to just let this happen? The Rebecca I knew would have still put up a fight, even knowing that it might do nothing.

Which meant she wanted to be captured.

Why would she want this? What was going on? I glanced over to Jonathan. He didn't seem surprised but watched, waiting for her to be taken away. I clenched my fist. So this was a plan, this is what they discussed the day before. And it also explained the sex.

The soldier patted her down, and when he got to her cargo pockets, he stopped. He pulled out her butterfly knife.The soldier said nothing but pocketed it. A few moments later another three guards came, their guns pointed at Rebecca.

"Hey, do you think I'm that dangerous that you need an entire army to take me down?" she joked. "I mean, was I even putting up a fight?"

"Your file says to take as high of security measures as possible—I'm just following orders."

For some reason I understood that. Rebecca wasn't your normal criminal. She wasn't even a criminal, but a soldier. A very, very talented soldier.

"Well, well, I wonder who put those orders through. Does his first name start with an *S* and last name start with a *W*?"

"We aren't at liberty to say."

She laughed. "So what you're saying is that I'm

right." Rebecca looked over to me and winked. "Well, can't wait to see his face when I smash it in with my fist."

The soldier turned her around and punched her straight in the stomach. Rebecca collapsed to her knees.

"Hey." I stepped forward. "That was uncalled for!"

One soldier pointed their gun at me. "Stand back or we will detain you."

I frowned. I felt powerless against them, powerless to help Rebecca. Why did she always have to back-talk everyone she met? She needed to learn how to keep her mouth shut. I had told her that again and again.

Watching as they pulled her up and cuffed her wrists behind her back, it took everything inside me not to go running after her, to get myself arrested so she wouldn't have to be alone. So she wouldn't have to face Sebastien alone. I had a feeling Jonathan wanted her to do this to bring him out into the open, then she could get close to him and find something about the human experiments. Of the three of us, she was the only one who was wanted alive, where our files said dead or alive. It was the safest option to have her sacrifice herself, but I couldn't bear to think what he might do to her.

But I knew there was nothing I could do except stand there and watch as the soldiers dragged her away.

CHAPTER FIFTEEN

Rebecca

So that happened.

I walked between the four soldiers, their guns ready to fire if I even made a slight movement to run away, not that I would. I wasn't stupid. It was much easier to escape during transportation than when stationary, such as at the border prison. Especially at the border prison. I knew Sebastien wanted me moved to a planet before retrieving me. He knew that these soldiers would question me and I might reveal some information that he doesn't want known.

My heart raced at the thought of him. It wouldn't be long now that I would come face-to-face with my worst nightmare once more. I scratched at my skin. His devilish smile, his heartless eyes; not a day went by when the image of him didn't come across my mind. I wished that this day hadn't come, that I wouldn't have to go back to the hell that he created for me.

But luck was never on my side. No matter how the cards played out, I would have still had to see him, still have him grab me and pull me back, kicking and screaming. Now I was going to him.

Well, sort of.

It was this or straight to prison—or at least a different prison. Admiral Bardon knew that I had ties through Bastien to the human experiments, and if Bastien was caught, then there would be evidence against me. However, if I let myself be captured by Bastien and gain intel, then the charges would be waived and Admiral Bardon would argue that I was an informant all along.

We'll see how that would hold up in court. I doubted he knew all the horrible things I had done under Bastien's thumb. Besides, I knew I didn't deserve a pass. Whatever was coming for Bastien, I earned as well.

But what I didn't deserve was having to face him on my own. Again.

Who knew the things he would do to me, or make me do, to earn his trust back? I had to wait until he took me to the facility, as the location always changed. Then, *Gott* permitting, he doesn't find the two tracking devices I have hidden in my shoe and inserted in my hand. I could activate the silent alarm on them, and Bardon would send in his soldiers to capture Bastien and everyone who was in the facility. And I would be saved.

That is, if all went according to plan.

He was always two steps ahead and could guess everyone's next move. I didn't know how he did it, how he could think like all his enemies, to see every attack before it happened, but he did. He always did.

This wasn't the first time someone tried to take him down either. Hell, it wasn't even the twentieth. And all those people disappeared shortly after. Though usually I was involved in their disappearance. Just like with Alexandra's parents.

That night kept playing in my mind. Bastien had wanted her parents, both excellent brain surgeons and scientists, to help him with his special little enterprise, but they refused. He tried to persuade them with threats, his threat of me, but they still held their moral ground. Good for them, but then I had to follow through with those threats and I killed them. Slowly. In front of Alexandra. That was ten years ago, and she had gone into the same specialization. She would stand out and find Bastien for herself. She was such a fool, thinking she could do anything to him.

I wondered if she told anyone about what had happened. She was a witness to her own parents' murder, yet Bastien was never brought in for trial. People knew not to cross him, and since it wasn't linked to the other crimes, they probably just swept it under the rug, or Bastien threatened some people to do that for him. Probably the latter, knowing him. And who would listen to a twelve-year-old girl? No one who wanted to face Bastien's wrath.

Fidgeting with my cuffs, I smiled. It had been a while since I had cuffs around my wrists, three years to be exact. They thought with the cuffs that I wouldn't be able to fight them. That thought was incorrect. Bastien had trained me well, after all.

We came to a stop, and two of the guards threw me into a concrete room. There was a bed and toilet inside. I found it ironic that the living space here was bigger than the one I had been staying in for the past three years. Then again, I could pace around in the ship wherever I wanted and here I was stuck.

"You will be escorted to Nouveau Départ as soon as we can secure a military ship. In the meantime, you are to remain here."

"Well, this place needs some sprucing up. Have any posters of whatever the latest music craze is? Or maybe of a cute kitten?"

The guard stepped forward and laid another one in my stomach. Damn, these Nreff soldiers didn't let up. Without another word they left me there. Alone, for the first time in what seemed like decades.

I sat there, in my cell, quiet, not sure what I was supposed to do. The soldiers had left my wrists bound, and I didn't have anything to fiddle with. They had taken away my butterfly knife, which sucked because that would have given me something to do. I just hoped that I would get it back at the end of all this. I liked that knife.

What felt like hours passed by as I stared at the wall, trying not to let my mind psych itself out about what was coming for me. There was a reason I was covered in scars, and they had nothing to do with being arrested for treason.

They had everything to do with him.

I knew I should have reported him. I had the evidence, but I was also so afraid. It wasn't until we'd broken up that he ever directed his anger and frustration out at me. When we were together, he was almost perfect, that is until I found out about the human experiments. I didn't know what to do then, as he treated me like a princess—his princess to be more exact. He was possessive, and it seemed like it was too late before I realized that. He was a sociopath and saw me as his. It didn't matter what he did, I was supposed to always be there with him, telling him how much I loved him and how he was my world.

But he wasn't that anymore; he hadn't been that for a very long time. I had tricked myself into believing his lies, and when I opened my eyes, I realized what kind of monster he was. But it was too late; I couldn't do anything. At least not without getting myself thrown in prison.

I was glad I took a dose of the morphine-B before we got to the border, otherwise I would have been in a shaking fit already. Although I felt on edge, it was nothing compared to what this scenario would have been like without the drug.

As I stayed deep in thought, wishing that I had taken some kind of online meditation course, the door to the cell slid open. The four soldiers from earlier stepped in.

I gave them a little smirk. "Guess my ride's here, eh?"

The soldier punched me in the stomach yet again. I guess it was his favorite thing to do. Didn't blame him. If I could punch someone I hated as much as I wanted, I would do it too. And by someone I hated, I meant Bastien.

"Traitor scum. You killed one of the best representatives that Nash Mir has ever had."

Ah, it was personal. Well, kind of. There were many

people who wanted my head for that same reason. And many other reasons. "I would beg to differ, but that's just me."

He punched me again, then grabbed me and shoved me out of the room.

The soldiers led me down the corridor and toward a small military transportation ship. It was the same as the ship Nik and I had, but it had two prisoner cells. Nik and I always had to handcuff someone in the hallway if we needed to transport someone, or threaten someone. Or just to teach someone a lesson.

"Ah, my chariot awaits. Would prefer a little nicer ship, but I guess I can't complain."

The head soldier slapped me in the face. "Shut up!"

You would think I would learn not to talk back or make sarcastic comments, but I never do. I've gotten so many slaps and punches over the years for just talking. Nik tells me I need to learn to be quiet—or that I was a masochist. I disagreed about needing to stay quiet for a couple of reasons. First off, it pissed off whoever I was up against and they would be distracted, and second, it made me feel more powerful, as none of them had me under their control. It was a powerful tool I had learned over the years and one that gave me the most scars.

As for the comment of being a masochist, I'm neither going to agree nor disagree.

I wondered how many people would be aboard the

ship or if it would just be me. Probably the latter, as I doubt many people got arrested at the border. No one was dumb enough to cross it when they were wanted for a crime—just me.

Nik was most likely throwing a shit fit now, as Jonathan hadn't told him about this part of the mission. Jonathan promised me he wouldn't tell Nik about my past. I didn't want him to know about all the things I did. At least not yet.

The guards shoved me into the cell, and I could hear the door lock behind me. Great, I was stuck in another cell for the time being. I glanced around to find that it was the same as the one at the border—small, quiet, lifeless. Couldn't wait to see what would happen next.

Oh, that's right, it would be Bastien's face, smiling.

I sat down and leaned against the wall, shutting my eyes and listening to the ship depart the border station. It was only a matter of time now.

CHAPTER SIXTEEN

Nik

What the fuck just happened?

Rebecca was gone—taken away—just like that. Jonathan didn't argue with them, I didn't argue, or at least not much. I only could say so much before they would double-check my papers and realize they wanted me too. My first instinct was not to care, to go to prison with her, but then this entire mission would have been for nothing. So I just stood there and watched.

And then she was gone.

The paperwork cleared since Rebecca had confessed she lied to us and that none of us seemed to be worthy of a search. I was a little surprised, but it had to do with

Burt's answers when he was questioned in the beginning. All the rest of the paperwork was fine, so I guess they cleared us to go. That, or Bardon pulled some strings to make sure we were in the clear.

But if that was the case, then why did Rebecca get caught? I let out a sigh. Probably because that was what they wanted to happen.

I was pissed at Jonathan. I could tell he was in on it since he didn't do anything to stop it. Then again, he could have just been quiet because he didn't want to jeopardize the mission just like me. But he had that look of intent on his face, not one of surprise.

Which was why I was going straight to the cockpit where Jonathan was.

Most of the crew was asleep or at their own duties. No one would hear the discussion that the two of us were about to have, which I was thankful for. I didn't need them to know the truth about the three of us nor think we were villains and turn us in just like Rebecca.

"Jonathan," I said as I stepped into the cockpit. "We need to talk."

He turned and glanced at me with a little smirk. "About time you showed up. Was thinking you hadn't put two and two together yet."

Taking a seat next to him, I tried not to let my anger get the better of me. I hated it when he did things like this and presumed I would just figure it out later. "So you were behind this."

"Oui."

I clenched my fist. "She's going straight to a holding cell, you know this right?"

"That's where you're wrong, *mon ami*. She's going straight to Sebastien."

"What?" I asked. That made little sense. That was the last thing I ever wanted.

"You remember that her wanted article said she's needed alive, yes? I suspect that Sebastien will receive word straightaway that she's alive and in a cell. Then he will come and retrieve her, taking her where we want him to go."

I let out a deep breath. I knew where he was going with this. "You mean you set her up as bait."

"You could say that. It was Jacques's idea, not mine. So if you have a problem with it, talk to him."

I knew it wasn't his fault, but that didn't mean I wasn't pissed. I was kept in the dark yet again. "But you could've at least told me."

"And would you have listened? No, amour has clouded your judgment." Jonathan clicked two buttons on the console. "And it was up to Rebecca, not you."

I didn't care that it was. I didn't want her near Sebastien without me. I slammed my hands on the console. "I just can't imagine what will happen to her once Sebastien has her—what if she is his next victim?"

"That won't happen. She has two tracking devices on her person. All she has to do is push a button and our men will be there. I'm hoping we will stay close enough to her that we can show up when the alert goes off, but either way someone will be there. Jacques is keeping a close eye on it as well. So don't worry, she's safe."

"If you can call being in Sebastien's hands safe." He didn't understand what kind of monster he was, otherwise she wouldn't have agreed to it. "I'll try not to think about it, but I hope she'll be okay."

Jonathan clicked a few more buttons. "Have you known Rebecca ever not to be fine? As long as she doesn't say something to piss people off, I think she will be okay."

I gave him a look. "Thanks. I didn't even think about that. She will provoke anyone she runs into to punch her. *Gott*, why does she have to make life so much more difficult?"

"Because she's Rebecca and that's her hobby."

I rubbed my forehead. She just liked to piss them off. I knew she did. I didn't like the thought of her getting punched for every word she said. I swear she was a masochist. "I just can't wait until this mission is over with."

"Neither can I, *mon ami*. Neither can I."

"Well," I began as I stood up. "I better get some shut-eye. That is, if I can sleep."

"Don't have Rebecca to tire you out, you mean?" He gave me a little wink.

I shook my head. "If she were here, she would have decked you for the comment."

"I'm sure she would have."

"*Gute nacht.*"

As I turned, I found Alexandra just outside the cockpit. "Oh, what is it, Alexandra?"

She appeared nervous, fiddling with the ends of her dark hair. "I wanted to speak to Jonathan about something."

I sat back down. "What is it? Maybe I can help."

She glanced at Jonathan. "How long have you two been friends?"

"Since the academy," Jonathan answered. "Why?"

She stepped in closer to the cockpit and shut the door behind her. "So his name isn't Gunther, is it Jonathan?"

I stared at Jonathan. After all that work, someone had figured it out. That, or she knew in the first place. "How does she know…?"

Jonathan explained, "Because Jacques was friends with her years ago. He has monitored her and knows she won't spoil our secret. So no, his name isn't Gunther, but for safety I'm not giving you his real name."

She didn't seem to care. "That's fine. However, I do

have a question that I want the answer to: How long have you known Rebecca?"

"Over fifteen years. Why?" I asked. I didn't see where this conversation was going, but I was getting a strange feeling in my gut.

"It's just that… I think I've seen her before."

Jonathan shook his head. "No, the probability of that is low; it was someone else."

Alexandra took a deep breath and bit her lip. "That's what I thought at first, but when I heard her name, it all clicked. You all once worked for Sebastien, isn't that correct? Along with Rebecca?"

I nodded. "Yes, but I still don't see your point."

"It's just that Sebastien was the man who killed my parents ten years ago. They were both doctors, and Sebastien wanted them to work for him. Well, you can guess their answer, so he had them killed. However, looking back to that night, I remembered a woman being with him. She looked a lot like Rebecca."

My mouth opened but nothing came out. That was impossible; she would never kill in cold blood. Not to mention that would mean she would have known about the experiments, and there was no way she would have just stood by and watched them happen.

I mean, she couldn't have, right?

Jonathan was first to shake his head. "No, that couldn't have been her. She and Sebastien only worked together on missions the government authorized. We went through all the paperwork, and there was no way they would even have a spare moment to do anything like that."

Alexandra was quiet for a moment. "I remember him saying her name… I swore… I guess I could be wrong. It could have been someone else. It was a long time ago, and you two know her better than me."

"Yeah, she wouldn't hurt someone," I began as Jonathan gave me a side glance. "At least not without being provoked. And she wouldn't kill unless she had to."

She nodded. "I trust you two. It's just that now I can't get that night out of my head. I wish I could figure out who it was, then maybe I could get my revenge."

"We will get our revenge on the man behind it—Sebastien. Whoever was with him was probably forced and didn't have a choice, remember that."

"No, everyone has a choice. She could have said no even if that meant her death. All of us are risking our lives, she can too."

I knew she had a point, but I can only imagine what threats Sebastien could have given in order to make someone do what he wanted. I felt bad for whoever it was, especially since when the evidence and names came out, they would be on that list.

Unless it was Rebecca.

That couldn't be true; she couldn't have done that. I mean, I knew she had a dark side to her, but she wasn't a killer. She would never hurt someone like the way Sebastien did.

"I mean, I doubt he could force anyone to hang someone upside down and drown them in a sink. If someone was forced to kill, it would have been a little more humane."

My heart felt like it skipped a beat. There was only one person that I knew who would use that as a torture method, though it never ended in people's deaths, just to get information out of them.

And that was Rebecca.

I never knew where she picked up that technique, nor would she ever tell me. Was it from Sebastien? Was it her who helped him kill Alexandra's parents, among countless other things over the years? Had she known about the experiments all along?

That was impossible. She would have said something.

Alexandra went on. "Anyway, I better get going and take a sleep cycle. Mary needs me up to help cook since now we don't have a chef and all the men on this ship suck at preparing food."

Jonathan nodded quickly. "It's true. Gunther almost caused a big fire on a ship once."

I gave him a look. "You just have to bring that up

whenever you can, don't you?"

"Oui."

Alexandra left the cockpit, and now it was just Jonathan and me. He kept checking the navigation as I sat there, waiting for him to say something.

"It wasn't her, was it?" I asked in a whisper. It was something I didn't want to admit I was thinking, and I would have never thought it, but that was Rebecca's signature move. It was how she threatened people.

Jonathan let out a sigh. "We went through all those reports over the years. There is no way they are fake, and there is no way they could have done anything else. Besides, do you think Rebecca is a coldhearted killer?"

I paused. No, I didn't. She had a heart, and even if she didn't act like it, she cared for people in the long run. She wanted people to be safe, she wanted them to be happy.

Yet deep down I felt like it was all beginning to click.

I rubbed my temple. "I don't, but that was her signature move to get information from people. We've all seen her do it on some missions."

"Yes, but she never killed someone in cold blood doing that. It was always just slight torture to get information. And she could have picked it up from Sebastien, and then he could have taught someone else. It was easier for him to have done whatever he was doing when all four of us were on missions than when he was with Rebecca. You and I both know that."

"I know, but I can't help feeling like something else is going on with Rebecca. I'm regretting bringing her on this mission, I think it was a bad idea. If she has anything to do with it and ran away, Sebastien will want her head."

"Nik, I doubt he would hurt her. She will be fine. She can hold her own, remember? This is Rebecca we're talking about. She's capable of handling a sociopath."

I let out a small laugh. He had a point. She had handled many over the years. "And we're keeping a close eye on her?"

He nodded. "Of course. By the looks of it, they've already put her into a shuttle and it's heading to Nouveau Départ. Then Sebastien will retrieve her and the mission we have been on, for what seems like forever, will be over with."

"Yeah. I guess it will be."

CHAPTER SEVENTEEN

Rebecca

I was having some regrets.

And it wasn't just regret in turning myself in, it was more a regret of all the choices that had led up to this— mainly the one to become Bastien's agent. Had I taken Admiral Bardon's offer to work under him, none of this would have happened. I would be living the good life, or at least a better life. And maybe I still would have been with Nik. Or Walrum. Damn, it was strange to think that in another life I would have to choose between the two. I loved them both so much, and I couldn't imagine my life without Nik now.

Walrum had been gone for three years. It was odd to

think about that and how Nik and I had only been friends back then. I mean, he and I were close and shared almost everything, but now it was different—now we cared for each other. Now we maybe even loved each other.

Maybe wasn't the right word. I knew Nik loved me; he had even said it. The problem was I didn't know if I truly loved him. I had so much baggage in regard to Walrum and Bastien; I wasn't even sure if my heart could love again.

And now I was heading straight back to Bastien.

I wondered if I hadn't become Bastien's *Gott*-damned *Puppe*, whether he would have gotten this far. I mean, I was the vital key here in getting the location of the most recent facility. I sighed. I didn't want to go back there. I didn't want to see those things again.

Just the thought of him dragging me there, making me watch those people scream as doctors performed different experiments on them. It was grotesque. I didn't know how he could stand it. Oh right, because he was a sociopath who didn't understand that people weren't his playthings.

Like me. I was a human who had feelings and didn't want to be his *Puppe*.

I started scratching at my arms. The thought of the things I had done for him, the mental torture he put me through, I couldn't go back. I didn't want to go back.

Closing my eyes, I took deep breaths. This was the only way they would arrest him. This was the only way he would be behind bars.

Unless he saw it coming.

That *drecksau* knew it was coming and had a plan, a backup plan, and then another plan just in case. He was cunning like that. That was how he was so dangerous. He always knew. He always was a few steps ahead of anyone who dared try to cross him.

He was always steps ahead of me and everyone else.

I had tried to run away from him so many times that I had lost count. It wasn't until they arrested me that I got away from his clutches, with Nik and Jonathan's help. But on my own, I was never successful. He always found me.

And tried to persuade me to never run away again.

Why was I so stupid to decide that I wanted to work under him all those years ago? Probably because it seemed like a once-in-a-lifetime opportunity; he was one of the few admirals who rarely took on new blood, and I felt like I was special, that I had earned it. Never did I realize what would be in store for me.

I wasn't sure what it was I did in my life now to deserve all this, but apparently I was a horrible human being.

But either way, I was stuck on this ship, heading to my demise. They would transfer me to a secure holding cell until Bastien could pick me up. *Gott*, I wondered how long that would take or if he was already there waiting, as if he knew I was coming even before I did. It made me shudder.

The door slid open, and the soldiers came in to take me to the spaceport. I stood up before I noticed what was in the leader's hand.

My butterfly knife.

I grinned, analyzing the situation. The grin on *his* face was cocky. The other three didn't appear so sure as to what their leader wanted to do. "Want to make me pay for killing the Nash Mir representative, I take it? And with my knife too."

"You deserve a lot more than what our government will do to you," he said as he flipped the knife open in his hand.

I let out a laugh. "Oh, I doubt that. You sure you want to do this? I mean, you do realize that I'm Admiral Wilde's property, right? He will kill you if he finds out you tried to harm me."

The two other soldiers looked at their leader. "Admiral Wilde? I don't want to cross him—I've heard some horrible things about him."

The leader waved his hand. "Those are just rumors, and I doubt he cares that much for this girl, especially if we tell him she put up a fight and we had to use force to restrain her."

I shrugged. "Your funeral. He believes me more than anyone else in the system, even if I ran away. I wouldn't lie to him, not when he's as crazy as he is."

I could tell the other soldiers looked uneasy about that. They would be the easiest to overthrow; it was the leader that I would need to deal with. And I couldn't wait to see what Bastien would do to them.

"And you would also have to defeat me in order to hurt me, and unless you want me to stab you."

The leader let out a sharp laugh. "Like you can do anything. Your wrists are bound and you're outnumbered."

"Okay, I warned you…"

They surrounded me, which was typical. I only needed to worry about the one with the knife, as none of the others had their weapons out. Two of them grabbed both my arms and held me in place. I tugged on them a little, sensing their strength. Yeah, this would be easy. Ever since Admiral Bardon left the academy, I swore that the students coming out of there got weaker and less smart.

Like this dummkopf.

I leaned back and brought my leg up, kicking the knife straight out of his hand. He cursed as it dropped to the ground. Before the two men holding me could strengthen their hold, I rammed my body into him and he fumbled on top of the other soldier. They smacked heads and crashed onto the floor. Damn, that had to hurt, but it was two down and two to go. I quickly maneuvered so I could bring my bound wrists around my butt and legs and had them in front of me so I was at a better advantage. Thank goodness I stayed flexible all this time, mainly for this exact reason.

The leader scrambled for his gun, which I grabbed straight out of his hands and slammed the butt into his nose. Blood spilled out, and he hit the floor, grabbing his face. One more. This was way too easy. I wondered if someday I would meet someone who was a match.

Oh wait, that would be Bastien. Hopefully I would someday be his match or find someone who would help me.

I retrieved my knife and flipped it open. The soldier grabbed his gun and pointed it straight at me.

"Stop! Now! Put both weapons down!"

I raised an eyebrow. "You think that will stop me? Honestly? And what if you shoot me? Then you will have to deal with the wrath of Admiral Wilde, and we both know you don't want that."

He paused for a moment. "Y-you think he will do something?"

I laughed. "I doubt that he wouldn't. He's very, very protective of me. He doesn't like anyone else playing with his *Puppe*. So, if you want to live, drop your gun."

The man paused, as if thinking it through. I had made

a good argument. Anyone who has met Bastien would know that. I wasn't the only one who knew what a psycho he could be—and that was when he was doing things that were legal.

He dropped the gun. "Fine, but if anyone asks, you overpowered me."

"Oh," I commented, stepping forward and hitting the butt of the gun across his head. He hit the ground with a thud. "No one will doubt that."

Now I had four knocked-out soldiers on a ship docked to a spaceport—whatever was I going to do?

I know. I could run for it.

I flipped the knife closed and pocketed it. I threw the gun down. There would have been hell to pay if they caught me with one of those. Searching through the leader's pockets, I found the key to my cuffs. Unlocking them, I cuffed the leader to the bedpost and put the key in my pocket. At least that would slow them down.

I ran off the ship and toward the sky elevator. I didn't know where I was going or how long I could run for, but I knew I had to get out of there. If those soldiers woke up, they would be coming after me.

And that guy thought he was pissed about me assassinating the Nash Mir representative. Now he would be mad I knocked him out and made him look like a fool. I mean, I deserved to be killed, but that soldier didn't know the half of it.

So I hurried toward the exit as fast as I could. Jonathan would be angry, but I couldn't do it—I couldn't face Bastien again. Not right away. I needed to get out of there. I needed to breathe.

I needed my freedom.

And Bastien would do whatever it took to take that freedom away from me.

It wasn't my fault. I wouldn't have run away except those soldiers tried to attack me. And then so would the ones on the planet, and so on and so on. They were foolish, going against Bastien's orders. They hadn't worked as close to him as I had; they didn't know what lengths he went to make sure everyone understood who was in charge.

He was. He always was.

And it wasn't until I realized that, it was already too late.

I tried to keep a calm composure as I boarded the sky elevator down to Nouveau Départ. I couldn't let anyone notice who I was, notice that anything was wrong. I just had to get through this and I was free.

At least that's what I hoped.

CHAPTER EIGHTEEN

Nik

Some things still made little sense, but I knew that I wouldn't find answers, at least not right away.

I relieved Russ from engine duty and took a careful observation of the systems. It had been acting fine, but that didn't mean something couldn't happen. Rebecca and I had gone on many missions where the engine was acting fine until one moment it decided it wanted to have a freak-out and drop us out of hyperspace in the middle of nowhere. Those were the good ol' days and reminded us that life never worked the way we wanted it to, just like the hyperdrive.

Thinking about the hyperdrive reminded me of

Rebecca. I didn't know what to believe about her. I thought I knew her; I thought she told me everything. I couldn't believe that she had a part to play in the human experiments. I wouldn't believe it.

Yet it made sense.

She would go on missions alone with Sebastien, coming back a little detached, as if she had seen things she wanted to scrub out of her mind. I always thought it had to have been just a rough mission, but now I wasn't so sure. All the signs were there. I was just blind to them.

That and Sebastien hid his tracks well. He made it look like there was no way either of them were doing anything other than the mission assigned. I didn't know how he managed it, who he paid off or threatened, but they completely covered their tracks—that is, if Rebecca was a part of it.

None of that seemed like it was in her nature. She might not have been the most caring human being, but she wasn't a sociopath like Sebastien. Deep down she was nice and caring. There had to be more to it. She must have had a motivation.

Which meant Sebastien had threatened her.

How long did he do this? How long had he threatened her? I didn't want to think about it and didn't want to think about what he might have her do before we got there. Damn, she was brave to take this mission knowing all that could wait for her. It was no wonder that she was so hesitant in the beginning and why she was worrying so much.

If Alexandra was right, Rebecca had been the person who killed her parents. I still wasn't sure. I just wished Rebecca was here so I could talk to her about it, tell her that it would be all right and that we would figure something out.

That I would always be there for her.

I sighed as I clicked a few buttons, getting a reading on the hyperdrive speed. We were still maintaining a consistent velocity. This was a boring job for sure but one that needed to be done.

The door to the engine room slid open, and Mary stepped in with a plate of food. I smiled. "Thank you. You didn't have to bring me anything."

She shrugged. "Yeah, well, I know how boring this job can be, and if you're hungry, I know it sucks even more."

I let out a brief laugh. She had a point. "I guess that's true. How's the cooking coming?"

"Fine. I had some practice when I was younger. I wish Natascha, or I guess her name was Rebecca, left a recipe book. It would have made my life a lot easier."

I wished she hadn't brought Rebecca up. I had finally gotten my mind off her for a brief second. But it was true. Rebecca had some amazing recipes. And crappy ones, like the one with the peaches.

"I can't believe she was wanted for treason," Mary commented. "I mean, how was it even possible she could have gotten this far on her own?"

She didn't—she was with me. "She's crafty."

"Oh, I didn't mean to bring it up, *mi dispiace*. I knew you two were together. It must have been heartbreaking seeing her go like that, not knowing she was wanted for an assassination on a representative's life. It's crazy to even think about."

She didn't know that Jonathan and I were wanted for the same crime. It surprised me we didn't get more questions at the border patrol, but I had a feeling that Admiral Bardon was behind the scenes, pulling a few strings.

We were lucky that Sebastien wasn't cutting the strings and leaving us to fall. Just like he did when we got caught for assassinating the representative of Nash Mir.

Also, I knew very little Italian and wished Rebecca was here to help.

I shuffled around, acting like it was no big deal even though it really was. "Yeah, it was a surprise. It explained a lot though, like the fact she never wanted to return to Nreff Nation."

"I… I can't even believe she would do something like that. She had a cold exterior, yes, but deep down she had a warm heart. She let me help her cook."

Yeah, even that surprised me. She let no one in her kitchen, not even me. "I guess she thought you were helpful then. I can't imagine her letting anyone near her meals. I got smacked a few times when we were together."

She perked up. "Really?"

I nodded. "Yup. She even said if I tried to help her again that she would stab me with a kitchen knife."

"Oh," she said. "Now I feel bad that we let her get taken so easily, had we known—"

I shook my head, especially since I knew the truth behind the arrest. "There wouldn't have been anything any of us could do. When all this is over, we can try to go back for her or at least see what we can do. But meanwhile, we have an important mission to finish."

"Yeah, I guess you're right." She stood there for a moment in silence, as if trying to think of something else to say. "Anyway, I better get back to the mess hall. I have a feeling Russ has eaten all the leftovers already."

I laughed. "Yeah, probably."

With that, she left, and I was alone again. I took a bite of the meal she made, which looked like pesto pasta. It was fantastic, but I guess she mentioned that her parents were Italian and cooked homemade meals. It only made sense. It made me feel a little better too, as

I really liked pasta—especially when it was homemade.

Once I finished dinner, it would almost be my time for a break. I should have brought a book to read since I could monitor stuff while reading. Well, kind of. Half an eye at least. And there were so many good books out there that would keep my mind off Rebecca.

It surprised me that Rebecca didn't care to read though. I think it was because she couldn't sit still. She always had to do something with her hands. That was why she loved the butterfly knife. It was something constant she could do, along with cooking. They both involved movement.

Yeah, I definitely needed a book to read. Maybe Jonathan had something. I would have to check later.

I finished my pasta, and it was very impressive. If Mary ever wanted to stop being a mechanic, she could make it as a chef. Her and Rebecca. Damn, how I would love to see that. But Mary had talent, especially at such a young age, both as a mechanic and as a cook. I supposed being a mechanic was her passion though, and cooking was just something to pass the time. Too bad. I knew many people who would give a lot of money for meals as good as the one I just had.

Russ showed up, and I asked him if Jonathan had gone to sleep yet or if he was still up. He said that Jonathan was taking a call in the mess hall while everyone else was on duty or sleeping. I figured it must have been Admiral Bardon since he was the only person Jonathan would be contacting.

That or maybe some secret lover. Yeah, that would be the day.

I headed straight there, wanting to see what Jonathan would report to Admiral Bardon and whether it had to do with what Alexandra had said about Rebecca. I hoped it didn't—I didn't want more suspicion on her head nor her to be tried for any of this.

Because then I probably would never see her again.

Sebastien deserved the punishment—not her—even if she played a hand in it. She must have been forced; there was no way otherwise. She wasn't a cold-blooded killer.

I slid open the door to the mess hall and stepped inside.

"*Je t'aime*, Jacques. See you later."

I froze right there. *Je t'aime?*—I love you? At first I thought maybe he was in fact talking to someone else and my joke had been correct, but he had said Jacques's name. What the hell was going on?

Jonathan clicked off the communicator and gave me a half smile. "Well, I didn't expect you to walk in. By the look on your face I'm guessing you had no idea."

I shook my head. "I'm not quite sure what I just heard."

He let out a short laugh. "Then I guess Rebecca was

telling the truth when she said she hadn't told anyone, if she didn't tell you."

"Wait, Rebecca knew? How?" Because that was definitely news to me. Why wouldn't she tell me about this? Hell, I figured she would have loved to tell me Jonathan's secrets.

Jonathan shrugged. "Who knows? She probably saw us together one night or something."

"So you and Jacques…," I began, still surprised about it all.

"Are *les amoureux*? *Oui*."

"Since when?" I asked, still trying to put it all together. He was our mentor at the academy and like a father to me.

"Since before we graduated from the academy."

Scheiße, that was over twenty years ago, not to mention he was under age and Bardon could have gotten into a lot of trouble if someone found out. But that meant they had to keep it a secret all this time since Sebastien couldn't know about our connection to Admiral Bardon. "What the hell? I'm sorry you've had to stay quiet about it for the mission—"

He put his hand up. "It's fine. We got to spend some time together on breaks and if we were on the same planet. Believe me, it was more often than you would care to think about, not to mention these past three years he's kept me hidden from the government. That's been quite exciting, if you know what I mean."

I didn't want to know what he meant, not that I cared they were a couple. "But he's like…"

"A decade older? Not much of a difference when you get down to it. Believe me, he still has spunk."

I rubbed my temples, trying to get the images to go away. "He was one of our mentors. *Gott*, I don't want to know, Jonathan."

He laughed. "I can't help it. I haven't been able to talk to anyone about him. He's an amazing guy, Nik. I can't wait until this mission is over so we can do things together, in public."

I could see the sorrow in his eyes. This had to have been bothering him for years. I couldn't believe that he didn't tell Walrum or I. We wouldn't have said anything. I wonder if they had kept it a secret in the beginning because of his being an advisor or instructor of the academy for a while, and that would have been against school policy. Then when time passed and we were on the mission together, he just never found the right time to say something.

"I'm sorry that you've had to keep it a secret."

"Thanks, *mon ami*. I'm glad to have friends like y—"

The communicator buzzed. Jonathan glanced at it, confused, then answered. "Hello?"

I watched as Jonathan frowned. "I understand. We will go down to the planet immediately when we arrive." He clicked the communicator off.

"What is it?" I asked.

"Rebecca. She knocked out the soldiers and ran for it. Apparently she is loose on the planet."

I couldn't believe what I was hearing. "But she knew it was the only way to get to Sebastien. Why would she do that?"

"I don't know. It makes you wonder what scared her enough to run."

I frowned. Then maybe it was true. Sebastien had tortured her to the point where she would do anything he said.

And now she was afraid to go back.

CHAPTER NINETEEN

Rebecca

Nouveau Départ had changed very little. It was still the place that I remembered, filled with all the same scenes, smells, types of people, and buildings. It had been a little over three years since I had last visited, on my last paired mission with Bastien himself. My heart skipped a beat at the thought. What if he was here already, waiting? He shouldn't be, but I wouldn't be surprised if he was. It was a stupid idea to pick this planet to try to run away on, after everything, but I didn't have a choice. Now I just needed to blend in with the crowd and go unnoticed, just like I always dreamed.

I knew this would come back and bite me in the

arsch—stuff like this always did. I just hoped that maybe this time it would work. This time I would get to taste freedom. I always lied to myself when I ran away from home that the academy was my freedom, but it wasn't. I didn't have a free day in my life.

And he reminded me of that every single day.

My hands started shaking, recalling all the memories of the things I had done to those people—people who could have been innocent, I knew now. I used to think that no one was innocent, as that was what Bastien had always said. Now I wasn't so sure.

That was a lie. I knew those people had been innocent. I knew even when I did everything Bastien told me to. I just lied to myself again and again because I thought he knew what was right and I wanted him to never leave me.

What a stupid fool I was. Why had I cared so much? Why did I want him to care?

Because he was such a good liar. He knew how to craft his words, how to make everyone like him, fear him, want him to care. And I fell victim to that. But I changed. I learned better. Now I just wanted to be free.

I stopped in front of a produce stand, but I couldn't focus on the present, all I saw was the blood dripping from my hands, onto the table, and rolling off, staining the ground. Bodies lay in masses, the stench of death always following me.

"Are you all right, *Fräulein*?"

I looked up to see an elderly man concerned why I was just standing in front of his booth, staring off into space. I gathered myself and gave him a nod.

"I'm fine, *Herr. Danke.*"

With that, I left him and moved on down the street. There was only one thing I needed and that was a way to clear my mind.

I would have to find a dealer.

The problem was I had no money. I would either have to steal the drug, kill everyone that was making the deal with me, or pick someone's pocket and use that to buy just one vial.

Ugh. Choices.

I held out my arm, and I could see it shaking. The more I thought about the fact Bastien would send all his men out to find me, the more my heart raced and I felt I would go into a fit. He would find out about the morphine one way or another, so it wasn't like it mattered, if he hadn't already. I had a feeling if Bardon knew, then Bastien definitely knew.

I couldn't believe Admiral Bardon wanted to stick his neck out like this in order for me to not get the same punishment as Bastien. It made little sense to be honest, although I wondered if it was because if I helped him, he could pull some strings to make sure I stayed safe and didn't get arrested. I didn't understand why he always favored me and felt as if he needed to look out for me, although I was touched. If it wasn't for him, I would never have been able to stay in the military academy, especially since I forged most of the paperwork. And he knew that but still wouldn't let them dismiss me. I never thanked him for that.

But he didn't understand that I was as guilty as Bastien, that I had committed those crimes, even if it was under Bastien's thumb. I could have done something. I could have been stronger. I could have told someone what was happening.

And watch them die.

Deciding to pick the pocket of someone with nice clothes, I glanced around. There was a lady with a designer purse, thick makeup, and a leather jacket, looking around, not paying attention to those around her.

Perfect.

I started toward her, then watched a little boy about the age of seven reach into her purse and take her wallet. I was right to think she was oblivious and an easy mark, as she didn't even notice the kid.

But now I had to chase a kid. I sighed and followed him as he turned down an alleyway. There was no one around when he stopped and opened the wallet. I grabbed him by the collar and lifted him up.

"My, my, what do we have here? A little thief?"

He struggled, but I was a little stronger. "Let me go, you old hag!"

I frowned. "Who are you calling old?"

"Just let me go!"

"Look, kid, you have two options. You can either give me half of what you found, or I can turn you in to the police right now. It's your choice."

I wouldn't have turned him in to the police, as I was sure there were a bunch of pictures of me sent in within the past hour, but the kid didn't know that.

"Fine! I'll give you half! Just let me down!"

I set him down, and he gave me one credit that was in the bag. I checked it. It had at least a thousand credits on it, which would get me what I needed, if not a few more.

The kid ran off with the rest of the purse, and I pocketed the credit. Now I would just have to find me a dealer.

It wasn't that hard to find what I was looking for, not after three years of learning how to look. Apparently this guy's code name was Dr. Klatsch. I wasn't even going to ask because I did not want to know.

His lackeys brought me in. This time, instead of a laundromat, it was in the back of a *pączki* shop. It smelled heavenly, and I knew I had to buy a couple to enjoy after this transaction.

Dr. Klatsch was on the tall side, with a goatee and blondish-brown hair. He appeared to be the same age as Nik and had the same build. His clothes were plain, different from what I was used to, just a T-shirt, jeans that were a little on the tight side, and shoes that looked like something a dad would wear. I noticed a wolf pendant that made his chest look even broader. Strange.

"So, what is your poison?"

Such a cliché line. "Missy-B. And not the contaminated stuff, I can tell the difference." Shit, I didn't have my drops on me. I hoped he wouldn't call my bluff.

He raised an eyebrow. "You expect me to contaminate?"

I shrugged. "It would surprise you how many people do, even ones that say they are professional. I have enough credits and just need two vials."

He held out his hand for the credits. I handed them to him. Examining the card, he nodded. "This seems legit. And how will you tell the difference?"

"I have drops. They just aren't on my person, but I can check when I get back to my lodging and come back to make you understand I don't like to be played with."

Dr. Klatsch smiled, then let out a laugh. "All right. Let me go back and retrieve it for you. Wait here a moment."

His men watched me as he went back to get the drug. It surprised me, as usually they had the lackeys doing such work. Nothing seemed off though, so I waited.

He came back out with a small case and opened it. "Does this appear to your liking?"

It was four bottles, which surprised me as the credits should have only covered two. "What's the catch?"

He shook his head. "No catch, this is the amount they go for on this side of the border."

I nodded and took the case. Just as I did, the door opened and a man with a tablet came in.

"Is she still here?" the man yelled.

All of us froze. Shit, I should have figured dealers got postings.

"What is it?" Dr. Klatsch asked.

"The woman is wanted for murdering the Nash Mir representative, on top of just breaking out of the border jail!"

Why couldn't this ever be easy?

Before the four men in the room could pull out their guns, I pulled out my butterfly knife and stabbed the closest man next to me in the chest. As he went down, I stabbed the other. That just left the informant and Dr. Klatsch.

The informant was faster than I thought he would be and kicked my knife out of my hand. He pointed his gun at me.

"Freeze!"

I raised my hands, and Dr. Klatsch also pulled out his gun.

"Great, now we will get that reward and your credits. This was definitely a deal in my favor."

I sighed and judged how I would do this. There were a few syringes on the crates next to me. If I could get them, I could inject the two and run. Hopefully whatever the drug was, it was quick acting.

As Dr. Klatsch moved back to his desk to get to his communicator, I kicked the gun out of the informant's hand, grabbed the syringe, and injected him. The man screamed and started seizing.

Now I just had to get to Dr. Klatsch.

He crouched under his desk and started firing at me, but I was quick to jump behind a crate. Why these men always emptied their guns so quickly, I did not understand. But it was lucky for me.

I counted until the gun was empty and jumped to where he hid and injected the man in the neck. He also started seizing and collapsed. Curious, I checked the label on the syringe. Yohimbine. I had never heard of it.

Grabbing the case of morphine-B and the informant's gun, I ran out of there.

However, not before others noticed.

Sirens were closing in from every direction. I cursed under my breath, damning my luck for the billionth time. I never caught a break, not once. I should just give up, but there was an instinctual side of me that kept me running, that didn't want me to stop and give in. Whether that was a good thing, I wasn't sure.

"Get her!" I heard a voice call out behind me. Great, some of the people at the dealer had followed me. Damn it.

I heard more voices as people joined in the chase. No one in front of me reacted enough to catch me as I pushed past them toward the port elevator. I would reroute so it didn't seem I was going straight there, but I needed to get there before an alert went out with my face on it. And to do that, I had to pull a few tricks out of my sleeve.

Mentally counting how many shots I had left in the gun, I figured at least twenty for this type. I looked back to find no more than fifteen people chasing after me. I could, theoretically, shoot them all if I wanted to. My face, though, would be plastered on every screen if I did, as the sound of gunfire would bring any sensor that was in the area toward me. I was surprised there had been none already.

I needed a diversion. Glancing around, I saw nothing sticking out as a good way to divert attention long enough where I could sneak away. More sirens. Shit, I had to think fast.

Rounding the corner, I found it. The perfect thing.

A circus.

I pushed back the thoughts of Walrum and how the first time I ever went to the circus had been the day when we started dating. No, I had to focus now, had to get out of this pronto.

I ran past the gates and toward the maze of tents. Hundreds, if not thousands, of people were attending this event, making it hard for me to stick out. It was crowded, loud, and only a matter of time before I lost the people behind me.

I slipped into one tent and hid under the filled bleachers. I looked out through the legs of people as I caught my breath. Aerobats danced through the air, impressively so. I hadn't been to a circus in quite a while, but I had to admit I enjoyed it. It was amazing what these people could do.

After taking a few more breaths, I peeked through the flap of the tent to see if any of the people were still out there looking for me. I didn't see anyone.

As I stepped out, I felt metal jam into my side. Damn, did everyone have a gun nowadays?

"Hold it," a young man said. "Don't make a move."

I let out a small sigh, furious at myself that I hadn't noticed him there.

"Turn around," he said.

I did just that and found the man to be quite younger than I had presumed. He had to have been eighteen, maybe nineteen years of age. Way too young to be killed by me.

"You don't want to do this," I whispered.

He shook his head. "I don't have a choice. I know who you are. I know what kind of money you would bring to my family. My wife and I have been starving for weeks. I can't go home empty-handed again."

"She also doesn't want you to come home in a coffin. Let me go, and I won't have to kill you. Then your wife will see you again."

"That's not how I see it. I see me turning you in for the reward. Now hands up."

I lifted my hands, and he reached for my gun in my hand. But he was too slow, and I used the butt of the gun to hit him in the side of the head. As he hit the ground, he dropped his gun. I retrieved it and held both guns at him.

"You should have listened," I said.

"Please." He held his hands up. "I beg you, my wife needs me."

"You should have thought of that before you went on an impossible quest."

"Are you going to kill me? I am helpless; you could get away. I won't come after you again."

"You came after me once before. I don't have any reason to trust you."

"Please." Tears rolled down his cheeks. "I beg you."

I waited for the aerobat to do her last trick in the air and land safe. The crowd cheered and clapped, the sound masking that of the gun that shot the man straight in the head.

But it wasn't my gun.

Before I could turn around, I felt a piece of cloth go over my mouth, and seconds later everything turned black.

CHAPTER TWENTY

Nik

The rest of the crew weren't told why Jonathan and I rushed to the planet's surface.

It wasn't like anyone knew about Rebecca's mission nor how Jonathan and I were connected to her. They just knew we were on a mission to gather evidence, but that was it. Their hand to play had to do with transporting us and verifying our paperwork, otherwise we would have never gotten across the border as easily as we did.

Either way, they didn't know about Rebecca.

My heart was racing, worrying that Rebecca would get into more trouble than what we had expected. I had noticed that her luck hadn't been that great in the past few weeks. I tried to take deep breaths to calm myself down, but I was beyond that point. I just wanted to punch something, but I couldn't make a scene. Damn, I wished I could find another way to calm myself down!

Jonathan was keeping a rather cool composure. Even after all these years, I didn't know how he did it. He was the only one to stay calm, always cracking a joke and making Rebecca angrier.

"Calm down, she's fine. She just got nervous and ran for it. That, or some soldiers attacked her."

"What? You think that happened?"

Jonathan shrugged. "According to Jacques, it sounded like the guards attacked her, but it wasn't clear. It would make sense if they did. We killed a nice representative, not to mention they might have come across her before. Or she just back-talked them enough times."

I rubbed my forehead. *Gott*, it must have been all those things combined. She needed to learn when to keep her mouth shut. It always landed us in heaps of trouble.

Like that time in YamaXie when we were almost caught by the authorities. All because of that stupid samurai.

"I just wish she told me the truth," I whispered.

"About the mission I gave her or whether she's

involved with the human experiments?"

I didn't answer. I didn't want to answer. There was so much going on that I didn't know what was up or down. For so many years we were getting nowhere, and now all this information was coming to us. I didn't know what was real and what were lies anymore.

"I just can't wait until this is over with, then maybe answers will be given."

Jonathan nodded but didn't say a word. I felt like he was still keeping something from me, but I knew not to press him. It wasn't his place to tell me, not when Admiral Bardon was calling the shots. Besides, I doubt he would even tell me anyway.

I still couldn't believe that he and the admiral were a couple. It was strange to think after all this time that Jonathan had someone and none of us knew that. He seemed like he hit on everyone, but now that I thought about it, I realized he never followed through with those comments. I never saw him take anyone back to his room. I just wished I had found out under different circumstances, then I would have been one to joke with him about it, especially if Walrum were still alive.

But then I wouldn't be able to love Rebecca.

I had a crush on her when she first got hired by Sebastien, but I never told a soul. Since we were on a mission, I didn't want to get involved, not to mention I would have felt like I was lying to her. It wasn't until years later that Walrum made his move. He didn't even ask us, nor did he warn us. It just happened one night when he and Rebecca stayed up late drinking after Jonathan and I left the bar to get some sleep.

If only it had been me who'd stayed behind instead of him.

I wondered what would have happened every day since that night, not that it mattered. Five years after that, they tried us for treason and Walrum died. I felt horrible, but my feelings for Rebecca never wavered. So that left the two of us in a complicated situation.

Banners for the upcoming TOWER signing littered the area, declaring peace for all the nations, not that the citizens cared. They knew nothing else, and it wasn't like they got to vote on it. It was just for the nations to go over, make sure no one was disobeying the laws, then sign it yet again. I didn't understand why they made such a fuss. It wasn't as if they just used it to gain political support. *Gott*, I hated politics.

"She's on the move again, heading toward the main park system. We better hurry, but by the sounds of it, she's being followed by some kind of mob," Jonathan said as he began to jog.

I wanted to ask him for more details, but I had a feeling that was all he knew. Rebecca wasn't kidding when she said the odds of her running into an enemy were high. Someone must have recognized her from the wanted bulletin and got a bunch of people to run after her. I just prayed that they wouldn't try to kill her. The bulletin had said they wanted her alive, but a raging mob didn't pay attention to details.

"If they used more resources, trying to catch the people behind the human experiments than they did advertising the TOWER, I think that Sebastien would have been caught by now," Jonathan commented as we hurried toward the park.

I laughed. "Yeah, ain't that the truth. I just can't wait until the signing is over and we can finally relax."

"Yeah, like that will ever happen."

He had a point there. Even if this mission succeeded, that didn't mean everything would be peaceful. There were plenty more missions out there. "I'm not sure what I want to do after they drop the charges on us— whether I want to stay in the military."

Jonathan glanced over. "You mean you don't know if Rebecca will want to stay and you will follow her to the ends of the universe?"

"And you'll just stay in the military to be with Bardon, so I guess we're even."

We were both silent for a moment. I didn't know if I crossed a line, but he definitely started it.

"Look, I'm sorry I didn't tell you…"

I shook my head. "No, I get it. You couldn't let Sebastien know about your relationship. It's fine."

"He is a great guy and helped me through a lot of stuff. It's just frustrating that we haven't been able to go out anywhere."

"I can understand that. Soon though."

He nodded. "*Oui*. Soon."

We arrived at the park, and it was full of people going to the circus that was taking place. It was no wonder Rebecca ran toward here, a crowd was a lot easier to disappear in. No one paid attention as we snuck through, searching for any disturbance.

As we searched, we tried not to be noticed. It was apparent that most of the people here were bringing their children and wouldn't recognize someone whose face had been plastered on screens everywhere three years before, but you could never be too careful.

The last time I had been to the circus had to be right before Rebecca and Walrum started dating, almost nine years ago. Rebecca had never gone before, so we dragged her to one. She had a lot of fun, and that marked the night when she and Walrum started getting close. Actually, it wasn't probably—I saw Walrum and her making out and stumbling toward his bedroom.

I hated circuses.

Jonathan grabbed my arm and pulled me behind the cotton candy stand. "Whoa, Jonathan, I like you as a friend but you know I don't swing that way. Besides, Bardon would have my head."

He gave me a look, then nodded down the walkway. "It's him."

I glanced around the cotton candy stand, and there he was, our old admiral, Sebastien Wilde.

Scheiße.

Turning back to Jonathan, I said, "He can't see us here. We're screwed if he does."

"I know. We have to be careful. He's here for Rebecca, so he might not be keeping an eye out for us."

Even though he said it, we both knew that wasn't true. That bastard always had an eye out for us. It was why we had to be so careful to sneak around, not to mention that he wanted us dead. He had it out for us for betraying him, and I doubted that just because he was looking for Rebecca that he would forget all that.

"Should we follow him? See if he finds her?" I asked.

Jonathan stood there, thinking. "We'd have to be careful; we can't let him see us. But we need to make sure she completes this part of the mission. And whatever happens, we can't intervene. You got that?"

I nodded. I knew what he meant; that if Wilde attacked Rebecca, we couldn't stop him. I mean, if she was on the brink of death, I would do something, because there was no way I would let him kill her. But he wouldn't do that, not after all this time, not when he had spent so much time trying to find her.

Once Sebastien was farther down the walkway, we followed. I could tell his intent by the way he walked, as if he was sick and tired of looking for Rebecca but knew she was within grasp. It was horrifying to see, to know what could be in store for her. I wished I could stop it, but I knew I couldn't.

He turned toward a tent and signaled a few men to follow. I had missed them, so Jonathan and I made sure that there weren't more men around us, that it was only those ahead. We both had a feeling that all of them had memorized our faces. After they disappeared and we counted to ten, we followed them into the tent.

Inside, an acrobatic performance was underway. They were almost to the end since the crazy things they were doing were quickening. Just as the crowd clapped, we heard a muffled gunshot. I saw Jonathan jump.

Both of us headed in the direction the sound came from. I prayed to *Gott* that it wasn't Rebecca, that Sebastian didn't kill her. That couldn't happen. He wouldn't do that.

We rounded the corner to find that it wasn't Rebecca but a young man, around eighteen, who was lying on the ground in a pool of his own blood. Rebecca was there with her gun at the ready. She appeared as confused as we did, not sure what happened.

Did she kill him?

Sebastien and his men were behind her, and

Sebastien had his own gun drawn. It had to have been him; he must have not wanted Rebecca to kill him or thought she was taking too long. Before Rebecca registered what happened, Sebastien pulled out a cloth and covered her mouth and nose with it. Seconds later Rebecca was knocked out cold.

Jonathan and I stayed hidden in the shadows, knowing that this needed to happen in order for Rebecca to get the location of the facility. It was hard to watch, hard to realize what could be coming for her. I wanted more than anything to be there with her, but I knew the moment Sebastien saw me, he would shoot me.

They took Rebecca away, leaving the body of the guy under the bleachers. The show was over, and everyone was leaving, so Sebastien could blend into the crowd. We waited a few moments, then went to inspect the body.

He had shot the man in the head. I guess Sebastien didn't want any witnesses to his kidnapping of Rebecca.

Jonathan pulled out his communicator and called Admiral Bardon.

"Jacques, he has Rebecca. There's also a dead body under the bleachers at the acrobatic tent at the park. I don't know if Sebastien will send someone out to cover it up." He paused. "Understood." With that he clicked off the communicator.

"What did he say?" I asked.

"That we should get out of here. He's sure Sebastien will send someone to get rid of the body, and we don't want to be around when that happens."

I nodded. "And he has her so we should try to stay close. She will contact us the moment she finds the facility, right?"

"*Oui*. Now hurry, I think I hear someone coming."

And with that, we left the poor soul there to disappear with the rest of Sebastien's victims. We couldn't do anything, not without alerting him of our existence. No, the only way to stop anything like this from happening again would be by destroying him once and for all.

Which was exactly what we were going to do.

CHAPTER TWENTY-ONE

Rebecca

When I woke up, I was lying on a cold, hard table.

My first instinct was to flee, to run away as fast as I could. But I couldn't move; my wrists and ankles were bound to the table. I struggled, hoping that maybe something would give, but it was no use. I was tied down as tight as one could be without losing feeling in a limb. I held back the tears, knowing what was coming for me.

I was on a surgery table, and I would be tortured.

No! No, I couldn't let this happen again! I had to figure something out. I had to get out of here!

My body shook, and I remembered I still needed a

dose of morphine.

The lights were bright, reflecting on the metal table and pieces of equipment that surrounded me. I couldn't make out anything, my eyes still not clear from coming out of the induced unconsciousness. I took deep breaths to calm myself down.

No, nothing I could do would make my heart stop racing. I was royally fucked.

I had no idea where I was, whether I was still on the planet, or if Bastien had transported me to a ship. All I knew was that he was nearby, watching me. I opened my mouth to say something, to curse him, but nothing came out. I was dizzy. I was confused. I just wanted out of there.

I was losing focus. Damn him, he knew how to play with my mind. I wanted out; that was all I knew. I couldn't go through this again. I couldn't lay there and let them slice me open, cut my innards. Bastien letting them experiment on me just to teach me a lesson. I couldn't—I wouldn't.

I pulled on the restraints again. There was no give. I could feel my wrists bruise, but I didn't care; I wouldn't let up. Fuck the bruises, I could deal with those, but letting them touch me again would be far worse than that.

"Anyone there? *Bitte*, help me! *Scheiße*, I can't do this! Please! *Je suis à tes pieds! Kudasai! Te lo ruego!*

Qĭng! Pozhaluysta! Anyone… *Bitte…*"

There was no response in the room. I heard nothing at all except my own quick breathing. I could feel sweat pour off my entire body. I didn't know where they were or when they would come in. I was helpless.

Just like he wanted me to be.

"Please…"

He was watching from the other side of the room, waiting to see what I would do, how much I would struggle, how much I would cry out for him to stop. Nothing had even happened yet, and I wanted to beg for his forgiveness, to tell him how wrong I was for running away, that I had made a huge mistake.

No. I wouldn't give him that satisfaction. I wouldn't let him hear me give up.

But what was the alternative? Be sliced open just because of my pride? Just because I couldn't bring myself to say those words even if I didn't believe him? He used mind tricks like this to get what he wanted, and I was damn tired of playing games.

What did I do in my life to deserve this?

Memories of all the things I had done came rushing back, things that would now be done to me if I didn't figure out a way out of this. I remembered the first time I captured someone for Bastien; him telling me it was an order from the nation, that the person deserved it and needed to be experimented on. He tried to convince me that it was to better our knowledge on mind control, that if the systems underwent a war, that it would be the only way to win, that we had to do this to prepare.

It was a bunch of lies—just a way for him to fulfill his sociopathic urges. His lust for power was like no other, and this was how he filled that hunger. It was too late for me by the time I figured that out, and I regretted it ever since that night when I delivered that man, when Bastien kept me in the other room and made me watch as they sliced him open, awake and screaming. I'd thrown up on Bastien's shoes, but he didn't care. It was the first step in torturing my mind and soul.

And he's tortured me ever since.

It wasn't just mentally. No, that was only how it started out. When I tried to run away from all this, get away from that *drecksau*, he found me and decided that he needed to teach me a lesson—one that I would learn from. He said that watching wasn't enough, that I needed to endure the pain to understand what he was capable of.

So he stood over me and watched as the doctors messed with my insides. Never had I experienced so much pain. And I hated him for that. I hated him with a burning passion. I wanted him killed. I wanted him out of my life.

I wanted to run away, far away, so he could never find me.

Why was I so foolish to think that it was a good idea to request to work under him? Why didn't I see the signs before it was too late? He was possessive of me even then, the moment he hired me. And I fell for it; I thought he truly loved me. I thought he cared and wanted me as a partner, not as a *Puppe*.

It would be a lie to say I never loved him, and that was why it hurt so much, why I hated him so much. I had trusted him. I had given him my heart. For three years everything was perfect. I was young and such a fool for falling for an admiral, especially one as fucked up as he was. Then three years passed, and he introduced me to his real self.

And I was ashamed to say that it took another four years until I broke it off with him. Or at least tried.

I tried to request another admiral so I could get out from under him, but for some reason that paperwork kept getting lost. It wasn't like I could go running to anyone, not after what I had done. After I'd broken it off though, he stopped taking me on his little missions, and I thought I was finally free. It wasn't until he found out I was dating Walrum that he dragged me back, kicking and screaming. That was when I tried to run away, and that was the beginning of my scars.

Or at least my physical scars. I had plenty of mental and emotional ones before then. Ones that would never heal, no matter how hard Walrum and Nik tried to calm me down. They didn't know how many times I almost killed them whenever they'd try to wake me up, thinking that they would hurt me. Thank *Gott* I had some self-control.

My eyes didn't adjust to the darkness, but everything felt like it was turning a blood red. I wanted to cry out for Nik to help me, but I knew he was nowhere near. He couldn't save me from this, no matter what he did. It was coming for me, and I knew that the moment we ran away three years ago.

But three years with Nik was worth it. Spending time with him would be worth the pain Bastien would bring upon me. Bastien didn't understand what it was like to have true friends, to care for someone. He couldn't take that away from me. He couldn't take away the feelings Nik and I shared.

Unless he killed Nik.

The thought of something happening to Nik made me shake even more. I wished I could give myself another dose, but I couldn't even move. I could take anything that Bastien would bring except for that. I took a deep breath, trying to keep my heart rate down, but it wasn't working. I was panicking, and there was nothing that would stop this.

The memory of the pain from last time came flooding back. It had been a long time, but it felt like just a moment ago. My whole body ached, and I didn't know whether it was from being tense for such a long time or if it was the memory of it all.

Whatever it was, I was screwed.

He had slept with so many girls while we were together, and he didn't even see it as a problem when I found out. It seemed like he didn't care, as if I was just another one of them. Never did I realize that with me it was different—it wasn't about the sex, it was about the control.

It was about me doing whatever he asked without question or resistance.

I couldn't stand it, just lying there with no one coming to save me. I knew it was how all Bastien's victims felt. I could see it in their eyes while they were lying on the table during the procedure. They screamed and tried to fight back, but it was no use, because I wasn't there to stop the doctors.

A tear left my eye and ran down the side of my face. I deserved this after everything I witnessed and did nothing about. I deserved to die.

I heard steps in the room, and a shadow of a figure stood over me. Although my eyes didn't adjust, I knew that outline anywhere.

Bastien was standing over me. He reached down and touched the tear on my face. "Really, are you that weak to cry before my doctors come in and do anything to you?"

No air was coming into my lungs. I couldn't breathe. I couldn't do anything. More tears came pouring out of my eyes.

"Please, I'm sorry… *Bitte*…"

He bent down closer so I could see his face. He still had that same fucking satisfied smile as he had all those years ago. "I'm not here to hurt you. Not if you cooperate."

I shook my head. "Some reason I don't believe that."

"But it's true. I let you get away with sins you have committed against me. All you have to do is tell me what you've been up to for the past three years."

It couldn't be that easy. It was never that easy with him. "Nothing. Just running and then more running. You know me, I can't stay still for a moment."

"I'm not a fool!" he screamed into my face. "Tell me where you were."

It wasn't like he didn't know. He had people on the lookout for me. I had barely gotten away from an attempt to get me back a year ago. That would have been an interesting conversation with Nik. "Anywhere that wasn't the Nreff Nation. Let's be honest, if I showed my face here, they would have killed me."

He caressed my face. And just a minute ago he was screaming down at me. Fucking crazy *arschloch*.

"No, you wouldn't have. I have given specific orders that I wanted you alive."

So it was Bastien who wanted me alive, but why did he want Nik and Jonathan dead but not me?

"You should have told that to the soldiers who tried to teach me a lesson on the spaceport, not to mention the mob that chased me."

"I will deal with those soldiers, I assure you. As for the man who chased you to the circus, well, you were soft. You should have killed him when you had the chance."

"I'm sorry to have disappointed you."

Bastien pulled a knife out of the drawer next to me. "Do I sense sarcasm in that comment?"

"*N-nein.*" My voice squeaked.

"Well, that's good, because you know how I hate it when you are sarcastic with me."

He did. He really did. I had forgotten. "Sorry, sir."

"That is *meine liebchen.*"

I tried not to cringe, to not let the memories of him calling me that word come flooding back. He used it in such a way that made me want to vomit. It was a name he called me when he was trying to exhibit control while talking, while torturing me, in the middle of sex. It didn't matter, it was all the same to him. He was constricting me through his words.

He leaned against the table, setting the knife down next to my face. "Now, explain to me why you ran away."

"I… Because I was a wanted criminal. Because I was up for treason because someone sabotaged the mission. I would have been killed if I stayed."

"I wouldn't have let you die, and you knew that. I care far too much for you. You're *meine Puppe*."

If I threw up, I wondered if he would take offense to that. Probably, but hearing him talk about me after all these years still made my stomach churn. "Well, it sure as hell didn't feel like that. I felt like I was being punished for something I didn't know about."

A flicker of a smile appeared on his lips. "You know there is plenty I should punish you for."

My body shook more violently. Shit, I was going into a fit. I should have taken the morphine-B when I could, although I still wasn't sure if something contaminated it. Shit.

Bastien glanced at my body as it shook. "Well, well, what do we have here? Is this why I found a case full of morphine-B in your pocket? Are you an addict?"

I glared at him but didn't say a word, mainly because in this state I couldn't talk.

"Should I give my little Puppe her drug so she can calm down? Or should I let her suffer the withdrawals?"

I couldn't respond and didn't know which choice he would pick. He was a sadist, to say the least, so watching me suffer for a mistake I had made would bring him a lot of pleasure, but he also wanted me back. He could pick either choice.

Or he could give me something else to mess me up even more.

He pulled out a black case, opened it, and took out a vial. "Are you sure this is pure and not some laced drug?"

It was frustrating me that he thought I could respond, not to mention he had access to drops that could answer that question very easily.

"Well, I guess we will find out."

He put the liquid in my mouth. It tasted the same as normal, bitter and almost acidic, but even with contaminants, it would have the same bitterness. I would just have to hope for the best.

A few moments later, the shaking stopped, but I still felt as if I was in a panic. I didn't think there was enough morphine in the world to help me deal with the fact Bastien was here in front of my face.

"Now that you are back, I have some questions for you." He sat on the table, stroking my hair. "What about the other two in your squad?"

"Jonathan and Nik? What about them?" I had to play it simple. I couldn't let him know about Nik and me. It would be hard, especially since he was good at seeing through lies. Damn good at it.

"Where are they?"

I shrugged. "No clue. I haven't seen them in a while. We went our separate ways."

He tapped his finger on the table. Yeah, that was a bad lie. "Why do I have this suspicion that you aren't telling me the truth?"

"Because you are so untrustworthy that you think everyone else is a liar just like you."

He jabbed the knife straight into my left shoulder. I let out a scream, more out of surprise than pain. I should have seen it coming, especially after my last comment. I had pushed him too far. At least I had the morphine.

Bastien twisted the knife. I bit back another scream. All I wanted to do was fight back, but I couldn't. Not yet. No, I had to make him pay for all the things he had done. I had to get him on trial so that people saw him for the monster he was.

Leaning forward, he whispered into my ear, "Let's just stop playing these games, Rebecca. Neither of us enjoy going in these circles. Why don't you just, for once, tell me the truth?"

I narrowed my eyes. "For once? You're the one who always lied to me."

"That was a long time ago."

"Doesn't mean you don't still manipulate me, that you go above and beyond to torture me."

He gave me his most innocent smile, the one that

everyone else believed. But not me. Never again. "Everything I do has been for your own good, don't you see that? I am the one who has made you who you are today. You owe everything to me."

I shook my head. "You are sadistic and only care for yourself."

His face went dark in an instant, his eyes full of anger. I bit my lip as he pulled out the knife and waved it at my face, blood dripping onto my cheek. "I would die for you! Don't you understand? I am only trying to protect you and make you into the woman you wanted to be. I have done everything for you!"

I didn't say a word as he kept the knife in front of my face. He stood there for what felt like minutes, taking deep breaths, not letting his anger get the better of him. I had seen him like that once before, a long time ago when I found him cheating on me—when I saw him for the *schwein* he truly was. We fought, and I told him we were through, and knowing him as I do now, I realized how much he must have had to hold back from hurting me that night. I never thought he would ever hurt me. It wasn't until a couple of years later when I tried to run away and had seen his darkest nature.

I couldn't believe he thought that all the things he had done was for my benefit. The torture, the pain he had caused me. All the lies and secrets he had kept from me and those that I would never find out.

I took in a deep breath, trying to keep calm as I answered his accusation. "That isn't what you said nine years ago. You told me that you never loved me. You told me to walk out of that room because I was just another girl to you. You slept with countless women while you were with me and countless then after." I took another breath. "Why didn't you tell me the truth that night? At least then maybe all this mess would have never happened."

That was a total lie. Or at least I hoped that I would have realized what kind of monster he was. Why didn't I run away sooner? Maybe, deep down, I wanted him to love me so much that I neglected to accept what I was seeing in front of me. A sociopathic egotist who treated everything like some kind of game, a game he had to be the winner of.

But now it didn't matter—now the love I once possessed was replaced with fear and anger. Nothing he could say would change that. I knew his true colors. I had seen the things he had done, and I'd gone through more torture by his hands than I cared to admit.

He shook his head as he set the knife down. "None of those other girls mattered to me, only you did." He grabbed my jaw, making it so I couldn't turn away. "I lied to you back then. I didn't know what to do. I loved you, and I still do. Nothing will ever change that. I just was waiting for you to calm down. I didn't want to act rash. But before I knew it, you were with Walrum and I couldn't do anything about it. I figured it wouldn't last —"

I held his sharp gaze and didn't back down. "Then he proposed, and we were engaged. He didn't treat me like some object to be played with, to torment and see how far he could hurt me before I reacted."

"You are the strongest, most loyal soldier I know. Was that not your dream you told me the first time we met?"

"You mean the day you tried to get me to sleep with you? And I said no, which is why you made it your mission to sabotage my life."

A sly smile appeared on his face. "You gave in eventually, but no. You told me you wanted to be the strongest soldier, and I promised you I would teach you everything I knew. Did I not fulfill that promise?"

"Unfortunately, yes."

"Then, *meine liebchen*, tell me what mission you're on for Admiral Bardon."

How did he know? I had no ties to Admiral Bardon, at least not after graduating from the academy. And there was no way he'd found out about Jonathan's affair with him. I made sure of that. Did he know Jonathan and Nik were with me? And if so, why weren't they arrested at the border. "I'm not on any mission."

He slammed his fist down on the table next to my

head. "Liar! Tell me or I will force it out of you."

I turned and stared at him right in the eyes. "I'm not on a mission. I was just hired to transport merchandise for a good sum of money."

"Oh really? You would risk all this for some money?" he asked.

"It was enough to live off of for the rest of my life. I could go buy an island where no one could find me and disappear. So yeah, it would have been worth it."

He let out a deep breath. "Then you wouldn't have any problem with me searching you for a tracking device?"

I shook my head but cringed at the thought. I had one in my hand and another in my shoe. I prayed to *Gott* that he only found one. "Not at all. I have nothing to hide."

Bastien smiled. "We will see about that."

Going to a drawer, he pulled out a metal scanner. Starting at my pants pockets, he waved the machine up my torso. Then my right arm and hand. Then my left…

The scanner beeped. I cursed under my breath. I had hoped that Jonathan had found ones a scanner couldn't detect. A smile appeared on Bastien's face as he put the scanner down.

He grabbed the knife and traced my hand with the blunt edge. "Tell me now, Rebecca, who put the tracker on you? Who are you working for?"

I didn't say a word. I couldn't say a word. Anything I could say he would hurt me for anyway. He would hurt Nik. Bastien started pushing the tip of the knife against the flesh between my thumb and pointer finger. "Don't… don't, please!"

"I can't have anyone tracking us, now can I? Now don't move or it will hurt a lot more than it has to."

I wished I could struggle, but the leather straps made it impossible. "That's not fair. You have other ways to deactivate it."

"Then tell me the truth."

I turned my head away from him and waited for him to stab my hand and dig the tracking device out. It would hurt, yes, but I had the scars to prove that pain stopped bothering me long ago. I clenched my teeth as he sliced the side of my hand open, ever so slowly, wanting me to give in to him, wanting me to let him win.

He pulled out the tracking device, blood all over the knife, his hands, and table. I was feeling light-headed from the loss of blood from the shoulder wound and this. I glared up at him.

"If you just cooperated, none of this would have happened. You should have just told me the truth."

"Yeah, well, I should have just stayed in prison three years ago," I mumbled.

"You failed your mission. You paid the

consequences. I warned you," he said.

"I know, but it wasn't my fault someone sabotaged the mission. They knew we were coming."

Bastien raised an eyebrow. "Oh?"

"One of them alerted the official. I know it wasn't…" I left off, not wanting to bring Walrum to him. I didn't want to start that argument up.

"Walrum? Because he's dead. So who do you think it was?"

"Had to've been Jonathan. I think he did it, not knowing they would capture us though."

"Not Nik?" he inquired with a bit of suspicion.

"I don't think it was Nik. Then again, I could be wrong."

"And why do you think it wasn't Nik?" Bastien pressed further.

Scheiße, I shouldn't have let that slip. "I just don't think it was him. I knew him better than anyone else."

"Do you now?" He let out a little laugh. "So you know they were spies for Admiral Bardon? All three of them, ever since they left the academy."

"What? Why would…?" I would ask why Bardon would send spies against Bastien, but that was a stupid question. I knew why he would do that. A lot of the admirals suspected him, but Bastien covered his tracks well.

"You know the answer to that. They wanted

evidence. Bardon hired them before they left the academy. He knew I would look for Special Forces agents, and then he got them to spy on me. They'd hoped I would trust them enough to show them the experiments and then they'd arrest me."

This entire time, they had known. And they lied to me. They never told me the monster our admiral was. If they had just told me the truth, maybe this would have never happened. Then maybe I could have helped them and he would be locked up somewhere for the rest of his life. "How did you figure it out?"

Bastien laughed. "Please, it was obvious. And I learned not to trust anyone over the years."

"You trusted me to help you."

He stroked the side of my face. "That's because I saw the innocence in your eyes. I knew I could trust you, and I knew I had to make you see the cold hard facts about life."

If I could, I would have slapped him. I didn't know what he would have done to me then. "How much did they find out?"

"Nothing. They never found a trace. Don't worry, *liebchen*, they don't know what your hand is in all this either."

But they did. Admiral Bardon had suspicions that I was involved, and he told Jonathan. That was why I was selected for this mission, because I was the only one he would trust in showing the location. Then I could alert them to where it was. Then I could have my revenge on Bastien.

I would do anything for that to happen.

I wondered, after all this was over, would they regard me as a hero? Taking down the man who had caused so much chaos in the nation? Or would I be sitting there next to him on trial for all the things I had done? Would they even care that I helped to capture him? Or would all this be for nothing? Jonathan had said Bardon would pull some strings, but once the knowledge was out there, would they just let it slide? I had a feeling they wouldn't.

Over the years, I learned that Bastien had control over so many people. Even if he got caught and put on trial, that didn't mean he wouldn't somehow get away. No, there was no guarantee that capturing him would mean they would bring him to justice. There was only one way to take him down.

To earn his trust back and then stab him in the heart. And I don't mean that metaphorically.

I had to get close to him. I had to make him believe I was on his side again. I would have to do everything he asks for, do everything he ever wanted me to do. I would regret it, but it was the only way to take him down. It was the only way to make him suffer like I had suffered.

"So, you have one last chance to tell me. Who hired you to find me?"

And here was my chance. I let out a sigh, as if I had given up. "Jonathan. It was Jonathan. He's working for Admiral Bardon, though I didn't know that they had been all this time. I was told the mission was to carry a large sum of money to a contact on Regenwelt for evidence against you, though for some reason I have a feeling that wasn't the full mission, that it was to lure you out, using me as bait."

Bastien leaned down and kissed my forehead. "That's a *gute mädchen*. Now I will send the doctor in to look at those nasty wounds in your hand and shoulder. Wouldn't want them to get infected."

I glared at him as he walked out of the room. There had to be more he wanted, not just a name. Especially since he already knew who was behind this mission.

CHAPTER TWENTY-TWO

Nik

Sebastien was taking Rebecca somewhere in the Nreff system, but we weren't sure where.

Jonathan and I both figured it would be Regenwelt. That was the location of most of the rumors about the human experiments and probably for a reason. I wondered how long it would take Rebecca to get him to take her there, if she could get him to trust her right away or if he would torture her.

I didn't want to think about it. I snuck into the mess hall and took a swig of the schnapps that Rebecca and I had taken from the store. It felt like so long ago now. I missed her, and although I tried not to think about it, I wanted more than anything to save her from whatever Sebastien had in store for her.

Because he was one sick, demented *schwein*.

Taking a seat in the mess hall, I took another swig of the schnapps. I hoped everything would turn out, knowing I wouldn't be able to handle it if it didn't. First it was Walrum, one of my best friends, now Rebecca.

No, Sebastien wouldn't kill her. If he was going to kill her, he would have done it already. She had to be kept alive; that was what all the reports said. And if Alexandra was right, if she was part of the experiments, then he would keep her close to make sure she didn't talk.

I didn't want to believe that Rebecca had anything to do with the experiments, killing innocent people like Alexandra's parents, but after everything going on, I didn't know what to believe anymore. Jonathan was keeping secrets from me. Rebecca didn't tell me about getting arrested at the border—hell, who knew what secrets all the rest of the crew had? I wasn't even sure why Bardon hired them. I felt they knew a lot more about all this than they were telling me, especially when it came to Rebecca.

Why didn't Rebecca say anything to us? Was it because she didn't think we could help? *Gott*, if we had said that we were trying to find evidence all those years ago, maybe she would have come clean. Maybe she would have wanted to help us.

Or maybe she would have told Sebastien and he would have killed us all.

No, there was no way Rebecca would do that to us. Hell, even Jonathan had said she kept his secret for a while. She didn't even tell me about his relationship with Bardon. I wondered how she'd known, when she'd only seen them one time. I was pretty surprised she didn't tell me, especially after three years together. What was the point of keeping that secret when we didn't even know where Sebastien was?

I guess when one was so used to secrets they just become natural.

The door slid open and Mary and Burt stepped in. I screwed the bottle closed.

Burt gave me a look. "I thought there was some rule against having alcohol on a ship."

I shrugged. "I'm off duty. It's fine."

"Give him some slack," Mary commented. "He just found out his girlfriend was a wanted criminal."

I tried not to let out a laugh. They didn't even know half of it, thank *Gott*.

"Yeah, like that was a real big surprise," Burt added. "She's coldhearted and always looking over her shoulder. I personally thought it answered a lot of questions."

That it did. I stood up to put the bottle away. "She

might have seemed that way, but she cared about people. She didn't deserve what happened."

"Other than she killed the representative of Nash Mir. I would have to say that she did in fact deserve what's coming for her."

I tried not to lash out and say something stupid, like confess that I was there too and all of us had no idea that was who we had killed. He didn't know what Sebastien would do to her. He didn't know how much of a horrible creature that man was. "Yeah, well, when this mission is over, I will see if I can get her out somehow."

Burt went behind the counter and grabbed a drink. "Good luck with that. Nreff military is one of the hardest to make budge. Believe me, I would know."

I decided that it would be best if I left before I punched Burt for his comments. It was no wonder he drove Rebecca insane. As I stepped forward, the ship quaked and I slammed to the deck. It took me a moment to regain myself and realize what happened, although I figured it out faster than most since Rebecca and I had this problem before.

We had just been taken out of hyperspace.

I slammed my fist on the ground. *"Verdammt!"*

"What was that?" Mary asked as she stood back up.

I stumbled to the comm system. "Samuel!"

"We were taken out of hyperspace."

"No shit! What do you see?"

It took a few moments for him to answer my question. "It was a net, set up to take anyone who traveled through it out of hyperspace. Engine is down, scanners are down. We're blind and can't move."

A net? Damn it. It was an electronic trap that could stop even the fastest of ships. It wasn't something that was easily created, and one had to have a lot of money and connections to get the parts to make one. And if they found you out, they gave authorities permission to kill on the spot. I punched the wall. "Pirates. Bloody fucking pirates!"

Mary clasped her hand over her mouth. *"Dio mio."*

Burt shook his head. "That's not possible. I thought the system was clear. All the systems have worked hard at ridding the sky of them."

Thanks to me, Jonathan, Walrum, and Rebecca; we had destroyed many of them a while back. "Yeah, well, that doesn't mean they still aren't out there." I took a deep breath and pressed the comm button. "Samuel, get navigation and scanners back on pronto. I will head to the engine room." I turned to Mary. "This is your time to shine; show me why you were picked for this mission."

"All right."

Although she appeared anxious, I could tell she was determined to get the job done. She and I both hurried to the engine room where Russ was.

He was already on it, his head under the control panel, figuring out the damage. He cussed, *"Pezzo di merda!"*

So I took that as not doing good. He didn't notice as we stood there.

I bent down next to him. "What do you have so far?"

He jumped up, smacking his head on the control panel. "Wires to the navigation and scanners are completely burned out. So are communications to anyone outside the ship. The only way to repair them is to replace them."

"Do we have any extras onboard?" I bent down to look. He was right. They were completely destroyed.

He shrugged. "There are some, but it will not be enough. We're sitting ducks right now."

Mary bent down, mumbling in Italian. She scratched her head as if trying to figure all this out.

I bit my lip, trying to think of something we could do. "What if we ripped out the wires to the communications between rooms of the ship? Will we have enough for at least the navigation and scanners?"

Mary and Russ glanced at each other. Russ shrugged. "Perhaps, but that takes time."

"We don't have time," I said. "We will be boarded by pirates any moment now. Jonathan and I will stall them while you figure all this out."

His eyes widened. "Pirates, you can't be—"

"I am. Now get to work and don't stop. The moment you get everything back online, call for help."

I turned and left them. They could manage without me—especially since someone needed to hold off the pirates. Jonathan was already coming down the hallway with Burt.

"Status?" Jonathan asked.

"*Scheiße*. Got some guns?"

He nodded. *"Oui."*

"There is only one thing to do. We let them board and wipe them clean. Then we can take out their system and put it into ours. Simple as that."

"Simple as that?" Burt exclaimed, joining in the conversation. "You have to be kidding me!"

Jonathan stared at me for a moment, then nodded. "We've done it before. Granted, last time we didn't have civilians on board, but it shouldn't be a problem. We won't let them get on this ship."

Burt just stared at me, not sure how to take the information I had just given them. He shook his head. "You two are crazy!"

"*Oui*, but it's the only thing we can do. Now you can join us, or you can stay here. Your choice."

He paused for a moment, then nodded. "Fine, I will help you. We can't let them on the ship."

I pointed at him. "And you'll follow our orders

exactly. You got that? No questioning, no deciding to do your own thing. We have innocent lives on board, and we can't fuck this up."

"Yes, sir."

Jonathan and I both nodded to each other. I let out a sigh. "Great. Now let's go wipe out some pirates."

"*Que Dieu ait pitié de nos âmes*," Jonathan added. "May God have mercy on our souls."

Ain't that the truth.

CHAPTER TWENTY-THREE

Rebecca

The doctors patched me up a lot quicker than I expected. I thought for sure Bastien would stop them in the middle and stab me once more, just for fun, but he didn't.

He didn't hurt me, at least not like I thought he was going to. Sure, he stabbed me in the shoulder, and sure he dug that tracking device out of my hand, though I blamed that one more on Jonathan than Bastien. Next time I saw that bastard I would punch him for suggesting to put it in my hand. Punch him straight in his chiseled jaw.

Hours had passed since my interrogation, and they

gave me a room where I could rest. I stayed there, lying on the small cot and staring up at the ceiling, wondering when he would come for me.

I couldn't sleep, not after everything that had happened. My chest was hurting too much over Bastien telling me that all this was for my own good and finding out that the two closest people I cared about had been lying to me. Jonathan, well, that wasn't much of a surprise. It explained why he hid his relationship with Admiral Bardon. He just didn't want Bastien to know how close they were. But Nik and Walrum, they never told me anything. Walrum and I would be married. Nik and I were… Well, I didn't know what we were. Either way it hurt.

But was I any different? I had been lying about everything with Bastien. I could have been a witness. I could have testified against Bastien. We didn't need all this; we just needed for me to say where everything was held, everyone involved.

And then I would be arrested.

It kept coming back to how much trouble I was in. I couldn't be seen as innocent, not that I ever considered myself innocent. I wondered if I could get away and hide after all this was through. Maybe then I would finally have a life.

Like the one Nik and I had.

I didn't want to imagine how Nik would view me

once this was through, how he would see the monster I truly was. It was my fear all this time. Now I didn't have a choice; now he would know the truth about everything. So I guess it was petty of me to be mad at him for keeping a secret when I had the worst secret of all.

The commlink's buzzer went off. "Commander Kompen, the admiral wants to see you."

Commander? Really? Had my rank been reinstated already? And the soldier sounded calm, as if it was just a simple request. No request was ever simple from Bastien. What he wanted, I didn't want to think about. I just knew it couldn't be good.

The door to my bunk opened, and I followed the soldier to wherever Bastien was waiting for me. I didn't recognize him, probably a recruit from the academy. He appeared younger than me, of which the number of younger-than-me officers seemed to keep multiplying. *Gott*, I hated it.

This ship was bigger than the ship I was on with Nik and Jonathan and also had more people on it. I calculated at least thirty soldiers, if not more. Even if I wanted to run away, there was no way I could.

Well, that's not true. I had done it before. But that was under different circumstances.

As we approached the room where Bastien was waiting, I cursed under my breath. "You have to be fucking kidding me."

Bastien was waiting for me in the mess hall. No one was in there. I presumed he made them all leave and ordered them not to come back for a bit. I stood there, just inside the doorway, wanting to stab him with my butterfly knife, wherever that was.

"Thank you, you may leave."

The soldier nodded and left us. I felt like begging him to stay—or begging him to shoot me, I wasn't sure. The door slid closed behind him.

Bastien sat at one table, smiling at me.

"You can't be serious," I whispered.

"What are you saying, *meine liebchen*? I saw that you were the cook on that ship of yours before they arrested you, and I'm just dying to see how much better you have gotten in the culinary arts since the last time you cooked for me."

I clenched my fist, holding back the urge to want to smack him. "That's because last time I cooked for you, you said that you had eaten better food in a backwater pub on Charlottetown."

"I wouldn't lie. Your cooking was horrible back then. But to be a cook on a ship, well, you must have achieved something worth sharing with people. And here I thought you only cooked for me."

Deep breathing. Deep breathing. And people wondered why I was so fucked up inside—because of this *arschloch*. No, most definitely.

"Well." He gestured to the kitchen. "I'm waiting."

I walked over to what he had waiting for me in the kitchen. Vegan tagliatelle pasta, onion, carrots, celery, garlic, tomatoes, and a bunch of mushrooms. *Gott*, I hated mushrooms. Next to the bag of mushrooms was ground beef.

"Presume you want me to make you mushroom bolognese pasta?" I asked.

"Of course. My favorite dish by my favorite girl."

Which meant I would screw this up big time because nothing I did was ever good enough for him. All the meals I ever cooked for him, even though I knew they were perfect, he said tasted like *scheiße*. After a while I gave up and stopped cooking for him and lost the urge to cook for everyone else—that is until Walrum figured it out. He said my cooking tasted like a gift from an angel, and it was only then did I have confidence in something that I used to love. Bastien was just doing this again to get in my stupid little head. I wouldn't let him though. Not this time.

I started washing the vegetables. I would have to get the tomatoes ready first, so I grabbed a pot and filled it with water. I'd need to boil it and set the tomatoes in to help get the skins off. It was the easiest way.

While the water was boiling, I chopped up the rest of the vegetables. My arm was still throbbing, but I ignored it. I even sliced up the disgusting mushrooms. Nik liked mushrooms a little, but I never let them on our ship. I told him I hated them, everyone knew I hated them, but they never realized why. They never realized that it was because it was Bastien's favorite food, that he had it with everything he could. The mere sight of them reminded me of him, and I just couldn't take it any longer.

I wondered how far away Nik was and how long until Bastien took me to the base so I could push the other tracking device that was in my boot. I just prayed to *Gott* that Bastien wouldn't find it and remove it like he did the other one.

The tomatoes were peeled and the seeds extracted, so I started heating the frying pan, adding a bit of olive oil, parsley, garlic, oregano, basil, and, of course, salt and pepper. Normally with a marinara sauce I would add onion, but since I was adding more vegetables to it later, with the mushrooms, I decided to sauté them later. I added the tomatoes and covered it on low while I started the rest of the sauce.

Bastien stood from where he was sitting and came up behind me. He wrapped his arms around my waist, and it took everything to not flip him over onto the stove. Mostly I just didn't want to mess up the dish by doing so.

"So tell me, what were you doing on that ship?" he

whispered into my ear.

I mixed the vegetables around so they wouldn't burn. "I told you, Jonathan hired me to lead the ship to Regenwelt to trade credits for evidence against you and the experiments."

"That's not what I meant. I meant what were you doing on the ship? Why did Jonathan look for you in particular?"

That was a good question. I thought it was because Nik was with me, but at the moment I wasn't too sure. Bardon had suspected my involvement with Bastien, but I had a feeling that this mission was entirely centered on me.

Either way, I wouldn't tell Bastien that it was because Nik was with me. I would never tell him that because, well, he would kill him.

I picked up the lid and gave the tomato sauce a quick stir. "I don't know. He mentioned it was because out of the three of us, I was the only one who was wanted alive, that you wanted me back."

"The three of you? So you were with Nik then?"

"No," I lied. "I was alone."

"Oh, Rebecca, you know how I get when people lie to me. Now tell me, were you and Nik together for the past three years?"

I didn't know how I would answer that. If I said yes, then he would ask more questions, and if he knew what we did together, all would go to hell. "We weren't together for the past three years. Nik found me a few weeks ago on Tierra Prometida and convinced me to travel to Unité. There, Jonathan convinced us to take the mission, though I have a feeling that was why Nik found me on Tierra Prometida. They were tracking me, but you took the device out of my hand and destroyed it, so they are at a loss. But I wasn't with Nik for three years, no."

He pulled me in tighter, hurting my ribs. "Then why was your ship registered under both your names?"

"We did that before I left for the mission so that he could sell the ship."

Bastien forced me around and slammed my back against the edge of the counter, pinning my wrists back. The wooden spoon was still in my hand, and the few pieces of vegetable dropped to the floor. His eyes were dark, and I could tell he was restraining himself from hurting me. "Liar. Tell me the truth, Rebecca. I'm getting tired of your nonsense."

"Fine." I cringed at his tight grip. "We were traveling together the entire time. Happy?"

"And your relationship with him?"

"Is that necessary—?"

"Rebecca, don't make me ask again."

I sighed. "You fucked me up to the point where I don't know how to love anymore."

Without warning, he let go of my wrists and pulled my head to him, kissing me straight on the lips. As a knee-jerk reaction, I started to grab the nearest chopping knife but stopped myself. No, I had to fulfill this mission. I couldn't let anger get the better of me. He had to pay for all that he did—it was the only way I could wash my hands of all the blood.

So I let him kiss me, like I was his little *Puppe* all over again.

He backed away with a smile. "That's better. Now, you better stir those vegetables or they will burn, and you wouldn't want that."

Turning around, I stirred them, regretting my decision not to kill him.

"Why haven't you added the ground beef yet?" he asked as he watched.

I shook my head. "You know I don't cook with meat."

"Are you still on that stupid diet? You do far worse to humans than any animal has had to suffer in the farming industry, that is, if my presumption of your fear of it being an actual animal harvested is correct."

"I don't care. Just give me this one thing," I whispered.

He leaned in and kissed my cheek. "Fine. I will. Just don't disappoint."

I wasn't sure if he meant the meal or something else,

so I just focused on the meal.

About another twenty minutes passed before the food was ready. I had boiled and cooked the pasta as well and mixed the sauce in once it cooled down just a tad. I scooped some up onto a plate and took it to Bastien where he was waiting.

He smiled. "Smells good. Now let's just see if it tastes the same."

I wanted to smack that stupid smile off his fucking face as I stood next to him.

He took a bite and laughed. "Just as I thought. You still can't cook."

Setting the fork and spoon down, he let out a sigh. He was silent for a moment, and I stood there, not sure what would happen next. Suddenly he stood up and pinned me straight into the wall, his elbow in my chest, making it hard to breathe.

But at least he wasn't choking me.

"Damn it, *liebchen*, why do you always screw this up? It was the same then as it is now."

I couldn't move, terrified that if I did, he might hurt me.

"I expected more from you. I expect you to follow everything, just like you did when you were under me. You got that? You follow my every order from here on out. Not just in the kitchen, but outside. You are mine, you got that? Don't you dare think differently."

I nodded as much as I could while still panicking. He kept me there for a moment longer, then let go.

Bending forward, I started coughing—able to breathe in air again. I gasped, trying not to hyperventilate.

"Now, *meine liebchen*." He turned away from me. "Clean this up, try the recipe again, and I will get us something to drink from my room. I also have two pieces of chocolate, so if you do a little better next time, you might even get a reward."

I heard the door slide open and close, and it took all my strength not to sob.

CHAPTER TWENTY-FOUR

Nik

Everything was going to bloody hell.

It had been years since I was in a fight this bad. Then again it had been a long time since I had fought against so many people. Sure, Rebecca and I had gotten into a few scrapes, but nothing of this magnitude. Usually it was just a few men, a dozen at most, and Rebecca was a lot scrappier than I was. And we also were on land and didn't have to worry about where our bullets hit. One wrong move here could cause us to be sucked out of the ship, and none of us would come out of it alive. No, neither side wanted that to happen.

I knew that this battle hadn't lasted long, but it felt

like a century.

The ship was large—a bit bigger than the ship we were on. It could fit at least twenty people, and that was if they only needed the minimum crew to keep it flying. It was typical in Nreff design to have corridors leading from the front to the back of the ship and a few perpendicular corridors that led to various rooms. Then there was a second floor with the same layout.

We had entered through one of those perpendicular corridors, waiting for Jonathan to go ahead. The first thing we needed to do was get to the engine room, which was in the back, on the bottom floor, and then to the cockpit on the top floor.

Why was it always on the other side of the ship?

I wasn't used to working with men I didn't know. I mean, I got to know a little about Burt, but that didn't mean I knew how he fought, what his strategy was. At least he was Nreff Nation trained, so I knew what tactics he learned in school, and knowing that if I shouted out in German, he would understand. We were so used to our admiral commanding us in German that when we worked without him, we still communicated in that language.

Jonathan was just ahead, fist-fighting with a pirate. They must have both lost their weapons in the battle. The pirate stood no chance; Jonathan was the best fighter that I had ever known.

And I was right. Within ten seconds, Jonathan had him down on the ground.

So how many did that leave? How many more pirates were on this ship? There could just be a handful, or there could be dozens upon dozens. It was always hard to tell; pirates were great at masking their numbers on a ship.

But I still couldn't get over the fact that there was a pirate ship out there.

What did it mean? And did Sebastien have something to do with it? I don't know how, not when he had caused so many of their deaths. Hell, I didn't even think there were pirates in these parts any longer. I had thought they had all gone, after what we did to them all those years ago, blowing a few holes in some ships, destroying bases.

The good ol' days.

I felt sort of strange, thinking of those days as fun. I was with friends. I was with Rebecca. But in reality, we were on a mission to take down one of the most feared men in all the Nreff Nation.

Sebastien Wilde.

And I was still on that mission and would be until that sociopath was dead. It wasn't like we could kill him either. We didn't want to be charged with another murder. No, we had to find proof for the crimes he committed and charge him according to the law. He knew that and kept it under the radar for a long time. He didn't even trust his own men with the information.

I raised my gun and shot a pirate who had his head turned away from me. He never saw his death coming, which was for the best, I always said. I've seen many men tortured who begged for death. This was much easier.

Even with the past two kills, there were many more pirates coming from the top floor. Burt was doing his best not to freak out in the situation, which I was thankful for. When we fought them years ago, I had been afraid. Pirates were notorious for killing people without reason, almost like monsters. Rumors spread throughout all the systems, fear causing the stories to be exaggerated, but I wondered what truth there was to sayings like "They will cut off your head and use your blood as paint" or "They will keep you alive and throw you out into space where you can suffocate and freeze to death." Great things to think about while fighting such monsters.

But Burt didn't let it get to his head. He didn't cower like some people did. I was happy that the crew selected for this mission were smart and strong. Bardon had done his research. They were great fighters and, from what I could tell, very reliable. I trusted that they would make it through this, as Jonathan and I had already made it through before. It just took careful thinking and planning throughout the entire takeover of the ship.

Our choices in life had never been easy. From the start of our mission to find evidence against Sebastien Wilde twenty-one years ago, to the present day, which was still the same mission. He was a sneaky bastard, one who never seemed to slip up until we found that Rebecca was wanted alive. I didn't understand how he knew it was only the three of us, and I didn't feel right about having to use Rebecca like that. But that was the choice we had to make.

Which brought us to this moment. And what to do about these bloody pirates.

Burt stabbed another pirate in the heart. He was great with a knife, and I didn't want to run into him in a dark alley. You wouldn't be able to tell by just looking at him though. He seemed younger than he was, and he was lengthy and slender, not your typical Nreff soldier. But after watching him with that knife, I could understand how he used to be a soldier.

We finished with the last two pirates who were in the area. We checked around each corridor. It was all clear. They had either gone back to the bridge or were guarding the engine room and waiting for us. I nodded to Jonathan to come over to Burt and me.

"I think we should split up and head to the bridge and engine. If we take down the engine room, we can stop the ship, and through the bridge we can see how many more life signs are on the ship and how many more pirates we need to capture," I explained.

Jonathan nodded. "I agree. I will go to the bridge, and you can take out the engine room with Burt. We will communicate via commlinks."

With that, Jonathan headed off toward the bridge. We both knew the layout of the ship as it was a common, well-packed Nreff ship. I headed in the other direction. "Come on, Burt, this way."

Another pirate appeared, and I shot him the moment I saw movement from the corner of my eye.

Heading down the main corridor, I saw that I was correct in my thinking that a group of pirates were waiting for us there. Burt and I turned down one of the perpendicular corridors before they could shoot at us. Peering around the corner, I got a better look.

There were four spread out, getting ready to throw smoke grenades. Burt and I had to act fast; we couldn't let them get past us or go after Jonathan. I signaled for Burt to follow me as I ran across the corridor. I motioned for him to shoot where I wanted him to shoot in order to take them all out. Did I have faith in him? Sure I did. But did I have faith that this would succeed? Not particularly, but it was worth a shot.

I held up my fingers—three, two, one—and ran out across the corridor, signaling where to shoot. Then a miracle happened. We did it. We succeeded. I watched as all four pirates fell to the ground, dead.

I hurried down the corridor and into the engine room, shooting the last pirate, who was about to pull out his weapon. "I'm in," I said into the comm device.

"Good for you," Jonathan replied as I heard someone scream in the background. "I'm getting there. Just have to clear away these bodies."

"I am hacking into the system now. Should have the ship down in no time."

"Sounds good." Another scream from Jonathan's side. "These *mauviettes* won't know what hit them."

I laughed as I pulled up the keyboard. Jonathan was a lot better when it came to fighting than hacking into a system like this one. Although he was going to the bridge, mainly he wanted to take down the captain before it was too late. The engine was easier to hack into because it didn't have all the fancy things going on that the bridge had. All I needed to do was get the ship to go offline, far easier to do from here.

Then the captain would have nothing to… captain, I guess the word would be.

Burt held guard at the door, making sure no pirates would come storming in. I heard him fire two shots, but I wasn't worried. We had the high ground now; we wouldn't lose.

After a few minutes, I was able to hack into the

mainframe. "Bingo," I whispered as I typed in the code. "System lockdown."

I heard the engine stop. There was no longer any power to the bridge. "Jonathan?" I asked.

"Yup, I'm still here. Only two pirates left. Any on your side? Can you hack into the scanners and see how many are left on board?"

I typed a few buttons and smiled. "Just the two in front of you."

"Well, that makes this easy," Jonathan said.

Something hit me after killing all the pirates—even though we had been out of the army, we were still killers. I knew they were pirates, but it was still hard to face. I didn't want to be a heartless killer, but after so many years of work, it was hard not to be. That was why the past three years had been the best in my life—because I didn't have to do the things ordered of me anymore. I didn't have to kill to keep on going.

Few people realized the things one did as a Special Forces agent. Just because there wasn't war against the other systems didn't mean that there weren't other problems that we faced. Terrorists, traitors, pirates, mass murderers, you name it. That was what we dealt with, and we were good at dealing with it.

Thinking about those things always made me wonder how Sebastien could have gotten involved with the experiments when he was working to defeat such people. He was psychotic, so that had something to do with it. He was the one who wanted us to kill instead of asking questions. He was why we were so good at killing pirates. But this felt…

Wrong.

Not only that, but I wanted to know if we could figure out who hired them. Jonathan could have kept them alive for us to at least question them, not that pirates would ever tell the truth, if the ones left even knew who hired them.

I turned the engines back on. "Coming to you."

"Roger that."

Still cautious, Burt and I went up to the bridge and didn't run into any pirates. So we had gotten rid of them once and for all.

Jonathan was searching through the electronic documents on the ship. I stepped up next to him and peered over his shoulder.

"Who do you think sent them?" I asked.

Jonathan shrugged. "Hard to tell, could just be new pirates. I don't see any clues in their manifest."

"Hm."

"Exactly."

I didn't know what to believe—pirates haven't been talked about in years. So there was only one way they could have survived, one way they could have stopped us.

Sebastien had lured them out there. They had somehow been under his thumb.

CHAPTER TWENTY-FIVE

Rebecca

It took me three tries to get the recipe to be adequate. The chocolate wasn't a lie either, and as I nibbled on it in my bunk, I thought about all the ways I could kill him. There were so many ways—knife, gun, acid, my own bare hands. But first I had to betray him to shatter his ivory tower. I had to destroy everything he worked so hard to create.

I was being selfish, but at this point I didn't care. I was the one he had dragged through it all. I was the one who was made to be his little *Puppe*. I wouldn't have it any longer. Even if the Nreff Nation captured him and he went on trial, I guaranteed he would get away somehow. He had connections everywhere, and people feared him even if he was behind bars. No, I had to outsmart him. I had to do the worst possible thing.

I had to think like him.

It was the only way to catch him, to make everything just disappear from his grasp. I loathed ever having a thought close to his, especially since I knew I could, but it was the only way to have my revenge. It was the only way to bring him down.

I couldn't let anything stop me at that point. I had to be in it all or nothing. I knew the things he would make me do to see if I had given him my trust again, to see if I was his. It wasn't like things I hadn't done before, which was why I knew what to cringe or vomit about. But I had to take it, and in the end, it would feel so satisfying.

I sensed the ship come out of hyperspace. We were at Regenwelt. I took in a deep breath. This was it. I could let the Nreff Nation take him down or take him down myself. The choice was already made, but first I had to go along with whatever his plan was.

And I had a feeling he wanted to get caught. As to why, well, I would find out soon.

It could most definitely be because he wanted to kill Nik and Jonathan. I wouldn't let him do that. No, not even getting my revenge would be worth someone else's life. Especially Nik's.

The buzz of the commlink sounded, and Bastien's voice came out. "Rebecca, it's time to go planet side."

I opened the door to my bunk and climbed out. Bastien was standing there, patiently, as I straightened up.

"Are you ready, *meine liebchen*?"

I nodded. "Yes."

He smiled as he grabbed my arm. "That's a *gutes mädchen*. Can I trust you won't make a scene as we go through the spaceport and down to the planet?"

"I won't if you don't," I answered with a little smile. His grip tightened around my wrist.

"I don't make scenes. I just have to keep everyone in line all the time. And you know how I get when people aren't obeying their commands."

"Y-yes, sir."

"Now, don't say a word to anyone and stay next to me where you belong."

I didn't answer because, well, it would have been a sarcastic reply and he would have just gotten angrier. He didn't think I would obey his every word. I wanted to run for it the moment we got off the ship, but there was nowhere to go. Besides, I had to end this once and for all.

It would take a bit to get Bastien to trust me again, if he ever would. He didn't trust anyone, as everyone would just disappoint him. No, I would have to see what his plan was, what his true intentions for all of this was. Then I would destroy it, everything he worked so hard to accomplish, just like he destroyed my life.

Nik wasn't far behind, that I knew. I had no idea what Bastien's plan for him was. I hoped that they would think the mission was a failure and that they wouldn't come for me. I didn't need anyone else's blood on my hands because of Bastien's possessiveness.

I hated seeing him like that. It reminded me too much of what kind of monster he made me into. I would be lying if I didn't think I was as bad as he was. Killing became second nature to me, at least it did when I worked under Bastien. I got more hesitant after I was with Walrum though, and he knew that. Which was why he put me on the worst missions, ones where I couldn't leave any witnesses no matter who they were or how old they were.

It had been so long, yet those memories still haunted my dreams.

We got onto the sky elevator and headed down toward the planet. I looked out the window at Regenwelt, my home world, the world I was stationed on for most of my life. It had been so long since I had been there, and I never realized I had grown so attached to it. Though the moment I saw it, memories of Walrum came rushing back, all the times we traveled down the sky elevator. I turned away, not wanting Bastien to notice my emotional response. Who knew to what advantage he would use that?

"What's wrong, *meine liebchen*?"

Damn, he noticed. "Just been a long time, sir. I have a lot of memories on this world."

"That you've had."

I wasn't sure what he meant by that comment, if he was trying to refer to all the missions he forced me on, the ones that happened in the deepest and darkest of streets. If I could do anything, I would erase those memories out of my mind. I just prayed that he wouldn't drag me there when we landed.

No, there's no way, not with Nik and Jonathan just behind us… Right?

I doubted it, but I could feel my heart rate quicken. I didn't want to do any of that ever again. I wasn't the same person. I wouldn't let him use me like that, to kill and torture. I had grown stronger and I could say no even if it meant torture or being strapped down to a table. I would never hurt an innocent person.

And there were plenty of other things I never wanted to do with Bastien again as well. But I had a feeling in order for him to believe I was wrapped around his finger once more, I would have to. I tried to push back the sour taste that filled my mouth. Damn, I didn't want to be reminded of his foul taste in sexual acts.

We landed, and I took a deep breath. It smelled just

like I remembered—metallic, dirty, full of people and perfume. So many smells, so many sources, mixing together to give it the unique odor that I had learned to love. Many people hated the smell of the city, but I always found it to be the best—or at least this city. I didn't care for any other city if I were honest.

The place was crowded. It was strange, standing in a crowd and feeling so alone, so afraid. It was as if no one noticed anything around them, making everyone almost in their own little world. One could get away with a lot in public when no one cared. I just wished people took notice of what was going on around them more. Then maybe these cities all would be a little safer.

As we stepped outside, I saw a familiar face. *Scheiße*, what was Bardon doing here? Did he think it was a good idea to show his face at a time like this?

He glanced over to us, his eyes meeting mine. Why he was here, I did not know. He knew the tracking device was still on me. Did he just want to make sure I was still alive?

Stepping forward, Bardon smiled. "Admiral Wilde, I see you have found your commander who's been wanted for three years. Do you need assistance escorting her to the nearest holding cell?"

That was it. He was making it seem like he had nothing to do with me. It would not work. I had already told him that I was on a mission, although I guess he didn't know that. Either way, this couldn't end well.

"Sorry, Admiral Bardon, to inform you that Commander Kompen has been reinstated under my supervision. She is no longer wanted for treason. It was a big misunderstanding. It's been a few months, actually. I can show you the orders myself."

Admiral Bardon's eyes never left mine. "There's no need for that. I trust a fellow admiral. I'm just glad everything else has been straightened out. What about the others who were under your wing? Are they reinstated as well?"

Bastien shook his head. "No, those three were the traitors to the nation, while Rebecca was just at the wrong place at the wrong time. They should have never arrested her."

I could tell Admiral Bardon wanted to comment on that, but he didn't. "Well, I'm glad that has been cleared up. I would hate for someone innocent to get hurt. It's great to see you around again, Commander Kompen."

"Likewise," I said as I stayed close to Bastien. If I messed this up, I would be in even worse trouble.

"Good day, Admiral. Until next time."

Bastien grinned. "Yes, until next time."

Escorting me away from Admiral Bardon, Bastien took me toward the street where a car was waiting for us. I took a deep breath when my door was closed. He would contact Jonathan and Nik the moment we were gone and tell them we had landed. He had to be keeping an eye on us, just to make sure all went according to their plan.

Well, at least Bastien didn't kill him right then and there. I was pretty surprised, though I guess Bastien would rather use me to get to Bardon.

Bastien got in the car beside me. "Well, it looks like he's spying on us, doesn't it, *meine liebchen*?"

"Yes, it does."

He scooted over closer to me and wrapped his arm around my shoulder. With his free hand, he lifted my chin to face him. "What's wrong?"

A lot of things, namely you. I wanted to say that so badly, but I also didn't want to pay the price for such a comment. I couldn't believe he was asking such a stupid question either, as if he didn't know. But I had to think of something to answer with, then it hit me. "Is it true my commander status has been reinstated? And my arrest for treason has been lifted?"

"Yes, for the time being. You know I can pull as many strings as need be to get you where I need you."

Of course he could. He could have done that years ago. I guess he just let me sit in that prison because he wanted me to learn my lesson. What that lesson had to do with, I didn't know nor care. It was all in his mind anyway.

I wondered if I was there were others he played games like this with or if I was just that special. It didn't make me feel special but almost as if I was being punished for something I had forgotten about. I wouldn't wish this on any other person. Other than Bastien, that was.

And I would make a special little hell for him. I would guarantee it.

We ventured through the streets, and I watched as all the places I used to visit, places that carried memories of better times, flashed by. It felt almost like I was looking back on my past, seeing all the things that once made me happy. On one corner I even thought I saw Walrum, standing there, waiting for me like he always used to, but I knew I was wrong, that my mind was just playing tricks on me.

We came to a stop. Bastien got out and opened my door, and I found myself standing outside an apartment complex. It was the same apartment he had three years ago, the same old-fashioned tall building with dozens of apartments ranging from studios to luxury penthouses. Bastien always just kept a studio, not needing much. That, and I think he enjoyed having the bed in the same room as everything else. My heart started beating fast, wondering what was coming for me next. *Gott*, I didn't want to know.

He opened the door and ushered me in. I glanced

around. It was the same—simple, colorless, no evidence of any personality. I hated it there, always had. It looked like a stupid hotel room.

The door closed behind me, and I turned to find him still standing there, smiling. "Been a while since you've been here, hasn't it?"

I nodded. "That it has."

"Well," he said as he took his jacket off. "Make yourself at home. I have a few errands to run, but I will be back. I presume I can trust that you won't run?"

I wanted to. "I won't."

"*Gute*, because if you did, I would be very upset." He buttoned up a new jacket. It was still one of his admiral uniforms, so whatever it was, it was legal.

Bastien stepped toward me, and I flinched. He grinned as he grabbed my jaw and kissed me. "I will be back later tonight. Make yourself something for dinner. I doubt I will be back that early."

I didn't say a word as he put one of my vials on the table and left me there. I was alone at last, and I collapsed to my knees and shook uncontrollably.

"It will be okay," I whispered to myself as I took the drug. "I will bring him down once and for all."

CHAPTER TWENTY-SIX

Nik

"You sure you need nothing for the pain?" Alexandra asked as she poured some alcohol into a cotton pad.

"*Nein*. I'm fine," I said.

She shook her head. "Why are men such *duraki*?"

I shrugged, not sure what she said but figured it meant something along the lines of an idiot. "I blame society myself. Also, you have no idea how many stab wounds I've had over the years."

"Along with whatever happened to your eye?"

"Exactly. Fun stuff. This knife wound is but a scratch."

She let out a soft laugh. "A four-inch long, one-inch

deep stab wound in your shoulder is just a scratch."

"Jawohl."

"As I said earlier, *duraki*." She put the alcohol swab on the wound. My body tensed, pain jolting through my nerves.

Fuck that hurt more than I remembered.

"Want something for the pain now?"

I shook my head, not letting my agony show. "Nope."

She finished cleaning out the wound, and I wished I had some good whiskey to drink. Usually when I was getting a wound treated, I had something to drink to dull the pain, since Rebecca and I couldn't afford real painkillers. Damn, I wish I had thought of that before I stepped in here—that is, if Jonathan hadn't already finished up the schnapps.

Alexandra threaded the needle to put in the stitches. "I can't help notice that the wound is on the same side as your eye patch. Didn't see him coming, did you?"

"That, and I haven't fought pirates in quite some time. They are sneaky little *scheißer* if you didn't know. Come out of nowhere and destroy ships, like a space version of termites. Except more deadly."

She stuck the needle in and I took a deep breath. I hated stitches; they were the worst. "You do have a point, but I wonder if your eye patch gives you some trouble. Why haven't you gotten your eye fixed?"

"Just never had time." I didn't know how much she

knew about Rebecca and me, but I didn't want to push it. I didn't know this woman, and I had learned over the years never to assume innocence. It never ended well.

"Maybe your partner didn't want to go in a hospital, and so you never went to one. I wonder why that would be."

I stayed silent. She had a point. Rebecca feared hospitals like no other. I had always thought she didn't enjoy them because she wasn't in control and because she had a problem with being impatient. What if it had more to do with the human experiments?

After Alexandra finished stitching me up, I headed straight to the engine room. We needed to get going so we could follow Rebecca. I had a feeling she was in more danger than any of us realized.

I peeked my head in to find Russ and Mary tinkering with the engine. Sure, I knew how to work with one for a bit, but that didn't mean I knew how to rewire as much as they needed. Fucking pirates.

"When do you think you will have the ship up and running?"

Russ peered up and wiped the sweat off his brow. "Probably another two hours. Luckily the pirate ship's systems are compatible with ours and we can take what we need from theirs."

I nodded. Yes, that was fortunate. Otherwise, we would have been totally screwed for a while or would have had to call for help, which I didn't want to do. If word got out about this, Sebastien would have found out and known we were coming for him.

That is, if he wasn't the one behind the pirate attack. I wouldn't have put it past him. I just did not understand how he got them to do what he said. It wasn't like they took any orders from anyone except themselves. That was the pirate way.

"Hand me the wire stripper, *per favore*."

Mary handed him the wire stripper, and Russ went back to work while Mary tinkered on the communications panel. I found it incredible that the two of them could be so talented under extreme pressure, yet the rest of the time they acted like typical teenagers. Inspiring, really, and it made me think of the time I wasted as a child.

Then again, I was preparing for a mission that wouldn't ever seem to end.

I turned on my heel. "Let me know what you need and I can retrieve it. Burt is monitoring the ship to make sure no one was hiding anywhere, but we doubt it. Better safe than sorry though."

Mary answered. "Can you tell Samuel to check the communicators? That way we can see if things are working up there."

"Yeah, I will."

I hurried out the door and toward the cockpit. Two

hours wasn't that long; not much could happen in two hours.

I knew that was a lie, but I had to keep telling myself that.

I stepped into the cockpit. "Samuel, got the communicators up and running?"

"Almost, was just about to check them." He clicked a button. "Russ, Mary, can you hear me?"

"*Favoloso!*" was the response from Russ, a big grin appearing on his face. "Got some things I want to switch on and try. Are you ready?"

Samuel answered. "Ready."

Something made a clicking noise, and there was a loud kapow noise.

"*Mannaggia!*" Both Russ and Mary's voice came from down the corridor. Samuel and I glanced at each other, both afraid to ask.

I clicked the communicator. "What happened?"

"We will be done in three hours tops."

I rubbed my forehead. That was just great. I knew that Bardon had backups to take out Sebastien, but I wanted to be there when the deed was done—I wanted to watch that *arschloch* fall. And to make sure Rebecca was all right.

"Even in three hours, they are performing a miracle." Samuel clicked a few buttons on the console. "I have been on a few ships that ran into trouble. One of them we were stuck in space for two whole days. Three hours is nothing, especially with the damage we sustained."

"I know. And they are just kids."

He laughed. "Yeah, I guess they are. Though, compared to you, we're all kids, aren't we?"

I shot him a look. "What was that?"

Samuel held up his hands in defense. "I'm just stating the obvious. No need to get pissed. I just mean you have more experience than me."

Letting out a breath, I let the comment slide. "Tell that to Jonathan. I bet he would take it lightly. I swear he dyes his hair."

"I think gray suits you, makes you look more distinguished."

I raised my eyebrow, trying not to clench my fist. "I'm not that gray. Shut up."

He laughed. "Keep lying to yourself, man."

"I'll go check on Jonathan before I do something I regret," I murmured.

I wasn't that old, and I could understand why Rebecca hated traveling with such children. I just made her feel old.

Two more years and I would be forty. *Gott*, I didn't even want to think about that.

At least Jonathan and I were in the same boat. Rebecca would poke fun at us until it was her turn to hit that number, then she would shut up. I couldn't wait for that day.

Heading to the mess hall, I found Jonathan contacting Bardon, which was what I was hoping for.

"Any word?" I asked as I stood behind him, waiting for a response on the communicator.

"Well, *bonjour* Nik, I haven't heard your voice in quite some time," Bardon replied. "Though it's nice to know you're doing well, I had hoped to talk to Jonathan alone."

"Which means something happened," I commented. "That or you two wanted to do things that I never ever want to know about. I pray to *Gott* that I was right in my first guess."

He let out a short laugh. "Don't worry, you are."

Jonathan added. "Nik, please leave."

I couldn't believe they were doing this to me. It was our mission. What had changed over the twenty years to make them want to exclude me? I didn't understand. "No. I want to know what happened."

"Nothing happened, per se. But I ran into them at the sky elevator. I wanted to make sure Rebecca was fine."

"Well?" I asked.

Jonathan gave me a look but said nothing.

"She's alive and didn't appear to be harmed, or at least not much. She had bandages on her hand and seemed to not favor the arm in pain. However, it wasn't the physical things I saw but the way she looked at me.

She appeared horrified."

It took everything not to break something, and it was because Bardon would think so little of me. "And what are we going to do? Are you sending your men in?"

"No."

I slammed my fist on the table. Thank *Gott* it was metal. "And why not?"

"Because she knew her mission and took it. He will take her where we need to arrest him; it will just take some time. She had her chance. She could have said something right there if she needed help, but she didn't. Her tracking device is still active in her boot, and we're keeping a close watch. It's up to her now."

Taking a deep breath, I tried to calm myself down. Jonathan put his hand on my back. "She's strong, she will make it through this. Then he can't hurt anyone ever again."

He had a point. I couldn't wait until this was over, and I swore I would punch him even if I got in trouble for it. He deserved it after everything.

"I just want to see that *schwein* hanged."

"Don't we all," Bardon commented. "And don't worry, we will get him this time. I'm just sorry we had to use Rebecca to do it."

As was I. But she knew the risk, or at least I thought so. If she had a hand in all this, if Sebastien had been manipulating her, then she knew what was coming for her. And that she was the only one who could lead us there.

"I will contact you when the ship is up and running again," Jonathan said. "Should be about…" He looked over at me.

"Three hours."

"*Trois heures*," Jonathan replied. *"Je t'aime."* With that, he clicked off the communicator.

"So," I said. "We just have to wait then?"

He nodded. "Looks like it."

I sat down and sighed. Three hours would pass by very slowly.

Yup, I was right. The three hours passed by slower than a snail stuck in molasses.

At least our engineers could repair it. Damn, I would buy them a beer when this was over—I didn't care they were underage. They deserved it.

Even though I knew the logistics of engine repair, especially since Rebecca didn't want to deal with it, that didn't mean I could have rewired and gotten the engine to work. And in three hours.

We were on our way. Jonathan was keeping an eye in the cockpit while I watched over the engine room and Burt and Alexandra had dinner duty. The two engineers needed a break. I sat there, leaning against the backboard, trying not to touch any of the wires they rerouted. It was a crazy layout, but it worked. It just needed to get us a day's ride to Regenwelt.

As I sat there, thinking of all the pain I would bring Sebastien, the door opened. It was Burt.

"What is it?" I asked. "Did something happen?"

He shook his head. "Oh no. I just wanted to ask you something."

"Well, go ahead, just be careful not to electrocute yourself."

Burt let out a little laugh. "I'll try not to. I just wanted to know, you and Jonathan aren't just some typical military men, are you? I mean, typical men don't just kill others, even if they are pirates."

I would have begged to differ, especially after fighting pirates beforehand. I had killed quite a few over the years. "What is your point?"

He shrugged. "Don't know, just everything going on seems weird. First Natascha getting arrested, then the way you two act in combat—it's as if all of you have had a lot of action through the years. Almost as if you all could have worked together."

I stared at him. The mission was almost finished, and I didn't understand why he was bringing it up. "And why do I have a feeling your background isn't as simple either? Admiral Bardon picked us for a reason, so if I were you, I would stop questioning everything."

Burt had a little grin on his face that I wanted to

smack off. "I guess it just makes me curious what else everyone on this ship can do."

"I can see why you were discharged now. You ask too many questions."

"I just enjoy putting all the pieces together, not one to follow things blindly."

"Well, sometimes the only way to succeed is to not know what's going on around you." And that was true. There were many missions that if we had known all the details, we would have messed up. Then again, sometimes ignorance in a mission could lead to more problems.

Like committing treason for example.

"Kind of like with Rebecca? Or did you know?"

I didn't answer. I didn't want to deal with some stupid kid's comments. "Get out of here and go help Alexandra."

"That's what I thought. Well then, I will leave you to your thoughts."

With that, he left, and I wondered if he was right and whether everyone on this ship had some great secret to hide.

CHAPTER TWENTY-SEVEN

Rebecca

I huddled in a ball, my arms around my legs, rocking back and forth, waiting for Bastien to return. I knew I could have turned the TV on, drowned out the thoughts that were filling my mind, making my heart race. But I didn't. I sat there in the silence, hoping that maybe, just maybe, I would wake up from this nightmare and everything would be fine.

But I knew that wouldn't happen.

This was my reality—I was stuck, waiting for Bastien to show up and treat me like his *Puppe*. He would try to make it like it was before I caught him cheating on me before I realized what kind of *schwein* he was. Was this the punishment I deserved for falling for him? For not realizing what kind of monster he was in the beginning?

No. No one deserved this. Not even me.

I needed to keep telling myself that I was better than him, that I didn't deserve such horror. He had said he loved me, but I didn't believe him. I knew his dark heart could love only one person, and that was himself.

But was I any different?

I didn't deny the fact that I was the monster that he had created. I let him do it to me. I let him manipulate me until there was no going back. I should have known from the start what I was getting into. I should have known he just wanted a toy to play with.

Yet I did nothing to stop it; simply lied to myself about everything, trying to justify his actions. Why did I keep letting myself get into these situations? Why did I put up with this kind of torture?

Right, because he promised to show me everything he knew.

Looking back, I felt so stupid that I believed the lies that had come out of his mouth. However, it didn't stop me from falling in love with him all those years ago, a hidden affair that he didn't want anyone to know about. I should have known then that was because he didn't want anyone to tell me what kind of human he was.

Then I found him sleeping with another woman, a

younger one of course. If I remember, she had just graduated out of the academy. That was what he did; waited until they had just graduated, promised them he would put in a good word with his colleagues, saying he could get them into Special Forces, but never under his command, oh no. That would complicate things. Then he would sleep with them and never talk to them again. That was what he tried to do with me, and I told him off. Then he hired me.

I should have just slept with him that night, then it would have been a one-night stand and I would have never had to see him again. Instead, however, he hired me and made me his goal, —made me his *Puppe*.

Whether he fulfilled his promise and got them jobs elsewhere, I didn't know nor did I care. When I'd found out, I was furious.

That was nine years ago, when he saw me standing outside his door as a girl left his room. He told me that the entire time we were together meant nothing to him. We were just a fling, helping each other out. He said it was to train me, to help me learn the ways of the world. Then I slapped him. His eyes became dark, and he made me leave before he did something he would regret. I told myself I would never look back to that moment, that I would move on. Granted, I saw his fucking face every day, but we never talked about it. Then I became closer to Walrum, someone who didn't play with my thoughts and feelings.

But then Walrum died.

And now here I was, back in Bastien's clutches.

There was nothing Bastien could do to make me love him—no, I was far from ever falling for the *drecksau* ever again. But there I was, sitting on his bed, rocking back and forth, knowing what he wanted from me, thinking that I would want it in return.

I rubbed my forehead. Was this all worth it? It would be, in the end. But getting there hurt. It hurt like a son of a bitch. But at least I would watch him die at my hands. At least I knew I was getting closer every moment I was there.

At least I knew the pain would be worth it.

I could work through the pain, become numb to its hold. I had learned to do that long ago. Back then it had been worth it to just be around Walrum. Granted, I tried to run away a few times. That was before we got too serious though, before he asked me to marry him. Before everything changed.

A day didn't go by now where I didn't miss Walrum. He cared about me so much and I him. He treated me like a princess, always thinking about me before himself. I had never been treated like that before, not by my parents, not by anyone in the academy whom I had a relationship with, and definitely not by Bastien.

The door opened, and I stood up to find Bastien

standing there, his coat unbuttoned but his knife and gun still strapped to his leg. I stayed there, in silence, not sure what would happen next.

"How's your wounds?" he asked as the door slid shut behind him.

"F-fine. They don't hurt anymore."

He pulled off his coat and threw it in the corner. "That's good. I didn't want you to be in pain."

"I find that a little hard to believe."

He shook his head as he stepped toward me. I took a couple of steps back and found myself against the wall. Bastien smiled as he placed his left hand against the wall by my head, trapping me in the spot. His eyes looked down at my lips, and with his free hand, he touched my lip with his finger.

My heart was pounding in my chest. "What are you doing?" I whispered.

Bastien leaned in and kissed me, his lips warm against mine. It took me a second to gather my thoughts, to realize this was not what I wanted.

I shoved him back. "No. Not again."

He shook his head. "Don't deny you came back to be with me. It was always me."

Did he really believe that? Did he tell himself all these lies because it was what he wanted to hear and therefore to him the truth? He was the most *aufgeblasen, überheblich arschloch* I had ever met.

Bastien kissed me again, this time harder and with less compassion. I tried to shove him back, but he didn't budge. I had forgotten how much stronger he was than me, even if I exercised every day. I tried to smack him as he moved to my cheek and down my neck. As I hit him, I felt the knife still attached to his belt.

I pulled out his knife and brought my arm up to stab him in the back. He stopped kissing me but didn't move from my neck. I thought hard about what to do. I could kill him right then and there—he was going to let me. All this would be over, I could get the satisfaction of killing him, and I wouldn't have to sacrifice myself.

Or would I? Let's be honest, he had a plan. There was no way he would let me kill him like this. There was someone waiting outside, someone who would kill me if I did this. But would I have cared? Would it be worth it just to kill him? It was all or nothing. There would be no other way.

But it wouldn't be now. No, there was so much more pain I wanted to rain down on him. He would understand what it was like to suffer by my hand. Besides, I doubted stabbing him in the back would kill him. He was like a cockroach; it would take more than that to bring him down.

So it was a test. It was all just a test to see if I would give in to him or if I would hurt him. He didn't think I could do it. He was that positive I would give in. I wanted to hurt him for that so bad.

But I had to keep my mind on my mission. I couldn't let him win.

I dropped the knife, the clunk as it hit the ground echoing through the silent room. The only noise left was my deep breaths as I tried to calm myself down.

Bastien laughed as he kissed my neck once more and then backed his head away to look me in the eyes.

"I hate you," I whispered.

"You do, huh?" He kissed my lips. "Then show me."

I shoved him back down against the bed in his apartment. The look of surprise appeared on his face for a moment, then it was filled with excitement and satisfaction that he had broken me.

I yanked off his holster and threw it to the ground, appearing as if I wanted more, but in reality I just wanted this to be over with. Tugging at his shirt, ripping the buttons off, I tossed it to the ground.

All of this was to make him believe I was his again, to get him to trust me. After that, the mission would be over with and I could give him the torture that he deserved. I could watch his ivory tower come crashing down.

I ran my hands through his hair as I locked lips with him. I started down his neck and nibbled at the base of his throat. He pulled me closer, my chest heavy against his. I dug my nails into the skin of his bare chest.

Bastien pulled me closer and whispered into my ear. "That's *meine Puppe*."

Pulling my shirt over my head, I watched as he eyed the dog tag that was around my neck. He didn't say a word as he inspected it. He smiled as he read that it was Walrum's, and he lifted it over my head. Bastien threw it across the room with a satisfied look, then pulled me closer, his hellish skin heating my own.

I bit at his lip, the metallic taste of blood filling both our mouths, as he slipped his hands underneath the back of my pants. I unbuttoned them, jerked them off, and straddled my legs around his hips. He ran his hands over my scars—the scars that he himself gave, an assuaging simper on his lips. He flipped me over, letting no one have a dominant pose over him, and started kissing my neck.

"Now tell me," he whispered in my ear. He traced the edge with his tongue. "What does Admiral Bardon want?"

My heart was beating fast as his lips traced my neck. Did he think they knew about me? "You know that he's been suspicious. He wanted me to get the information out of you, I told you that."

His hand traced my side and went down farther and farther. "What about you having a hand in all this?"

"What do you mean?"

Bastien grinned. "So they know then? Well, isn't that

a surprise?"

"If that was the case, then I would have just confessed to it and named you as the mastermind behind it all."

"Oh really? You would confess about all the crimes you have committed over the years? I doubt that, and besides, you have no proof against me."

I paused. I didn't want to answer, but his hand had made it all the way down between my thighs. "You're right, I wouldn't have been able to confess."

"Because you don't want to be arrested, or because you don't want Nik to know the truth about you?"

I paused, and apparently I took too long to answer his question.

His hand left my leg and traced my cheek. "Well then, I will have to kill him, won't I?"

"I didn't say—"

"Then why didn't you say anything the first time I asked, if nothing happened?" He kissed my neck, nibbling my skin. I wanted to pass out, to not remember any of this. I wished I had more morphine-B, at least I could dull the thought of being with him, maybe even forget it all in the morning.

Bastien straddled my hips and straightened up to face me. He smiled as his smooth hands slid across my skin.

And around my neck.

I didn't react fast enough, and his fingers closed

around my throat. I tried to gasp for air, bashing my hands on his arms. Nothing helped. He had a firm hold.

Air had already escaped my lungs, and I couldn't breathe. I knew it had only been a matter of seconds, but it felt like minutes had passed. My mind panicked, wanting him to get off me, as it commanded my body to thrash around. I knew it would just end worse though, as the energy would be wasted.

I clawed at his arms, trying to get him to let go. Blood droplets ran down the side of his arms, but he didn't flinch, staring down at me with those dark eyes. After a moment, he let up a bit, letting me get one tiny breath before closing off my windpipe again.

Bastien leaned in close to my ear. "You will never betray me again, do you hear me? Never. You are mine. You do what I say or I will hurt you far worse than I have ever hurt you. Don't think the scars you have were pain. I will bring you pain far worse. Got it?"

I nodded, hoping it would make him stop. He held my throat for another moment, making his point, then released his grip. I leaned over the side of the bed, coughing, trying to bring air back into my lungs, but he only gave me a second before pulling me back onto the bed. *Gott* I wished I could reach the knife on the floor and stab it through his heart, if he even had a heart.

I wish I could say this was the first time he strangled me during sex, though this time it was out of pure hatred and not because he was sadistic. I debated for a moment whether to end this here and now, tell him everything, and get him the hell off me, but then it would have all been for nothing. No, I would finish this, and to do that I had to give him what he wanted.

Me.

Many would think I was weak for this decision, but on the contrary. I felt the power of knowing that I alone could defeat him. No one else had ever been this close to him, been able to get one step ahead of him. Now I could. So that was why I agreed to let him touch my body like that and why I could go through with it—because I would see him die.

Bastien licked the blood off his arm and pressed his lips against mine, his tongue tasting metallic. *Gott* he had some weird pleasure thing with blood, which was fine with me since I could make him bleed as much as I want.

"Now." He pulled off his boxers. "What games shall we play, *meine liebchen*?"

CHAPTER TWENTY-EIGHT

Nik

We landed on Regenwelt, and now I wanted the mission over with. Jonathan and I reported straight to Admiral Bardon, hoping that they hadn't raided the facility yet. I didn't know whether I was relieved or afraid for Rebecca when I found out she hadn't set the tracking device alert off. I just prayed she wasn't in a position where she couldn't set it off, needing our help and we just sat here, waiting.

Admiral Bardon was the only one awake when we landed in the middle of the night. The rest of our crew had also retired, but Jonathan and I wanted to know all that had happened before we would get any rest.

We met Bardon in his office. The moment I saw them together, I could tell they were in love. Jonathan was quick to give him a kiss on the lips, and I turned away, still feeling awkward that they were a couple. He was our mentor and instructor in the academy. It was still weird to think about. A ten-year difference—I always saw him as a cool uncle-like figure. Now one of my best friends was kissing him.

"Well, Nik, long time, no see. I'm glad you are doing well," Bardon said as he took a seat. "Please, sit down."

I took a seat beside Jonathan, still not quite looking either of them in the eyes. "To say I'm doing well would be an understatement, but yes, I'm alive."

He nodded. "I suppose that is true. Jonathan said pirates attacked you. Do you think they had anything to do with Admiral Wilde?"

Jonathan and I exchanged glances. We hadn't come to a definite answer, but all the signs had been there. Sebastien had to have played some part in it. "It was convenient for him that we were attacked and pushed back. It makes me wonder if Rebecca is all right."

Bardon steepled his fingers together, pondering on this newfound information. "I can understand your concern, but do realize that she is a commander and can handle herself. I gave her the chance to call it off by running into them, to make sure she was okay, and although she was afraid, she didn't make any gesture to say that she needed to be taken away. She knew the dangers of this mission, and I believe she will do anything in order for this to be a success."

I let out a deep breath. I knew he had a point, but that didn't mean I didn't still fear for her. She had gone through a lot over the years, and with this feeling like a complete mess, I didn't know how much danger she was in anymore. I felt like holding her, keeping her close until everything blew over. Damn, I got attached after our three years together. I tapped my foot on the ground, waiting to hear what he had next.

"Did you keep any of the pirates alive?"

Jonathan shook his head. "No, not when they could jeopardize the safety of the crew we were with. If it had been just the two of us, then maybe. They didn't seem like they would really want to cooperate either."

Bardon let the answer sink in. "All right, I will have someone go pick up the abandoned ship after this is over. I presume you have the coordinates?"

"Yes."

Turning to me, he gestured to the eye patch. "What happened to your eye?"

I had forgotten about it and the fact he didn't know. "That was when we ran away three years ago. I damaged my eye, and it wasn't like I could go to a hospital when my face was plastered everywhere."

"What about when you crossed the border? Why

didn't you go then?"

"Just was always afraid to, and I grew used to the patch." I didn't want to mention Rebecca's fear of hospitals—kind of felt like it might have had to do with all that was going on, and I didn't want to bring it up.

"Our doctors can still fix it, might take a little time though."

I hadn't thought about that. Since our charges of treason would be lifted, I could see a doctor. Getting my eyesight back seemed grand. "That would be great, at least after we get Rebecca back."

"What is the rundown for attacking the facility once she is in?" Jonathan asked.

Bardon pulled out two tablets. "We have men ready to go straight into the facility. We have enough men to surround it and make sure no one will escape. I have ordered the men not to kill unless they have to. We want everyone alive."

I glanced over the orders. Sure enough, Sebastien was the key person wanted alive. "What about Rebecca? Did you mention that she was to be kept safe?"

"Yes, and I presume she won't be fighting us. As long as she keeps her hands up, she should be fine."

I couldn't see her doing that, but I also knew she wasn't stupid. She needed to show her innocence in this in order for it to go smoothly. "And what Alexandra said?"

"Excuse me?" Bardon inquired.

"I presume Jonathan told you what Alexandra said about Rebecca. Also, I was surprised to hear that she knew who Jonathan was. She mentioned that she had a part to play in capturing Sebastien, and I have been scratching my head as to what that could be."

Bardon let out a breath before answering. For some reason he didn't want to tell me the whole truth, and I was getting a little fed up with it. "I knew that Sebastien had murdered her parents, and I know that she made it her life's dedication to undo any brain trauma that those experiments might do to a person, if they had survived. I wanted her on this mission so when we raided the facility she could examine the patients."

"And what about Rebecca? Alexandra said that Rebecca killed her parents."

Jonathan and Bardon exchanged glances. "We don't know if it was her."

And yet they had to look at each other for the right answer. There was something they weren't telling me, something they knew but kept secret.

"But you expect that it is. So I want to know, what is your plan for her after all this is over? Are you going to put her on trial, or are you going to tell the court that she was a mole? That she was the reason you could catch Sebastien, and that she is innocent?"

"Nik—" Jonathan began, but Bardon gestured with his hand.

"No, he should know now. Yes, I have a feeling she was in on the experiments, and yes that's why she was picked for this mission. He has some kind of grasp on her that I can't even begin to comprehend. As for putting her on trial, I will see what I can do. I promised her if she helped us, I would do whatever I could to waive her of all charges, that is if anyone raises a voice against her. For all we know, all those she ever worked with her and Sebastien are gone and out of the picture. The only person who might raise a voice would be Admiral Wilde, and his word won't seem very promising, especially since she is the reason we arrested him."

I clenched my fist. No, there was no *Gott*damn way she was involved. I couldn't believe it. Even if something seemed to go on between her and Sebastien, even if whoever killed Alexandra's parents used the same maneuver as Rebecca, that didn't mean we should assume she had something to do with the experiments.

Who was I kidding? Even I was having my doubts.

However, we didn't know the whole truth about her involvement. I just wished she said something in the beginning before going on this suicide mission. Actually, I took that back—I wished that my team would have told me the truth.

Standing up, I left the office.

"Nik, wait!" Jonathan called after.

"Don't worry," I said. "I'm just going to my quarters to cool off. If you hear any word about Rebecca, come get me. I'm not letting that *drecksau* string her around anymore."

With that, I left them there.

I knew I couldn't stay in that office. It had been so many years, yet they treated me like I was still in the academy. There was so much I wanted to say about this mission, stuff I knew I would regret saying, so I left. I wouldn't go far, straight to my quarters, knowing at any moment Rebecca might need me.

On top of everything, I had to hold back the urge to barge straight into Sebastien's apartment and kill him myself. He had been leading us down rabbit holes for far too long, and I was sick of it. If I wanted to solve some stupid puzzle, I would have picked up a fucking sudoku.

I wondered what his motivation for all this was, if he had an end goal or if he just did it as a hobby. How he graduated through the academy and had not questioned his sanity, I did not understand. They all thought he would be some great admiral, only to be a sociopathic killer instead.

I guess they were the same thing.

Many leaders and people who changed the systems

for the better had been odd, so would anyone be able to tell until it was too late? I guess I had never thought of it that way before. I just hoped that we could stop him before he brought even more chaos throughout the systems.

And brought more chaos into Rebecca's life.

Gott, I wanted him to die. I just prayed that I could pull the trigger when that day came, or at least help. Hell, I hoped I could just shoot his body after the fact.

I know quite a few people who would join me, Rebecca being one of them.

I arrived at my quarters and smacked my head on the door. Why had we found ourselves in such a bind? Why did all this have to happen to us?

When I entered the military academy, I did it because my father had also served in the military. I just did it because they expected it of me. I thought Special Forces would be different, and so I took that track.

Never did I imagine what that would entail. So much *scheiße* happened throughout the Nreff Nation, I couldn't believe that my parents would let me walk home alone when I was little.

Stepping into my quarters, I collapsed on my bed. It was nice to spread out on a bed, no walls to smack your arms with and a bed made for comfort. I let out a deep sigh.

How much longer until all this would be over?

CHAPTER TWENTY-NINE

I had blood under my nails. I had slashed at his back as hard as I could, wanting him to feel more pain than I had through the years. I knew that he found pleasure in pain, but the thought of scarring his body made me grin with delight. Most of the scars on his back were from me, after all.

I stepped into the shower, wanting to wash everything away. I scrubbed hard, my skin almost raw, as I didn't want the feeling of his body lingering any longer. I hated him with a passion and wanted more than anything to watch him cease to exist. The thought of it was the only way I could climax last night.

I knew he didn't trust me, nor did I think he would ever trust me again. I had to use that to my advantage though and let him think he was holding all the cards when I was the one with the ace up my sleeve. He had no idea about the second tracking device, no idea that I wouldn't even have to leave his sight to trigger it. I would see my nightmare end—I would be rid of him.

I finished getting dressed in the clothes he had prepared for me. How long he had been holding on to these clothes was anyone's guess. Either he always had them, or he knew I would be needing them and ordered them. I didn't know which answer I preferred.

As I entered where Bastien waited for me, I kept my head tall, trying to act like my old self, even though I despised the situation I was in. I knew where he would be taking me that day, straight to the facility. Then I could trigger the tracking device, then I could watch his stupid face as soldiers came for him.

He wrapped his arms around me. "So, I see the clothes fit."

"They do. How did you know I didn't need a different size?"

Bastien let out a small laugh. "Like you would change. Other than your hair. Fiery, just like your personality. I like it."

I needed to remind myself to change it when this was over. "And here I thought you hated my fiery personality. You sure don't like it when I talk back to you."

Did I regret saying that? Maybe just a tad. He raised his arm for a moment and I flinched. With a satisfied smile, he set his arm back down. "Now, we should get out of here soon. We have a long day ahead of us."

He had no idea. Trying as hard as I could to not let him see the satisfaction on my face, I went to slip on my shoes.

"Wait, *liebchen*, I have new shoes for you."

Scheiße. Why did something always happen when I thought all was going according to plan? "What do you mean? These are fine. You don't need to spoil me."

He grabbed a brand-new pair of boots that had been sitting next to the doorway. "Those are old and worn. You don't want those, especially with your new uniform."

I opened my mouth to say something, but nothing came out. I needed those shoes, especially since the tracking device was in them. "Oh, I suppose you're right. I just broke these in. You know how military shoes can be."

"Don't worry, I have what you want right here." With a smile, he held up the tracking device.

I froze. No, that wasn't possible—he couldn't have known! How did he know? He took the other one out of my hand and paraded me in front of Admiral Bardon, knowing I was still working for him. He knew I was bait.

He let out a laugh. "Oh, Rebecca, do you think I was really that naive? I knew they were using you to get the location of the facility. I didn't think you would ever come back to me."

I didn't know what to say—all I knew was my freedom was in that tracking device and now he held it in his hand. Everything had been for nothing.

And he had sex with me knowing all that. Such a *pute*.

"What are you going to do to me?" I whispered, now fearing for my life. I had hope with the tracking device. I believed that someone would come for me. Now he had all of that. I was screwed.

"I'm taking you to the facility. Can't have Admiral Bardon thinking something has happened."

I couldn't believe what I was hearing. He would let himself get caught. "I don't—"

"Of course you don't. I'm two steps ahead of all of you. I need to be captured for the rest of my plan to be fulfilled. And you will help me with that. Now come, *liebchen*, let's get out of here." He buttoned his coat. "Oh, I almost forgot."

Pulling my butterfly knife out of his pocket, he handed it to me. "I found this on you when we captured you. I figured you wanted it back."

I stared at it, wishing it was a gun instead. Then I could either blow out his brain, or mine. Either way, all this would be over.

Swinging it open and then closed, I stuffed it into my pocket and followed him out onto the streets.

The facility always changed places. I remembered that when I was working under him. Now it was in the warehouse district two cities over. No one wanted to deal with the crime in that area, so I could understand why Bastien thought it was a good idea to hide out there for a while.

He didn't say a word as we traveled there. I had no idea what his plan was and what he thought he would gain by getting arrested. It scared me, as I did not know how far he had thought all this through.

And how much he would hurt me to get his point across.

The streets were quiet, which surprised me. Sure, there were a few thugs here and there, this being the high-crime neighborhood, but I didn't see any workers. I didn't know whether it was always like that or if Bastien had paid them off,. All I knew was that no one would hear me scream as the doctors poked and prodded at my brain.

We arrived at the facility, and I couldn't believe I was back there after all this time. I dreamed of the day I wouldn't have to see so much blood, smell the grotesque stench in the air. The depressing part of it all was that the smell didn't even bother me anymore. I had grown used to it.

The doctors looked like drones, doing everything Bastien said so that they could keep their lives or so that their family could keep their lives. I knew the feeling all too well. He had threatened my sanity many times, and the truth was that I didn't know if he had destroyed it.

He shoved me into an office. I could still hear the screams of the victims being cut open and having their brain poked at. It wasn't like any of the experiments worked; they were all just for torture, to prove a point.

That he was one evil, fucked-up bastard.

"So, you are wondering why I haven't destroyed the tracking device," he commented as he sat down.

"To torture me? To make me think that I have some chance of escape when I don't."

He shook his head. "You know all this is for your own good, *meine liebchen*. But no, it's not for you. I need to get close to the head of the Nreff military, along with the other systems' members."

I gave him a look. "Why? That makes little sense."

"But doesn't it? If I am put on trial for human experimentations, the other systems will want to see my trial, to make sure they have taken the right action—death, to be quite frank."

And I prayed to *Gott* I could witness that. Hell, I

wanted to pull the trigger, flip the switch, whatever they would use. It didn't matter.

"And on the day they determine my sentence, you will be there and you will kill them all."

I let out a laugh. "You're joking, right? There's no way I would do that—it would be suicide, not to mention wrong, if you even know what that means anymore."

Placing his hands on the table, he leaned forward. His eyes were dark, just like they always were. "You either help me with this or I will have one of my men do it."

I was silent for a moment, putting the pieces together. This was his plan all along. It had nothing to do with experimenting with humans, it had nothing to do with mind control—no, he wanted something else. "You want to start a war."

He smiled. "Now you see. Yes, I will start a war. And if you don't do as I say, I will have the doctors outside do to you what they have already done to another commander. Brainwash you into doing everything I say."

I couldn't believe what I was hearing. After all this time, after what I thought was utter nonsense. It had worked. He had succeeded. "What? It worked?"

He nodded. "It did, on one. Haven't been able to get any others to work, but one will suffice. So either you help or I will have the doctors try to perform the same surgery on you, and not only that, but before I do, I will have him kill everyone you ever cared about."

I was silent. There was no way I would help start a war, but if I agreed, I could at least figure something out before the day of his trial. Then we could stop him for good. "What if I say yes and don't do as you say when you need me?"

"Oh, my man will still do as I say. He'll be there with you every moment."

"Then why do you need me?"

"Because, *meine liebchen*, I can't imagine starting all this without your help."

I didn't say a word, wanting to smack that smile off his lips. I could figure something out although there was no way I would let him get away with this.

"Fine. I will help you. What's our next move?"

He grinned and pulled out the tracking device. "We click this and let Admiral Bardon go through with his attack, but first I will introduce you to your partner who you will work with. Then we will go over the fine details of it all before they surround the place."

Bastien clicked the button. "Now, Rebecca, meet your partner."

I heard the door open behind me, and everything in my heart sank.

"Walrum," I whispered.

CHAPTER THIRTY

Nik

The tracking device alert went off.

After the device had shown Rebecca leaving the capital, we followed it out, surrounding the area, and waited for her to give the signal. The morning light had now come out, and all of us found it surprising that he would risk being seen during the day, venturing out into the warehouse district. I guess he figured he was in the clear.

Or he couldn't wait to torture Rebecca.

I tried not to think about what we might find when we entered the facility. I swore, if he had Rebecca on a table, cutting her open, I would kill him. Hell, if he had even harmed her, I would kill him.

Jonathan's and my goal was to find Sebastien and Rebecca, retrieve them both, and leave. All Bardon's other men were to capture and take in any other person that they ran into. If someone tried to attack us, they would be the ones fighting, not us. Our sole purpose was to retrieve Sebastien and Rebecca. That was it.

Well, mine would be to find Rebecca. That was all I cared about at this point. I wanted nothing to happen to her. She didn't deserve any of this.

Alexandra's confession still bothered me, and how Bardon and Jonathan acted about it frightened me. I didn't know if they wanted to take her in, arrest her, and put her on trial just like Sebastien. I couldn't believe after all this time that they would suspect Rebecca, and if she had a hand in something, that it wasn't because Sebastien forced her to. No, I knew it had to be him; he had to have threatened her.

I tried to push all those thoughts behind me as we gathered around the facility. The silence that surrounded the warehouse district this early in the morning frightened me. Shouldn't a bunch of workers be out this early in the morning, gathering supplies from the warehouses? Wasn't that how it worked? With it being this quiet, I wondered how many were owned by Sebastien so that he could have some privacy or if they had simply abandoned them.

Either way I had a bad feeling about this.

Bardon motioned to the men and radioed the rest with his headset. Nodding, we knew the time had come.

On the count of three. Two. One.

Bardon's soldiers pulled out their bludgeons and smashed all the windows that surrounded the facility. So far no one had come out, no one had even seemed to guard it, which seemed a little fishy, though I supposed if you didn't want anyone to suspect anything, you wouldn't make it look like the place needed to have a guard stationed.

Chucking in some smoke grenades, each of us pulled on our masks and entered the facility, guns ready. No one would slip out past us; there would be no way. After the first line of defense entered, Jonathan and I followed suit.

Nothing in the systems could have prepared me for this.

If I didn't have the mask on, blocking all smells, I could only imagine what it smelled like in here. I had been on many missions, ones that had a lot of bodies lying dead on the ground, but this was far worse. Blood splatters covered the walls, appearing as if someone had tried to run away, a bloody hand used as support, but they had been shot down before they escaped. And it had happened at least fifty times.

How many people had they done this to? How many

people were killed in such a violent, vile way without the media or government knowing about it?

I gagged at the sight, trying not to vomit in my gas mask. The sour taste had already filled my mouth, and I thanked *Gott* that I had some experience with gore so that I could keep myself from throwing up. It still took a lot of strength though, and if I had to stay in here any longer, I just might hurl.

I wanted to keep my eyes down, not to peer into any of the rooms as the image would burn in my mind forever, but I had to—I had to find Rebecca.

Bodies lay on metal tables, sliced open, some of them still breathing, many others not. I did not understand why anyone would do this, how they could do this. I guess if Sebastien knew what to threaten them with, he could make anyone do anything.

Just like when he killed Alexandra's parents.

It made sense now; he killed them because they said no and they knew too much. I doubt any doctor who wanted to leave this place got to leave with their lives. It seemed almost like a butcher shop in the old days, back when animals were killed for meat.

And now I understood why Rebecca didn't eat meat.

If it had been true, if she did in fact know of all this going on and witnessed it, her veganism made sense. I didn't think I would eat meat anytime soon even if it hadn't been made of animal.

I watched as the surrounding soldiers took down the rest of the guards that were supposed to be keeping this place secure. I guess Sebastien never thought a full-on raid would come, for he was outnumbered.

Unless he knew if a raid happened, the evidence had been obtained and he was screwed either way. I was just surprised that he didn't want to take down as many people with him by having more guards. Then again, that would mean more people to control and make sure they didn't squeal.

He had this all figured out.

Jonathan and I kept searching rooms, but there still was no sign of Rebecca.

I hurried faster through the corridors. How could we have not found her yet, how could we have not searched all the rooms? It seemed impossible, but I knew this place was a lot larger than it appeared. We just had to keep searching, had to not give up hope. Rebecca would be fine and this would all be over, I just had to keep believing that.

The smoke from the grenades subsided, and I could see clearer. Doctors were being taken away, their hands behind their head, blood staining their once pure jackets. I couldn't tell if they were afraid and angered by our raid or if they were relieved that someone had come to stop them performing deeds they never wished they had done. I felt pity for them, as they hadn't chosen this life, but Sebastien had chosen it for them. I wondered how exactly the trials would go for them and how they would be sentenced.

That's when I heard it—Rebecca screaming and yelling.

Jonathan and I ran straight to where we believed the noise was coming from. My heart was racing, and my skin felt sweaty. This was it, the moment I was dreading, having to find her being beaten by Sebastien. *Gott*, Jonathan would have to pull me off him before I killed him.

We pushed the door open to find quite the opposite of what we were expecting. Instead of Sebastien hurting Rebecca, she was in fact on top of him, punching him in the face.

"I loved him, you fucking bastard! I'll kill you!" She was crying, freaking out. I did not understand what was going on, why she would have such a reaction.

Until I looked up and saw him—the man trying to pull her off Sebastien. Walrum.

Jonathan and I just stood there for a moment, trying to process what we had just walked in on.

Walrum was alive. Walrum was standing right before us and trying to get his once fiancée off a man who had tried to kill him.

Exchanging glances, Jonathan and I tried to figure out what we should do. We hadn't planned on this and never in our wildest dreams thought this would be what we would find. Rebecca hurting Sebastien, Sebastien already defeated, and Walrum alive.

Rebecca shoved Walrum away and kept punching Sebastien, tears running down her face. "You bastard! You bastard!"

We had to do something. We couldn't let her kill Sebastien.

As I was just about to step to her, Walrum turned around and took a swing at me. I wasn't expecting it, but even then I could jump out of the way.

"What the f—?" I started, not sure as to why one of my best friends would want to hurt me or to stop me from getting Rebecca. Walrum took another swing at me. That's when I noticed his eyes. There was something wrong, something different about them. They appeared feral, as if he was some kind of rabid animal.

This was not the Walrum I used to know.

"They have brainwashed him," Jonathan commented as he pulled out his gun. "That's why Rebecca is trying to kill Sebastien. Now, Walrum, or whoever you are. Don't move."

Walrum raised his hands, glancing between the two of us, almost snarling. I didn't know what to make of it. I barely even knew what to do next. Then I remembered Rebecca was still there, beating the daylights out of

Sebastien.

I hurried over to her and tried to pull her off him. "Rebecca, calm down. We're here. I'm here."

"No, he needs to die! I need to kill him!" she screamed as she grabbed at his throat. Sebastien didn't even resist but lay there with a smirk on his face.

Sebastien gasped out a few words. "Do as he says. Follow your orders."

I grabbed her this time and pulled her off him before she could do any more damage. His face was bloody from a broken nose, jaw, and a few teeth. I understood her frustration and wanted to do the same to him, but we needed him on trial—we needed to show the other systems that we could handle this. And killing him like this wouldn't have been the wisest option even if he deserved it.

Rebecca thrashed in my arms, still screaming and yelling obscenities at Sebastien. He leaned on his arms, still grinning at her, blood covering his teeth. I had no idea why he could be so calm in this situation, especially since he would be on trial for violation of the TOWER. They could execute him for this.

Rebecca stopped fighting me and sank into my arms, sobbing. I stroked her hair. "Shh. It's okay. We're here. Everything will be okay. All this will be okay."

Walrum still stood there, watching us as we tried to figure out the situation. Jonathan kept his eyes locked on him, along with the barrel of his gun. We did not understand what Sebastien did to him or what he could be capable of.

Some soldiers came in, their guns all pointed at Sebastien and Walrum. None of them knew what to make of the situation either.

Bardon stepped in and gasped when he saw Walrum. "This isn't possible…"

"Oh, Admiral Bardon, I didn't think that I was worthy for you to come out for this mission. I must be special," Bastien commented.

Bardon shook his head. *"Va te faire voir."*

"Oh, don't worry, I know where I'm going, and I will drag anyone who has a hand in stopping me down with me."

Nodding to his men, he said, "Arrest him. Admiral Sebastien Wilde, you are under arrest for murder and violation of the TOWER."

I watched as they took him and Walrum away. Rebecca still shook in my arms, and I kept her close, letting her know I wouldn't let anyone else hurt her.

And that was it. All this was finally over.

CHAPTER THIRTY-ONE

Rebecca

I went directly to my quarters after we straightened most of it out. Admiral Bardon said I could rest up, take a long bath since I could keep my wounds out of the water easily, and do whatever I needed to do without getting bothered. I knew that Nik would come by eventually, but I didn't want to see him. I just needed isolation for a bit.

Starting the bath, I watched as it filled, trying to not let my mind wander toward what had just happened, a near impossible feat. Bastien had played his games yet again and at my expense. He thought he possessed me, that I was just a toy for him to play with. I couldn't let myself go down that path again. I wouldn't.

The bath almost overflowed as I let my mind get carried away. Damn it, I had to find a way for him not to wrap me around his finger again. This time had to end differently. It just had to. I couldn't let myself stumble down that road again. It would kill me.

Or I would just kill myself.

If I had to, I just might. Bastien wouldn't stop until I suffered or saw what he considered reason, which was just the opposite. After everything I had witnessed, had performed, had committed, I just wanted it to end.

I let out a sigh as I stepped into the bath. The warm water caressed my skin, and I just wished I could soak in the bath forever. Closing my eyes, I leaned back and tried my best not to start weeping at the scars that covered my body, along with the two new additions.

If I did end up killing myself, it would mean that he had won, and I couldn't have that. No, I had to see this to the end, make sure he suffered as much as I had over the years. I would stop at nothing for that to happen.

Especially after what he had done to Walrum.

He had tortured Walrum and made him a servant. I wondered how much of Walrum still existed inside, screaming to get out, or if he didn't survive at all. The latter seemed to make the most sense, but I didn't want to lose hope. Though if I let myself be honest, I already knew the truth. Walrum was gone and nothing I could do would bring him back.

The man that stood before me in that room no longer possessed any of Walrum's qualities. I could see it in his eyes—everything had been destroyed, just like Bastien wanted. He could keep telling himself that he did it because Walrum and the others had been sent to spy on him, but that was far from the truth. Bastien did it because he couldn't stand me with another man, that I had found someone else and didn't come running back to him.

So in the end, all this was my fault.

I would avenge Walrum's death even if it killed me. I wouldn't let anyone stop me—not Admiral Bardon, not Jonathan, not Bastien, not even Nik. *Gott* I didn't want to think about how Nik might react. He would probably want to stop me, but I wouldn't let him. He didn't understand the things I had gone through, the countless people he made me murder.

Bastien said that I wanted him to create me into a monster, that I just needed his help to become the perfect soldier I wished to be all those years ago. Damn, he could make my blood boil! I just wanted to strangle him.

Well, at least he let me get a few punches in before Nik yanked me off him. If only I could have had a couple more minutes, then maybe my wish would have been fulfilled. Though if I did that, then his mind-controlled servant would have slaughtered everyone I cared about. Who knew what Walrum was capable of at the moment if Bastien ordered it of him.

This bath didn't help me calm down—everything still rolled around in my head like a tornado. I felt like the three years Nik and I spent running meant nothing in the long run—I just found myself back where I started.

How could I let him do this to me all over again, use me like a *Puppe*? No, this time I made sure it differed; this time I had all the cards.

And I would defeat him once and for all.

I got out of the bath. I couldn't stand staying still any longer and needed to pace around. I thought about what Bastien had said, that Walrum would kill everyone I cared about if I stepped out of line for the next part of his little mission. I wondered how close Bastien would be watching me, whether I could stop what he wanted me to do and whether he had a backup plan. I knew he didn't fully trust me, that he wanted simply to see what I would do next. I had to outsmart him this time; it was the only way.

As I dried myself off, I heard a knock at the door, and I didn't even have to look to see who it was. "I don't want to be bothered, Nik."

Silence filled the air for a moment, and at first I thought maybe I had made a false presumption. Then he finally answered.

"Please, Rebecca, let me in."

I sat down on my sofa. Admiral Bardon had really spoiled me with this big of a room. I noted to thank him later, along with some other stuff that I had put off saying. But now wasn't the time as I needed to be left alone. And not even Nik could change my mind about that. "I need to be alone for a little while, *bitte*. I will come talk to you when I'm ready."

"Rebecca…" He paused, as if trying to find the right words. What he said next was barely audible, but I heard it loud and clear. "I saw your throat. Please, I want to make sure you are okay."

I touched the bruises that covered my throat. Damn Bastien and his sadism. This didn't mark the first time I had blemishes on my body because of his need for power during sex—but back then I actually wanted him to do it. *Gott*, I didn't want to be reminded. Why had I been such a blind fool when I was young? Either way, I was paying the price now.

"I said I want to be left alone, okay?"

Nik didn't answer, and after a few moments, I heard footsteps lead off down the hallway. I leaned forward, my elbows braced against my thighs, and stared down at my hands. Even after everything, I knew my innocence had long been shattered. I should be in prison with Bastien. The thought came to my mind, not because I felt sorry for him—far from it. But even if he had me wrapped around his finger, that didn't mean I had to do the things I did. No, I had committed those crimes knowing how sick and twisted they were, and for that I should be hanged.

Tears filled my eyes as I grabbed the vial of morphine-B Bardon left and took it. Letting the drug consume me, I curled myself up in a little ball. I didn't want to be there anymore. I didn't want to go through the torture he put me through ever again. What had I done to deserve this? Why couldn't it just disappear?

What was I going to do next?

Thank You For Reading!

Thank you so much for reading! Readers like you make it possible for authors like me to write stories! If you could spare a moment and leave a review on Amazon, Goodreads, BookBub, and wherever you like to buy books, that would mean the world to me! It really helps authors like me to succeed in the publishing world.

Book 2 is coming Summer 2021!

<u>Acknowledgements</u>

I want to thank everyone who helped me with this novel! This novel all started at ASU's Your Novel Year Program back in 2015. I want to say thank you to my mentors Mike, Joe, Chantelle, Kevin, and Paul who helped me with all my writing questions and taught me how to write. Thank you to everyone in the program who gave me feed back (dad, Cassie, Gil, Gina, Jeff, Laura, Marcel, Stacy, Deborah, Paul, Jasmine, and Tom), and to my writing group who also helped with this project (Traci, Rebecca, Bernie, and Christi). Thank you to my editor Anne Victory and cover artist Biserka Designs who made this book possible. Thank you to Kaleb who answered all my random questions. I swear it was for a book! Another thank you to my friends Earlene, Shayne, Faye, Veronica, Tom, Carl, Ruben, Justin, and all the others who have helped with this book over the years. Lastly, thank you to my parents who have always supported me, and to my husband who gets the privilege of reading all my books :).

About the Author

Lyra Thorsson is the sci-fi pen name for Dani Hoots. She is a science fiction, fantasy, romance, and young adult author who loves anything with a story. She has a B.S. in Anthropology, a Masters of Urban and Environmental Planning, a Certificate in Novel Writing from Arizona State University, and a BS in Herbal Science from Bastyr University.

Her hobbies include reading, watching anime, cooking, studying different languages, wire walking, hula hoop, and working with plants. She is also an herbalist and sells her concoctions on FoxCraft Apothecary. She lives in Phoenix with her husband and visits Seattle often.
Feel free to email her with any questions you might have!
danihootsauthor@gmail.com

www.ingramcontent.com/pod-product-compliance
Lightning Source LLC
Chambersburg PA
CBHW051010180726
48291CB00006B/2048